T0147817

NO TWO WAYS

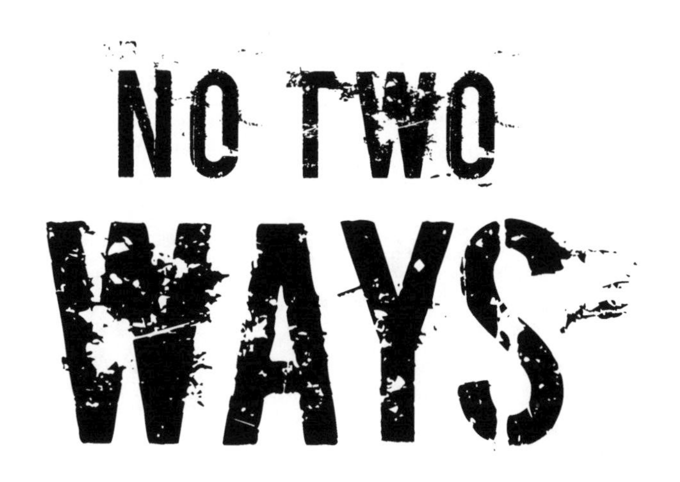

HOY VAN HORN

NO TWO WAYS

This is a work of fiction. All of the characters, names, incidents, organizations, and dialogue in this novel are either the products of the author's imagination or are used fictitiously.

iUniverse books may be ordered through booksellers or by contacting:

iUniverse
1663 Liberty Drive
Bloomington, IN 47403
www.iuniverse.com
1-800-Authors (1-800-288-4677)

ISBN: 978-1-5320-4997-2 (sc)
ISBN: 978-1-5320-4996-5 (e)

Library of Congress Control Number: 2018905883

Print information available on the last page.

iUniverse rev. date: 06/06/2018

DEDICATION

For my three daughters, with love…H.V.

CHAPTER 1

Have you ever wondered about the origin of the term "I've got your back"? It goes back to the military, where the term originated with the WWI fighter pilots referring to the rear of the aircraft at the six o'clock position.

If you picture yourself in the center of a clock face, the point directly in front of you would denote twelve o'clock and directly behind would be six o'clock. The six o' clock position is also the most vulnerable, unless you have eyes in the back of your head. Now, in the air battlefield, if another fighter pilot tells you he's got your "six", it means that he is watching your back. And, likewise, that pilot expects you to watch his "six" as well, in return, when the situation demanded. This certainly highlights how WWI fighter pilots looked out for each other.

Samuel Earl Trainer was lying on his back, staring at the suspended ceiling, sort of imagining himself as one of those fighter pilots. It was a Saturday in May and he had just added another year to his age. Yesterday, it was his birthday, May 20, 2018. He was now eighteen years old, a senior. This year, he would be graduating from the University High School. His thoughts traveled to the later part of the day, when he and his make-shift garage band were to play at the Community Center located on East Street in Morgantown, West Virginia. The band had been together for a couple of years and it was certainly high-time that they needed to introduce a little change in their look. He was thinking that his lead guitarist, William Zackery

"Zack" Taylor, and his forever friend and drummer, George Deacon Fritz, should always stay together, like a pack, and forever have each other's back. You know, like the WWI fighter pilots looking out for each other. He thought he should always keep that in mind. Today the three of them were going to meet with a gorgeous young lady who they were considering inducting into their garage band. She was a terrific base guitar player with a powerful singing voice. She would be the perfect addition to spice up the group, being a female and, indeed, a total knockout! Her name was Penelope Rose Daiquiri.

Samuel, being the originator of the band, could harmonize perfectly with both Zack and Deacon. They always sounded great. They mostly played Rock 'n Roll, a type of popular dance music originating in the 1950s, characterized by a heavy beat and simple melodies, usually based on a twelve-bar structure and an instrumentation of guitar, bass, and drums. It was pioneered by Chuck Berry, transformed by The Beatles, hardened by Led Zeppelin and AC/DC. Through the course of the 70's, it evolved into the pinnacle of musical glory. The name of the band was, "Sam E. Tra...Rock 'n Roll Band", and everyone referred to the band as just "Sammytra".

Sam loved rock 'n roll and always led off with a song written by George Jackson and recorded by Bob Seger, "Old time Rock 'n Roll". It all originated from his grandfather, Thurston Beltow, who loved that sort of music, and in turn Sam grew to love it.

Zack picked Sam up in his 1957 Chevy that he and his dad had rebuilt, powder blue, with a white convertible top. The three of them were planning golf and were meeting at Deacon's house. Deacon lived with his parents, on Downwood Drive, in Downwood Manor. "I'll leave my car here, Deacon," Zack said, as he pulled it next to Deacon's designer truck. Deacon was driving his father's new Nissan Altima SL to the Pines Country Club.

It was then, that Sam got a text on his iPhone from Penelope, asking about the interview. Sam sent a text back saying, "We will meet with you at 'The Fritz' on Clay Street, just off Beechurst Avenue at 2 pm."

Penny texted: "K"

Sam texted: "Don't be late; we have to make it to a gig later."

Penny texted: "O-ke-doke."

Deacon drove on Cheat Road, continued onto Point Marien Road, turned on Country Club Boulevard, and pulled into the parking lot at Pines Country Club. Sam and Zack went and brought back two golf carts and loaded up their golf clubs. Deacon ran into the pro shop and signed them up for 18 holes and they continued to the first tee. Zack came up with the game. "OK, we're playing dollar, dollar for the front, back and total. Best ball for each hole." It was indeed an interesting proposition. They all agreed and Sam teed off first and hit a perfect shot down the middle of the fairway. Deacon hit a long hook about 250 yards in the left hand rough and Zack hit his regular power fade in the right hand rough. They continued and when they got to the third hole, Deacon, on his second shot, hit a huge hook into the woods on the left.

"That ball probably landed on 'Butt-hole Road' or in the next county," Sam said. "Pretty much looks like you lost this hole, Deacon."

Barrowby Road, known to most people as the "Butt-Hole Road" was an old logging road that ran along the country club property. It leads absolutely nowhere and is seldom used.

"No way," Deacon said, not wanting to lose a stroke on the stinking hole, determined to find his ball and hit it out of there. The three of them went looking for his ball.

"We'll never find that ball, let's go," Zack yelled, chomping at the bit, as he kept looking towards the other side of Butt-Hole Road. "What the hell is going on over there?" On the other side of the road, about forty or fifty feet into the wooded area, there was something that looked like a man lying face down in a pile of dirt. They crossed Barrowby Road, and quietly walked up to see what was going on.

"Wonder what was happening here? Looks like the guy passed

out, must have been trying to dig a hole with that shovel." Sam replied, as he walked up. On a closer look, he saw a huge, thick leather bag with handles that looked like a getaway duffle; it was just next to the hole that the man had been digging and there was blood all over his shirt. He had been shot. Yikes. He was popped not only in the back of his head, but many times in the back as well. On a perpendicular path to the Butt-Hole Road, known as Rainy Road, a truck with heavily tinted windows sped away with the wheels spinning and the engine roaring, eventually disappearing down the Log Cabin Road.

"Did you see that pick-up?" Deacon yelled. "I saw three big dudes get in there. I couldn't see the license number. It had a dark film over it and they moved too fast. What do you say? Let's just get the hell out of here."

"Wait," Zack said, digging his hands into his huge leather bag. "Jesus, this bag is full of money. A whole, shitload of money! One hundred dollar bills, I'm talkin' C-notes!!"

"Holy crap!" Deacon yelped, as he grabbed the bag and looked for himself. "We have to call the cops. This is a bunch of bullshit. Let's go. Those thugs in that pick-up are going to come back, and then we are going to be three dead dorks." The three of them were absolutely dumbfounded and scared shitless, trying to get a good look at where the pick-up truck disappeared. They also spotted what looked like, maybe a 2000 Cadillac Escalade, close from where the black pick-up had zoomed away.

"Christ, we must have come right when this shit was going down. That man was trying to bury this money for some reason and was followed by those thugs. That leather bag is extremely heavy; I can see the path where he dragged it from his car. He did it all by himself I guess. Somehow this man was either a part of a drug cartel, a gaming establishment or was involved in some big robbery. Who knows? Anyway, whatever the circumstance, we are caught in the middle of it. We can't go to the police right now for obvious reasons, and maybe those thugs in the pick-up didn't get a good look at us.

I'm thinking that we just take the money and see if anything turns up in the news about a huge robbery or something, and then go to the police," Sam suggested, looking for some kind of backing from the other two.

"Are you crazy," Deacon yelled. "We should leave everything just the way we found it and get the hell out of here. I don't give a rat's ass about any of this. Piss on it."

"Our fingerprints are on that bag… and on the money," Zack whispered. "We are involved in this big time. That money has got to go with us, Deacon, no shit about it."

"Damn right it does, Deacon. We can figure out what to do with it later. Right now, we have to get it over to the golf carts and back to the car. We have to carry it because we can't leave a trail," Sam said, pointing at the bag of money. The three of them picked up the bag and struggled with it until they reached the golf carts, slung it on one of the carts and drove as fast as they could, back to the car. They threw the three golf bags in the trunk of the car, and put the huge leather bag in the back seat.

"Sum-bitch," Sam said. "Zack and I will drive the golf carts back, meet us by the cart barn Deacon, and we'll get the hell out of here. We have to meet Penny at your dad's place at two. So let's wrap this up. It's eleven AM already and we are going there right now."

Zack was riding in the back seat and opened up the bag of money. He absolutely couldn't believe what he was looking at. The bag was stuffed with packets and rolls of money, and it was making Zack believe that maybe they shouldn't have taken it. This was definitely drug money. Go figure. He thought: *This whole state was crawling with drugs* All three of them were living in the nucleus of it all, from Pittsburgh, Pennsylvania to Charleston, West Virginia.

West Virginia had the highest rate of drug-related deaths in the country. Like many of the Eastern states, West Virginia had always faced problems with marijuana cultivation, consumption and diversion as well as pharmaceutical drugs-abuse: Oxycodone, hydrocodone, methadone and Xanax (alprazolam). There is some cocaine in both its powder and crack cocaine forms, and definitely heroin. The nationwide opioid epidemic had been dubbed as "the biggest public health crisis since HIV/AIDS", and a United States Senator of West Virginia had even stated, "We need a drug czar leading the White House Office of national Drug Control Policy who has seen these devastating effects and is passionate about ending the opioid epidemic. We must protect the people, not the pharmaceutical industry."

A lot of the money was rolled into wads, with rubber bands around them. Zack couldn't imagine how much money it was. He picked up one of the wads, removed the rubber band and counted out fifty one hundred dollar bills, five thousand dollars, and that was not even the tip of the iceberg.

"Holy crap!" Zack yelled, as he threw the hundred dollar bills in the front seat with Deacon and Sam. "There's got to be at least a million dollars here. Are you sure no one is following us? If those thugs find us, they're going to mow down our asses. Drug money. This whole thing is going to shit…we are dead meat." They were heading to Chestnut Ridge Road and over to Patterson Drive on their way to Fritz's, a sports bar across the West Virginia University campus, owned by Deacon's father.

"Just cool it down at the moment, Zack. We'll go to Fritz's place, grab a sandwich and then think about where we can hide that bag, until we can figure out what to do." Sam said, as he was looking out the rear window. "What the hell, Deacon, look behind us, that black pick-up is following us. Get the hell moving; I was afraid of that, we must lose them!"

"How did they know this was us?" Deacon shouted, as he floored the gas pedal.

"They were waiting for us to come out, that's how, now they know what we're driving and they also know that we have the money!" Sam yelled.

"How about if I just throw the bag out and they can pick it up," Zack asked in panic.

"No good. They think we saw them. They don't want any witnesses. They are out to get us, and believe me, they can find us. Your dad's car has West Virginia designer plates. They won't be hard to trace with 'The Fritz' written on them, Sum-bitch, turn right and go past Star City and get out on I-79 south, Deacon, we can get rid of them on the four lane. They swung out on I-79 south, and were racing at 80 miles per hour, but the pick-up was keeping up and getting closer.

"I'm cutting off on I-68 east," Deacon said. "We can definitely lose them if I get off at the Cheat Lake exit. I know that area like the back of my hand."

"The shit is going to hit the fan," Zack bellowed.

"Shut that crap up, Zack. Those people aren't playing, they're out to kill us," Deacon said, as he looked out of the rearview mirror, the color had drained from his cheeks, he knew they were vulnerable, and that had scared him big time.

Racing on I-68 east, at 85 mph, the truck picked up some speed and pulled up along the side of the Nissan Altima as the dark tinted passenger side window rolled down. A double-barreled shot gun was aiming directly at Deacon.

"Sum-bitch! Look out, Deacon!" Sam cautioned.

"Danger, Will Robinson, Danger!" Zack yelped in utter fright.

"Those assholes are crazy," Deacon shouted, looking to his left, "He's going to shoot that son of a bitch!"

CHAPTER 2

Michael Desmond Trainer, Samuel's father, was a hard-working man with dreams of fortune and fame. Mike counted himself in the top ten percent of the good looking guys in Morgantown, West Virginia, and some of the girls on the West Virginia University campus would have agreed. He barely managed to make it on student loans and some money from his parents. He was taking classes and was in the market for the love of his life. He had his eye on a very attractive senior co-ed, Erica Beltow, who was two years ahead of him academically. He was a realistic man, however, and knew that he would never have a chance with her. Guys like him were a "dime a dozen". She had come to Morgantown from a predominant family in Stockton, Pennsylvania, who would have probably always wished for a highly-educated doctor or lawyer for their daughter.

Mike came from some predominance himself, considering that his father ran a successful construction business in Morgantown. His mother and father had moved to Michigan after selling the construction business, and then moved to Maui, Hawaii. Mike had attended High School in Maui. After completing High School, he was homesick and wanted to attend college back in Morgantown, West Virginia, at the West Virginia University. He decided to stay with his mother's brother, Robert Covington, who lived in Preston County near Cooper's Rock.

Mike was thinking of some kind of plan that could impress his gorgeous senior co-ed, and make her believe that he was a good prospect for dating. Mike was a divorcee and had been paying child support for his beautiful daughter, Allison, who lived with her mother.

Mike thought: "When it comes to going after what you want in life, don't take no for an answer."

Erica Anne Beltow had spent her freshman year cheerleading and another year rooming with her older sister, Catherine Michelle, in an apartment on the University Avenue, in the Evansdale Section of WVU. Thurston Beltow, their father, had taken care of their rent, books and tuitions back then. Now in her senior year, however, Erica was living in a small, rented house in Westover, and was driving the remains of a vehicle that she and her sister Cathy had shared. They called the car "Bernice". It was an old, used up Ford Escort. Cathy had graduated with a degree in soil science, and was home with their Mom and Dad in Stockton, PA for a short time while also planning her destination wedding with Jonathon Van Lorne, her boyfriend.

Mike had found Erica's rented house and had decided that he would do something humorous. He drove his beat-up, old pick-up truck to the front-door of her house, walked up to it and knocked. When Erica appeared, he told her that he had a truck load of watermelons and where did she want them unloaded. Erica could see that there were no watermelons, and trying not to display aloofness or disdain, said, "Either you are drunk, crazy or just pulling my leg."

"I'm not drunk, but I've been known to be a little crazy," Mike replied, apologetically.

"Well, I'll tell you one thing. You have more guts than most men I've seen over the years. I've seen you around the campus. What's your name?" Erica inquired, as she stepped out on the porch.

"Mike Trainer, I've been anxious to talk to you from the very first time that I spotted you, just didn't have the courage."

"Indeed! Now, I suppose you want to ask me on some exclusive date, and waste your money on flowers or candy."

"Something of that sort," Mike uttered, as he thought about

whatever little money he had. He had student loans and a partial grant that he was living on.

"I can tell you right now that I have allergies, and I don't like flowers. If you buy me candy, I'll throw it away. I don't like exclusive restaurants. But I do enjoy pizza and cola. I work part time at Shoney's. I'm finishing up my final year. I'm studying to become a Psychologist. And that's all the information you would have wanted, I suppose. So what now, Mike?"

"I actually grew up in Morgantown, but I graduated from high school in Hawaii," Mike responded "I don't know where this education is going to take me, and I may have to give it up and go to work. I'm an experienced carpenter. I could probable make a living out of it."

"Thank you for stopping by, Mike. My phone number is 555-5455, if you want to call and take me to Wendy's or something, OK, bye-bye. Oh, Mike, don't forget taking those watermelon back home with you."

Erica was elated; she had seen Mike Trainer around, and he was definitely a hunk. She was pretty excited that he built up enough nerve to do what he did. She had a strong feeling that a relationship would develop out of this. Erica and Mike dated for a short while and came to the conclusion that they had fallen in love. They decided to get married. After a small ceremony, with just a couple of Erica's friends and a few of Mike's friends as the witnesses, they became Mr. and Mrs. Michael Trainer. They moved into Erica's little house that she was renting. Erica received her degree in Psychology and passed her boards. Mike acquired a job as a carpenter with one of his old friends who paid him twenty dollars an hour. He now worked for a construction company named Huge Structural & Home Improvement in Morgantown, which was solely owned by an ambitious entrepreneur, Howard Huge. Howard would give estimates and take on projects that ranged from installing structural steel buildings to building apartments and doing designer improvements to building private residential homes.

Mike had his heart set on the desire to become a registered surveyor in the future, just like his father-in-law, Thurston Beltow III. Erica became pregnant right away and after nine agonizing months, she delivered a wonderful baby boy, Samuel Earl Trainer, at the Ruby Memorial Hospital in Morgantown. Judy and Thurston Beltow were naturally there, being the proudest grandparents ever.

The Ruby Memorial Hospital, the largest facility in the West Virginia University hospitals' family, was known for providing the most advanced level of care available to the citizens of West Virginia and the neighboring states. Ruby Memorial Hospital, the flagship hospital of WVUH, was named after the late J.W. Ruby. Ruby's late wife, Hazel Ruby McQuain, had donated $8 million toward the construction of the hospital.

The Virginia University Hospitals was a not-for-profit corporation operating the teaching hospitals of West Virginia University. These hospitals were as follows: Ruby Memorial Hospital in the Eastern Panhandle of West Virginia, City Hospital in Martinsburg, West Virginia and Jefferson Memorial Hospital in Ranson, Operating jointly as WVUH- East.

CHAPTER 3

Samuel Earl Trainer, born on May 20, 2000, in Morgantown, was very active boy right since his childhood, and always seemed to be brimming with energy. Samuel had always kept his mom, Erica Anne Trainer, on her toes, making her chase him right from the time he was crawling until his early toddler years, the terrible Two's, like his grandmother called it. His grandma Judith was also known as "Mimi" to all her grandchildren. Thurston Beltow III, known as "Fuge" to the grandchildren, was curious about Samuel's over activity, just like his wife. Judy believed that he had Attention Deficit Hyperactivity Disorder (ADHD).

"According to the 'Diagnostic and Statistical Manual of mental disorder', the symptoms emerge before the age of seven," said Judy, flipping through the manual.

"Samuel is energetic and it worries me for his school future. ADHD impacts school-aged children and results in restlessness, acting impulsively, and lack of focus which impairs their ability to learn properly," Erica replied, looking worried.

"He's acting like a normal toddler," Thurston barked, disagreeing. "That just tells me that he is going to be active in sports and accelerate in all the key positions. Get it. He doesn't need any help."

"Thurston, you know that aggravates me," Judy said. "Your lips are moving but all I hear is "blah, blah, blah…."

"Judy, I'm new, but I'm not brand new, I wasn't born yesterday, you know. I mean sure, I was born at night. But not last night," Thurston spouted, with a huge grin.

"Did you fall on your head when you were young, or were you just born stupid?"

"I resemble that remark," Thurston said. "Help Erica, this woman is killing me."

"You got yourself in trouble there, dad, you are trying to match wits with mom and she's too slick for you."

Attention deficit-hyperactivity disorder, also known as hyperkinetic disorder, is a mental disorder and neurobehavioral disorder, characterized by either significant difficulties of inattention or hyperactivity and impulsiveness or a combination of both.

"It's a good thing that you're a nurse, mom," Erica said. "I kind of wish dad was right about Samuel. It would be much easier that way, wouldn't it?"

Samuel was going to be a force to deal with. Mike and Erica were going to have difficulty in the future to burn up the energy that Samuel had stored. Who knows? Acrobatics, sports, cross country running. Not in his younger stages though. He could not sit still for one second; diving and jumping from couch to couch; rolling on the beds; running inside and outside; unconditionally unstoppable. He was burning energy from dawn to dusk; then not wanting to go to bed. This was going to be a trying time for Mike and Erica raising Samuel.

Then they heard this…

How many times have we heard from someone that knows someone, who told them something that sparked your interest? Well, this was one of those times. Thurston heard from a co-worker that his son spent over $700 at a nutritionist to discover that his son (who has ADHD and temper issues) needed a gluten-free diet, and after four days being gluten-free, the boy was much calmer and his anger issues were under control.

After hearing the success that Thurston's co-worker's grandson had, it seemed to make perfect sense to go gluten-free and try taking away Samuel's medication altogether. Erica would have never put two and two together because eating gluten -free is to help people who have Celiacs disease. She could have never, in a million years, thought that it could help someone with ADHD. Samuel's doctor did say that he had heard of success with this diet in treating ADHD. With that, Grandma Mimi and Erica decided they were going to give it a whirl. After a short while, they saw improvements in his behavior. Samuel was having focused reactions and was much calmer.

"I'm not a doctor," Thurston said proudly. "But I think we have found a cure for Samuel and we are saving a whole lot of money on the medication."

"I have to agree, Thurston, Samuel is much calmer and seems to be able to function without constant activity. I truly believe that other people with an ADHD problem should be made aware of this," Judith replied.

CHAPTER 4

Thurston Beltow III, Samuel's grandfather, who was the Vice President of a Nuclear Power Plant in Stockton, Pennsylvania, loved his times with his grandson. He was Thurston's second boy grandchild and he was going to spoil them because all he had ever been able to produce was three lovely girls. "Girls are easy to make," Thurston would boast. "You have the pattern right in front of you." His three daughters were Catherine Van Lorne, in Stockton, Pennsylvania, Erica Trainer, in Morgantown, and Victoria Erin Beltow, who was now at home. Vicky was an Elementary School Teacher and was trying to get into a District School in Pittsburgh, Pennsylvania. Cathy, the eldest, was running a greenhouse in Stockton, and Jon, her husband, was in-charge of security at the Stockton Nuclear Power Plant.

Mike had trashed school because he now had a wife and two children to support. He had Samuel, and his daughter, Allie, from a former marriage. Allie lived with her mother in a nearby town. Mike had also acquired some student loan debt, so things were a little tight for him. He had studied and trained as a rod man and an instrument man with a licensed Professional Land Surveyor, Francis James Paul, who was also employed by Huge Structural & Home Improvement. He was now applying for a Registered Professional Land Surveying (R.P.L.S.) for the State of West Virginia. Because of his education and experience, he had all the requirements and qualifications to be eligible for the state examination through the West Virginia Board of

Professional Surveyors, which would be due in April. He submitted five names for reference, of which at least three people were engaged in the practice of surveying, and were aware of his experience. He also had to be eighteen years of age; a citizen of the United States; hold a high school diploma; no conviction of crimes involving moral turpitude; of good moral character; paid all applicable fees; and he provided any other information the board prescribed as a surveying intern (SI). The licensing process typically followed two phases. First, the candidate would have to take the fundamentals of surveying exam, to be certified upon passing and meeting all requirements as a surveying intern. The second phase typically consisted of the Principles and Practice of land surveying exam along with a state-specific examination.

Surveying and land surveying is the technique, profession, and science of accurately determining position of points and the distances and angles between them. To accomplish their objective, surveyors use elements of mathematics (geometry and trigonometry), physics, engineering and law.

"Now the American Congress on Surveying and Mapping has an alternative definition. They say that surveying is the science and art of making all essential measurements to determine the relative position of points or physical and cultural details above, on, and under the surface of the earth, and to depict them in a usable form. Go figure. Sounds the same to me," Mike exclaimed, as he sat down at the table, explaining it to Erica. "That's the type of answers they want on the test," holding his throat and pretending like he was choking.

"Dad and his friend Dennis Crane have professional surveying certificates, don't they?" Erica asked, as she was warming some food on the range. "Can't they help you understand some of these practice questions?"

"Actually not," Mike replied. "They got their licenses on the 'Grandfather clause'. They received registration and certification through their experience, no testing. That is actually a thing of the past now, although I used them both as references. You have to almost be a genius today; because it keeps getting harder. They can't really help me with the examinations. Furthermore, land surveying is the detailed study or inspection, as by gathering information through observations, measuring in the field, or research of legal instruments, and data analysis in the support of planning, designing, and establishing of property boundaries."

"But Dennis Crane is a graduated Civil Engineer, isn't he Mike?"

"Yes, and so is your dad, but there work is industrial, surveying can include social services such as mapping and data accumulation, construction layout surveys, precision measurements of length, angle, elevation, area, and volume, as well as horizontal and vertical control surveys. Land surveying involves the re-establishment of cadastral surveys and land boundaries based on documents of record and historical evidence. It is a lot different. Dennis works at Weirton Steel Corporation, in a managerial capacity. They are into purchasing and installing new designs and structures. Thurston has a surveying license only because he is in the Pennsylvania National Guard and they use survey instruments to build bridges."

"I really wish I could help, Mike."

"We'll know by next week, after I complete my exams, whether I am successful or not. Fortunately though, I still have my carpentry occupation to fall back on; it can help keep us going."

"Guess what? Samuel is now starting to swing those golf clubs that my dad bought him. I must say, pretty well, for a two-year-old. He can actually hit the golf ball off of a tee. It's just a small child set with plastic balls, but he looks so professional. Dad got him some golf clothes and a hat.....So cute."

"Howard Huge and I are planning on teaching Samuel some tricks of the trade in golf when he gets a little older," Mike replied, "between Howard, Thurston and me, Samuel will receive plenty of training.

Howard belonged to the "Lakeview Golf Resort & Spa", set on 500 acres overlooking Cheat Lake; this golf resort is 8.5 miles south of the Pennsylvania border and 7.4 miles from the West Virginia University.

"Oh, Mike, I don't know if this is a good time to tell you or not, but I'm pregnant. I did a test and it came out positive, so we are going to have another little one. Mimi and Fuge are very excited about it. What do you think? I am very elated! We are all hoping it will be a girl."

"Wow, now that is a shocker," Mike replied. "How are we going to handle that? I am really lost for words. My God! That isn't good!"

Whoops. Your girlfriends and your parents jumped in joy when you told them your good news, so why is your partner looking at you like you had worms crawling out of your ears? Men don't always react to pregnancy the way women do. While many are over-the-moon excited, particularly if the pregnancy is planned and happily anticipated, others are flooded with worries. The best way to help your partner feel more comfortable about your pregnancy is to understand that men and women often look at pregnancy differently. Don't criticize him if he doesn't react the way you think he should. Give him space to experience the pregnancy in his own way. There are often legitimate reasons for men's reactions.

"Mike, not to worry, we'll work together to solve any problems and you'll most likely be an excellent father. Let's not worry about it until we have time to talk it over, alright. Time heals almost everything. Give time some time."

"I am just anxious about the upcoming expenses, our health insurance coverage, what life will be like with the five of us to support?" Mike said, looking stressed.

"My mom has no fear about us having another baby. She thinks it is wonderful. She says, 'You'll just know when it's right. It's something that just happens, and we should never compare our life with others. You have no idea what their journey is all about'."

"I was completely happy with our family as-is, with just one child. And there are plenty of logical reasons why our family should remain that size: we still have my daughter, Allie, who I am still supporting. My job and studies for this exam are growing more time-consuming and demanding with time. This is a nightmare! I am absolutely positive that I will pass that damn Land Surveying exam and receive a professional certificate. So for now, we'll just give it a rest," Mike replied, as he threw a cigarette butt down and stepped on it.

"Well, you better build a bridge and get over it, Mike, just take a deep breath because we have to look out for each other, regardless of the consequences. I am applying for a job at the Ruby Memorial Hospital tomorrow. I'm certain that I'll get the job with my Psychology degree."

"Alright, let's try to keep our chins up and hope for the best."

Anna Elaine Trainer was born on May 12, 2002. She was so much unlike her brother, Samuel, who was blond and blue eyes. She was lovely and elegant, yet distinguished like a princess. Anna had a glow about her, with curly, dark hair, a soft adorable face, with a smile to melt your heart. This little girl was a God-sent.

CHAPTER 5

LIFE ISN'T FAIR, BUT IT'S STILL GOOD…

"Slam the brakes Deacon!" Sam screamed, grabbing on to the handle above his head. "Slam on the freakin' brake!"

Deacon jumped on the brake with both his feet and the car skidded along the highway going from 85 miles per hour to 0 within just ten seconds, causing all kinds of havoc as the traffic was pretty heavy. Cars squealed, turning sideways and hitting each other. Some went crashing into the grass median. The black pick-up spun across the grass median and collided with a concrete manhole, instantly bursting into flames. Black smoke was spewed everywhere.

"Okay, Deacon, let's go, they will never be able to identify us in all this smoke. The State troopers' helicopter will be here any moment. I think we're going to make it. Get up to Cooper's Rock exit, and over to my parent's house, they're both at work," Sam said, as he pointed up the highway. "That pick-up will be burnt to a crisp. You alright Zack?"

"Un-freakin-believable, damn it to hell, I almost pissed my pants."

"You really are a piece of work, Zack. I am still scared shitless. What's next?" Deacon asked.

"Daaamn, crap, I don't know, we have to find a place to stash that duffle bag, and for now, we keep our mouths shut about this. We are in some really deep shit. We'll hide that duffle in a concrete crawlspace behind the house, we can move it later. Let's take your dad's car home. Zack and I will follow you in my van, *(Sam's van had "Sam E. Tra Rock n Roll Band" sprayed in large letters on both the doors)* and pick you up, Deacon. Then we shall head directly to Fritz's. Just remember, if anyone says anything, we know nothing," Sam explained.

They stashed the leather duffle bag in the crawlspace and returned to their vehicles.

"Ok, let's go," Sam said, flagging them to the vehicles.

Deacon was taking a back way to his father's house, off the Cheat Lake exit, and the van followed. There was no East-bound traffic, and there was a helicopter overhead, traffic was probably backed up five miles. Yikes.

"We should take some time to count that money, maybe tomorrow. If those characters in that black pick-up all became crispy critters, and the truck is a complete charred mess. No one will know that we have the money. How do you see it, Sam?" Zack asked, while he and Sam were following Deacon.

"Wow, Zack, I really didn't think of that, but eventually the authorities will find that body up on the Butt-hole Road," Sam replied. "We'll have to see what happens, but we need to lay low and keep things to ourselves. I would certainly like to know what is going down with all of this."

"It's the drug dealers, believe me. There is no way that money can be traced; the shit's wrapped with rubber bands. It's in a getaway duffle that the drug lords use to transport money to the islands, probably Nassau or Turks & Caicos Island, to launder it. From what I know, a small getaway duffle holds one million dollars in one hundred dollar bills, and weighs twenty three pounds. That large duffle weighs fifty or sixty pounds. Go figure. They call this dirty money! What do you think, Sam?"

"Come on, Zack," Sam laughed. "How do you know so much about that bullshit?"

"No bullshit, Sam. I heard my dad and some of his friends talking, and then I looked it up on the internet. The money is laundered at Nassau Life. They have made it a family business, they've even acquired a ten-year driver's license from Turks & Caicos Island. All perfectly legal. Some shit, huh. What do you think?"

"Hold that thought, Zack, here's Deacon. We have to talk some more about that. Don't say anything to Deacon about that Turk & Caicos crap, not yet. Sometimes he gets such a hair up his ass about questionable things. I'm starting to get a little more relaxed myself." Sam said, making a shushing noise.

"Got yeah, I got shotgun, Deacon," Zack yelled. "Get in the back."

"Don't even say the word shotgun around me, I'm still shittin' nails! That was the scariest thing that's ever happened to me, and if my dad knew what I did with his car, I would be grounded until I was at least twenty years old."

"That's not even funny." Sam chuckled. "We are lucky to be alive. Your father is fortunate he has a vehicle left at all. No kidding."

"Well," Zack spouted. "It is 12:30 PM now, we can finally get to Fritz's, grab something to eat, and figure what we are going to ask Penny in this interview that we have planned. I've only seen her once, gorgeous Penelope Daiquiri, tasty, with the varieties of delicious Cruzan Rum, a real cocktail project, yum, I'm in love."

"You are about a horny sucker, Zack," Deacon said. "You make me laugh; Penny wouldn't touch you even with a ten foot pole. You better wake up and come out of that dream. Regardless, Sam, we'll have to drive the back roads, to avoid the I-68 west, on Point Marion Drive."

"From what I've heard, her father, the attorney, Benjamin Franklin Daiquiri, is pretty wealthy, and spends most of his time in New York, New York." Zack explained. "He seldom comes to Morgantown to their home on the corner of Anchor Avenue and

Pinochle Way, I believe it is close to the Pines Country Club. I looked it up on the internet. She lives there with her mother. We should take a look. Drive past the Pines Country Club and turn left on Center Drive."

They went on Point Marion Drive, turned left on Center Drive and a left on Anchor Ave.

"Holy Mackerel!" Sam yelled. "That is a total mansion."

It was an Exquisite Estate. The home was tucked away on three acres and within a few miles of a hospital and downtown. It included nine bedrooms, six bathrooms, three fireplaces, hardwood floors throughout, indoor pool and spa, a detached sunroom with a fireplace, oversized six-car garage, and a workshop building. The grounds featured mature, manicured landscaping, fencing, patios, fire pit, flat yard, privacy and plenty of parking in the huge concreted area.

"And she wants to join our band? This is crazy! That has to be a million dollar estate. We are wasting our time talking to her," Deacon questioned. "That is my opinion."

"Opinions are like assholes, everyone has one, Deacon," Zack spouted.

"Ouch, shots received. Bite me, Zack," Deacon said, as he twirled his clinched fingers in the air. "Make a funny?"

"Come on, guys. Maybe she just wants to play in a band, no problem, we'll talk to her," Sam said. "Let's get going, alright?"

"Yeah, let's go!" Deacon answered.

They took the back way, naturally, so as to avoid I-68 west, where all hell was breaking loose. They headed to Chestnut Ridge Road and over to Patterson Drive on their way to Fritz's, going across the WVU campus. They took a left on Monongahela Boulevard, onto Beechhurst Avenue, and just past the Westover Bridge, on Don Knott's Boulevard, they turned right to Clay Street, and then reached Fritz's. The ride took about fifteen minutes.

"**The Fritz**", was a huge Sport's Bar owned by Deacon's father, George Francisco Fritz, a balding, heavy set and demanding proprietor who kept all his employees in line. It was known in Morgantown for its succulent & delicious, top-quality steaks. The food was fantastic to keep your belly satisfied, along with casual beer drinking. A little tacky but refined, with house brews and specialty cocktails. Out front were three lighted diagonal signs, top sign read, "**The Fritz",** middle sign, "***Take out or eat here***"**,** bottom, "***Welcome***". To the right of the doorway was a small plaque that read, *George F. Fritz, proprietor.* Walking in was a comical sign that read, Stop, Drop and Roll....which set people in a happy mode, just walking in.

As they turned into Fritz's parking lot, they spotted a police patrol car and an unmarked vehicle that they always knew belonged to the Chief of Police, Anton Calabrese. It was jet-black in color and had a spotlight mounted on the driver's side of the car.

"Can you even believe that," Sam screamed. "Damn it! We are sunk. Those no-good, drug- pushing bastards in that black pick-up must have got a hold of someone, and gave them a license-plate number of your father's car before they crashed, Deacon. They are in there talking to your father right now. Sum-bitch! We are what you call totally busted, man."

All Deacon could here was his heart pounding in his ear. He became petrified, "My dad is going to kill me."

"Crap," Zack cried out, hitting his fist on the dashboard. "They are going to hang us all. Period! We are all going to jail."

CHAPTER 6

In the summer of 2006, Michael & Erica Trainer decided to rent a small house on Bound's Circle in Westover, West Virginia. The house was absolutely, unconditionally, a perfect setting to raise Samuel and Anna. Samuel was now six years old and pretty well settled after being on a gluten-free diet, which is definitely saying something. Anna was four and had become a little chatter box, but she was still as cute as a button. Michael had acquired his professional survey certification and Erica was doing well with her job as a Psychologist at the Ruby Memorial Hospital. From the window of her office, she could see the West Virginia University Football Stadium. This was the place where she had attended a number of WVU football games. It certainly brought back a lot of memories. Erica remembered being a cheerleader, a flyer doing the air stunts, and casually dating a very attractive West Virginia University Mountaineer football player, who was the wide receiver and a captain of the team, Milton G. Underwood. She had been a cheerleader at Stockton High School at her home in Stockton, Pennsylvania. Milton was extremely big, strong and healthy, a six-footer, but wasn't the sharpest knife in the drawer. He was definitely lacking experience and was quite unsophisticated, but nonetheless a precious hunk of man. It was naïve of him to believe her when she said she loved him, because his family was rich, from Boston, Massachusetts, and he thought she was certainly taking advantage of that. He bought her sweaters and other paraphernalia, such as things needed for her cheerleading activity; equipment and shoes. There was absolutely no sex involved, not because he didn't want to try Erica on for size, but because she said no and meant it.

"Just forget it, Milton," Erica insisted, squeezing his cheek.

Erica had the best experience of her life, being a cheerleader for the 1996 WVU Mountaineer team. "Why not us... Why not now", was the rally call in 1996, the theme that fueled momentum in good times. Erica attended every game, their goal was to win and this was a year to remember. Coach Don Nehlen, who played his football at Bowling Green University as quarterback, before coaching at WVU, was in charge of the 1996 bunch, which represented West Virginia University in the 1996 NCAA Division 1-A football season. Along the way, fun was shaped, tears were shed and history was made on their journey to success, "Why not us...Why not now", was the cry of the entire cheering squad, and the thousands of students and fans, who were hungry for victory.

The Mountaineers' first game was called the "Back Yard Brawl" with Pittsburgh University, commonly known as just "Pitt". There whole season was measured by that game, and the result of the game was WVU 34-0 over Pitt, which was the biggest victory ever for West Virginia University. The defense was the best unit in WVU history. They went on to an 8-3 record, losing only to the Miami Hurricanes, Syracuse Orange and the Virginia Tech Hokies. WVU was invited to the Gator Bowl to play North Carolina on New Year's Day in Jacksonville, Florida. Unfortunately, they were defeated in the struggling battle with the Tar Heels.

Erica was so sad she cried the rest of that day and on the flight back home. Not only because they lost the game to North Carolina, but because West Virginia University throws the best victory parties in America. She also quit the cheerleading squad and dumped her wide receiver, Milton. Both had taken up too much of her time.

Michael Desmond Trainer was completely elated. Right on! He had finally passed the examination to acquire his West Virginia license and registration for land surveying. Amen. Now he would have been able to do certified surveys on properties and record them in the courthouse, which had in turn, also increased his salary at his workplace, Huge Structural & Home Improvement, owned by Howard Huge.

Samuel had started his school years at the Skyview Elementary in Westover, West Virginia, which was a brand new structure and was very pleasant for his parents and his grandparents, Judith and Thurston Beltow III (Mimi & Fuge).

"I'm so impressed with the school layout and the teachers we met are great. I think Samuel will certainly get a good education. I would sure like to see him get into the school band," Judy remarked.

"I believe they start them in the fifth or sixth grade at the University Middle School, for the band," Erica said. "We would like Samuel to do the trumpet."

"What about drums or a guitar?" Thurston questioned.

"Who rattled your chain, Thurston?" Judy said. "I'm sure Erica doesn't want Samuel banging on drums in their house, do you, Erica?"

"No way, are you kidding me, dad? Unless you want him to practice at your place."

"Yeah, right. You two are busted my chops! I'm new, but I'm not brand new, Erica."

"It's okay to let your children see you cry, Thurston," Judy said. "All you think about is getting Samuel on the golf course and getting him into Rock 'n Roll. He has plenty to do right now with school, so put a lid on that. Give it a rest."

CHAPTER 7

OLD DOORS CLOSE AND NEW ONES OPEN...

"Aright, let's get our stuff together, we'll just tell our story and hand over the money. No problem. Everything is cool, let's go," Sam said.

"In the name of the Father, the son, and..." Zack prayed.

All three of them walked into Fritz's, cool and slow. They all gave thumbs up to the Stop, Drop and Roll sign when they entered, which seemed to be the tradition when you walked into The Fritz. It sort of entertained people to no end. At the very first glance, they saw two uniformed officers sitting at a table. Calmly, Deacon saw his father standing behind the pay counter talking to his mother, Jennifer, who was working the cash register. Oh, Boy! Deacon walked up to them, while Sam and Zach hurried over and ducked into their favorite booth, adjacent to the officers. Deacon talked to his parents and then very smoothly, with a sway in his step, walked over and slipped into the booth.

"Everything is cool," Deacon said, showing excitement, and whispering so other people couldn't here. "My dad said that the Chief of Police and his two toads were there mooching a free lunch."

In unison, Sam & Zack gave a fist pump, and let out a rather silent cheer.

"What the Hell," Zack said. "That is so cool, we are now sitting pretty. All we have to do is read the papers tomorrow."

Just then, a man emerged out of the rest room, it was the Chief of Police, Anton Calabrese. He was a pasty, overweight and extraordinarily white man. He had on a pair of dress pants, a crisp white shirt without a tie and a wrinkled sports jacket. He sat down at the table with his two investigators, George Oliver, Chief Investigator for the Morgantown Police Department and Sparrow Alexander, the Assistant Investigator. George began bragging about his new outside grill, loud enough for the three of them to hear, acting like he was super serious. "My new 'Mega Meat-Monster 9000' is packing 100,000 BTUs and two side burners, the huge cooking space can feed an army."

Not to be outdone, the chief said, "Cute, I used to settle for 100,000 BTUs, also."

"What do you mean settle?" George questioned.

"My new 'Ginorma Gonza is crackin' 160 Gs of pure propane, it would make yours look like a toy!" the chief shouted, with a bit of laughter.

"Bite me, chief, and you're full of crap. You made that shit up." George replied. "I wonder what is happening out on I-68 east. That was one heck of a pile up out there, about ten cars. A pick-up veered into the grass median at a great speed and crashed into a manhole and blew it up. I guess there is nothing recognizable. There were possibly four people in the truck. Nothing left but the burnt end of a leather bag or suitcase and a double barreled shotgun near the passenger side of the car, everything else went to the ashes. The State Highway Patrol boys are taking care of it."

Sam and Zack did a quick high five, trying hard to hide their smiles. Keeping their voices low, Deacon said. "Is this crazy, or what? Nothing but the end of a leather bag or suitcase? This is totally unreal."

"No shit, Dick Tracy," Zack whispered, crossing him. "God is watching over us."

"We are definitely, now, out of the question, Deacon," Sam said, also crossing himself, "But we are not out of the dark yet, and there can be no smoke, without fire."

"What are you talking about, Sam?" Deacon whispered. "We are completely in the clear, aren't we?"

"Not entirely, Deacon," Sam said. "I'm thinking there is some kind of involvement with the law enforcement, especially those characters at that table, right there."

"Ya think?" Deacon asked.

"Oh my God, you are so right, Sam," Zack whispered. "My father says that he has heard things about the Morgantown Police Department…like… Anton Calabrese can't be trusted. He has been Chief of Police too long, thinks he is above the law."

Just then, the three law enforcement officers got up to leave, as the Chief ventured over to their booth and asked, "How are you boys doing this afternoon, staying out of trouble?"

"Oh, yes, Chief Calabrese," Sam said, smiling. "We have our band, and we have a gig at the community center at seven o'clock tonight."

"What's the name of your band?" Chief Calabrese asked.

"We're the 'Sam E. Tra Rock 'n Roll Band', Sam replied, keeping his smile. "Have you heard of us? We play old time Rock 'n Roll music."

"Not really, what does Sam E. Tra stand for?" Chief Calabrese inquired.

"It's short for my name, Samuel Earl Trainer."

"Well, I'm glad you don't play Heavy Metal… or Rap."

Zack jumped in and said, "The only think they left off of 'Rap' is the 'C', Mr. Calabrese."

"That is funny, 'Crap', I got it, and what's your name?" Chief Calabrese asked.

"My name is Zackery Taylor."

"Your father works at *Mylan* Pharmaceuticals, here in Morgantown. Am I right?"

"That's my father, Gregory," Zack replied. "He has worked there quite a few years, Mr. Calabrese."

Then looking over to Deacon, the Chief stated, "And you must be Francisco's son. The owner, I saw you talking to him earlier."

"Yup, I'm Deacon. My father really appreciates the fine job you are doing in Morgantown, keeping our town safe," Deacon answered, smiling faint smile on his face.

"I've tried to bring prosperity to this shithole town, and all I get in return is grief."

"Ah, yeah, grief. Got ya!" Deacon said, not really happy with that comment.

"OK, Boys. Nice talking to you," said the Chief, as he turned and walked directly out the door…without paying.

"Bastard," Sam blurted out.

"That son of a bitch," Zack said, almost yelling. "I got your shithole town, Chief, swinging."

"What a no-good prick," Deacon said. "That man needs to be busted… Damn."

"Guess what," said Zack. "My father was also talking about his sidekick, George Oliver, the big white haired, five foot nine, slob, who has had that Chief Investigator's job for too long. He also says Sparrow Alexander, the Assistant Investigating officer, with his shaggy head of dirty blonde hair, a rat tail mustache and his six-foot, 160 pound, raunchy body, is a total asshole."

"I like your dad, Zack," Sam laughed. "Why doesn't he say what he means to say?"

"Yeah, Zack," Deacon echoed, laughing and slapping his knee.

"This is the way I see it," Zack said. "You know the drug traffic and smuggling network. They work with corrupt police law enforcement in order to protect their trade. My guess is, those three toads are involved in that, how do you guys see it?"

"Freakin 'A' straight," Deacon answered. "Go figure."

"Creeps," Sam agreed.

"What time is it?" Sam asked.

"Five after two," Deacon said, looking at his Rolex.

"Where is Penelope Rose Daiquiri? I told her not to be late. She is starting to piss me off. I told her that we had a gig. We'll wait until quarter after. We're not going to play with this. She either wants in the band or not."

"We should just forget about her," Deacon said. "We're getting along just about fine."

"No way, Deacon," Zack said, "We need that base guitar and a female voice, and we also need someone that can do an organ. Sam can play a trumpet, and I can blow a saxophone, that is two woodwind instruments. We need to expand if we are going to stay alive in the music business, think about it."

"Zack's right, Deacon" Sam said. "You keep the rhythm with your systematic arrangement of musical sounds, get it! Everyone is important."

"Yeah, yeah, you're right...but, where is this girl?"

Before Deacon got that sass out, the front door opened and in stepped Penny, with what looked like two Hispanic or Puerto Rican dudes. She was definite the eye candy, at least between the three who gave thumbs up to the Stop, Drop and Roll sign. She had a wide beautiful smile and a top model's face; she was dressed in a tight sleeveless blouse and navy blue jeans. She was gorgeous and one look at her and you could tell she meant all business. The three approached the table and she pulled an extra chair over, while the two dudes stood. She was, fashionably, twenty minutes late and was hanging with her two friends.

"Hi," Penny said, showing her glowing white teeth. "Sorry I'm late, I am Penny, and these are my friends, Roberto "Weed" Fernandez and Mateo Martinez. Believe me, they're my only friends! We've seen your band play many times."

"Alright," Sam said. "I'm Sam Trainer, and these two complete the band, Zack Taylor and Deacon Fritz, I'm a little surprised that you brought your friends to this interview."

"These are the two that I have always jammed with, Weed, plays the piano or keyboard, and Mateo plays guitar, also does lighting and sound. I think the six of us could make it big time. You wanna give it a try? I can help with money to get everything started."

"We'll have to think that over, Penny," Sam said. "Why don't you give us a week or so?"

"Why a week, Sam, we know all of your songs, we'll do the gig with you, if we don't come up to your expectations, just throw us out. No pay!"

"I don't know, we have never even practiced together. "Sam said, looking for some help from Deacon and Zack. "What do you think?"

"I'm willing to give it a try, it might work; but if nothing ventured, nothing gained. It's as simple as that; what do you think, Deacon?" Zack said, with both arms outstretched.

"I definite don't like it," Deacon replied. "But let's do it, we do have some time to get set up. Maybe we can have a little practice session, alright?"

Everyone agreed and decided to meet at the Community Center at three o'clock. It was two thirty now.

"Pick up your instruments, Penny, and meet us there at three o'clock," Deacon said.

"We have our instruments with us, we're going there now."

Penelope Daiquairi drove a jet black Jeep Cherokee. It had charcoal grey interior with stitching and beautiful black and silver wheels. Weed and Mateo rode Harley Davidson Sportsters.

Once they all got to the Center, they set up, practiced for about two hours and later at seven o'clock, they brought the place down with their new look. Absolutely knocked their socks off. Everyone was excited, as they cheered and clapped. The "Sam E. Tra Rock 'n' Roll Band" was recreated and was definitely explosive. (Likely to shatter or burst with the music lovers)

CHAPTER 8

Penelope Rose Daiquairi was an only child; she had grown up in a Catholic environment and had enjoyed playing golf, which her mother, Mary Ann Daiquairi, taught her at the Pines Country Club, just off of Point Marion Drive. The Pines Country Club was just a stone's throw from where she was raised, on the corner of Anchor Avenue and Pinochle Way. Her father, Benjamin Franklin Daiquairi, was a very famous mass-tort litigation lawyer, working out in New York City, New York, and Washington, DC, extremely wealthy, dealing mostly with pharmaceutical companies. He was close friends with the President of the United States of America; both of them had one thing in common and that was that, they were "powerful and arrogant".

A tort, in common law jurisdictions, is a civil wrong that unfairly causes someone else to suffer loss or harm resulting in legal liability for the person who commits the tortious act, and is known as a tortfeasor. The victim of the harm can recover their loss as damages in a lawsuit, commonly referred to as the injured party. Of course, in order to prevail, the plaintiff must show that the actions, or in some cases, the lack of action, was the legally recognizable cause of the harm. Tort law is different from criminal law in that: (1) torts may result from negligent as well as intentional or criminal actions and (2) tort lawsuits have a lower burden of proof such as preponderance of evidence rather than beyond a reasonable doubt, indeed. Sometimes a plaintiff may prevail in a tort case even if the person who allegedly caused harm was acquitted in an earlier criminal trial, For example, a famous football player was acquitted in criminal court of murder but later found liable for the tort of wrongful death. Enough said.

Benjamin Franklin Daiquairi, known to his friends and associates as "Ben", was a powerful person with a heart of gold. He would come home on weekends, and sometimes invited friends and business associates, who wanted to try the "Pines Country Club".

Pines Country Club had filled up the void left by the closing of Morgantown Country Club. Its 18-hole championship course was laid out by pro designer Edmund Ault, and shaped by the rolling hills of West Virginia, This private golf club, incorporated in 1968, had officially opened to the shareholders in 1970, and Ben Daiquairi was one of the biggest shareholders. The Pines was considered to be the best golfing experience in the Morgantown area. In addition to its course, the Pines offered a driving range and putting green, a winter simulator, heated swimming pool, clubhouse facilities with lockers and showers, a restaurant, "The Clubhouse Grille", which serves lunch and dinner, and banquet facilities for special events.

Ben Daiquiri had attended The University of Law in London, United Kingdom, at 2 Bunhill Row. The Moorgate campus was brilliant. It was based right in the heart of the city and it was very fascinating to see what went within the magic circle of law firms, which was directly opposite the campus. Upon graduation, his father had loaned him approximately one-hundred and twenty million dollars, using which, he had built his fortune in the United States of America. He owned penthouse apartments in New York City, New York and Washington, DC.

Penelope had grown up in a different atmosphere, consisting of people much older than herself, such as her mom's golf friends and her dad's friends and associates. She had also done a lot of traveling, not just in the United States, but all over the World. Her family traveled a lot. She had met two Hispanic high teen boys in church, who sat at the 10 o'clock mass and made faces at her. She thought that they were so cute, that after mass she had asked them what the hell they were doing. Their names were Roberto and Mateo.

"You just looked so cute with your fancy clothes, setting with your powerful looking father and your gorgeous mother. We thought we would try entertaining you," Roberto said, with his arms outstretched.

"We didn't mean to offend you, but you were just too pretty, we're sorry," Mateo said.

"I'm not offended," Penny laughed. "I was quite entertained. Where do you two live?"

"We live at Country Squire Mobile Homes Park. We have off road quads, trail bikes, and street Harley Davidson Sportsters. You should come and see us sometime. We live with our parents who make us come to church with them. Keep us holy!" Mateo said, doing a high five with Roberto.

"I just may do that, you have an iPhone? I'll text you."

"I have a Galaxy S7," Roberto replied. "555-944-4444, and my friends call me 'Weed'."

"The 4's be with you, Samsung G57," Penny chuckled, covering her laugh. "And Weed?"

"Yeah right," Mateo said. "That is hilarious; we do call him 'Weed'."

They all had a good laugh; Penny put the number in her iPhone 7 that she had just purchased at Verizon. She said goodbye and later became best friends with *Roberto "Weed" Fernandez and Mateo Martinez.*

CHAPTER 9

It was eight o'clock the morning after the gig, and Sam had just picked up the Sunday paper. The top two articles were about an off-duty policeman being shot many times and a huge traffic accident on I-68 east. The first article in The Dominion Post read:

Off Duty Police Officer Shot

An off-duty Morgantown police officer was found dead on Barrowby Road, at the top of Log Cabin Road yesterday. The body of Sergeant Earnest Maxwell of the Morgantown Police Department was identified by Chief Investigator George Oliver, who stated that Maxwell was apparently in the process of digging a shallow grave. The investigators also found markings of a body having been dragged to the grave site from a Cadillac Escalade SUV that was parked on Barrowby Road. After Maxwell's murder, the anonymous murderer dragged the body, and carried it from the crime scene into another vehicle, which seemed to have left in a hurry because of the rubber burn marks on the road.

The chief of police, Anton Calabrese had no explanation about what had happened. He said that Sgt. Maxwell had served in the Vietnam War and was a veteran. Some of his fellow police officers said that he was suffering from a condition referred to as Posttraumatic Stress Disorder, commonly referred to as PTSD. He was told that people who suffer from this condition often relive the experiences through nightmares and flashbacks, and it significantly impairs the person's daily life. Sgt. Maxwell was never considered getting help or to receive treatment. An ongoing investigation is continuing to find more information about the shooting.

Sam couldn't believe what he was reading. He thought: *Holy crap* Calabrese thought Maxwell was digging a shallow grave and burying a body. Maxwell was actually a police officer; probably a corrupt one, working for Chief Calabrese. He was probably a money pick-up toad that got greedy, and was temporarily digging a hole to bury that huge leather duffle bag of stolen money, and planning on a very comfortable and rich retirement.

Sam had to get hold of Deacon and Zack. Meanwhile, He had to read that other article about the car pileup on I-68 east. The second article in The Dominion Post read:

Ten car pileup on I-68

Yesterday, around about noon, a ten-car pileup occurred on eastbound I-68 east. An eyewitness told John Tate of the West Virginia State Highway Patrol that he saw two vehicles racing side-by-side right in front of him. The cars were recognized as a huge, black Ford pick-up with dark tinted windows and a new car on the inside lane. Whoever was driving the car on the inside lane slammed on its brake and the pick-up veered left onto the grass median, hit something and exploded into flames. It appears that another driver was quick on the brakes and got rear-ended, which slid his car sideways blocking both lanes, which caused a huge chain reaction of havoc behind the car, involving several vehicles.

The Morgantown Fire Department arrived and doused the flames of what was left of the pick-up wreckage. Four unidentified bodies were in the trashed pick-up, three men and one woman. The bodies were burned beyond recognition. On the passenger side of the car, lying in the grass was a double-barreled shotgun and the remains of a burnt suitcase or bag and traces of burnt money. Other eyewitnesses, who were traumatized, shell-shocked and dumb struck, could not identify the vehicle that was racing with the pick-up. The vehicle, maybe a new Nissan, sped away. An ongoing investigation is in progress to find more information about the accident.

After reading the article, Sam sent a text message to Deacon and Zack: "Say nothing on text…need to meet today at Fritz's…10pm…"

Deacon texted: "K."

Zack texted: "K."

Sam thought: *This is the weirdest thing* First of all, that man digging in the woods turns out to be a corrupt cop, who the authorities think was digging a shallow grave, also impaired by the Vietnam War. Secondly, there is no clue of us being anywhere near the I-68 east crap, and finally, they had a bag full of money. They needed to check that duffel bag. They needed to get it out of that crawl space before my dad finds it by mistake. They needed to count the money.

Sam backed his van up to the garage of his mom and dad's attractive split level home situated on a mountain in the forest near Coopers Rock on the beautiful Laurel Drive, actually in Bruceton Mills, West Virginia, He unloaded the band equipment in the garage because he had school in the morning at the University High School, in Monongalia County. Sam and his sister Anna were allowed to maintain their schooling in Monongalia County, although their residence was in Preston County. The only reason behind this was that they had started their education in Monongalia County, and the Board of Education had therefore allowed them to continue further. Another week and they would be starting their summer vacations. Thank God! His sister Anna was staying overnight at a friend's house, and his mom and dad had gone to pick up some groceries and later have some lunch. He walked around to the back of the house and opened the door to the crawl space, looked inside and got into a total panic.

"What the fuck!" Sam cried out.

The huge leather duffle bag was gone. Standing up and looking all around the back yard, he absolutely couldn't believe what was happening.

"Who in the hell would take that sum-bitch."

CHAPTER 10

THE BEST IS YET TO COME...

Sam was still traumatized when he saw some text messages from his friends and thought: *I told those idiots* No Texting.

But when he looked at the ID, it was from his dad, Mike.

Mike had texted: "Sam...I don't know what the hell you had in that huge bag in the crawl space, but I had to get in there to check a pipe. I moved that heavy son of a bitch to the tool shed."

"Oh my God, Thank you, Dad," Sam yelled, as he sped over to the tool shed. "There you are. You big, beautiful bag of money!"

Sam looked inside to make sure everything was intact and dragged that heavy son of a bitch around to the front of the house, and somehow hoisted into the back of the van. It was twenty minutes until ten and Sam jumped in the van and got on his way to Fritz's. He got onto I-68 west heading west. His plan was to go on I-68 west, to I-79 north, get off the Westover exit, cut across Westover to Beechhurst avenue and over to Fritz's on Clay Street. He was cruising at around seventy mph as he passed the Cheat Lake exit and two motorcycles and a huge red dump truck came on to I-68 west, and began following Sam. The two motorcycles honked at Sam as they passed quickly and the red dump truck started to pass and when it was alongside Sam, it veered right, hitting the driver's side door of Sam's truck and forced him off the road.

"You asshole," Sam cried out, as he careened into a bank spun around and went backwards down a storm gutter for about one hundred yards. He was unhurt, having his seat belt on, but he was mighty pissed. He got out of the van and saw the red truck disappear. About fifteen seconds later the two motorcycles were back. It was weed and Mateo, Penny's two friends.

"You okay?" Weed asked, putting his arm around Sam's waist, holding him up.

"I'm alright; you have any idea who that was?" Sam asked, as a State Police car pulled up and the trooper was now coming over.

"My God," said the trooper. "I'm Sgt. John Tate. You alright? I've never seen anything like this before, your van slid about a hundred yards, backwards! Did you just run off the road, do you need an ambulance?"

"No," Sam said, "A big red dump truck forced me off, hit the door of my van. He kept going. These are two of my friends that stopped by to help."

"Come and get in the cruiser, I need to make a report and call a wrecker. What is that suitcase in the back?"

"Just some clothes and equipment from gym, I'm a senior at University High School."

"We Know Liam Hercules, the manager at Rockefeller Towing Services, he'll come right over," Mateo informed trooper Tate. "We can call him."

Rockefeller Towing Services was owned by Liam Hercules's cousins, Seth and Ethan Rockefeller, who were attorneys in their self-established Law Firm, Rockefeller and Rockefeller. They owned a shitload of property in Morgantown, WV. They let Liam completely run the towing and designer body shop, but they were in charge of the money and paid him a fruitful salary. Liam just loved running the business and making daily bank deposits in the Rockefeller account.

"Alright, as long as you're friends with him, I need to ask Sam some questions. Thanks."

"No problem Sgt. Tate," Mateo responded, as he punched in Liam's number.

"I've got to do a text, to my friend, alright, Officer Tate? I have to let him know what has happened," Sam said. He began texting Deacon: "Wrecked my van…get over to Rockefeller Towing Services and pick up the duffle bag out of the back…wait for it."

The report took about ten minutes and Sgt. Tate asked Sam if he had a ride.

"Those two will give me a ride." Sam said, pointing at weed and Mateo.

"OK, I'll hang around until the wrecker gets your van out of here; take it easy on those Harley's. This is a speedy highway. Be careful."

"Thanks, Sgt. Tate," Weed said, as he told Sam that he knows the guy in the red truck and he will tell him about it when they get to Fritz's.

They mounted weed's Sportster as Sam put on the extra helmet and prepared himself for the wildest ride in his life.

When they arrived at Fritz's they went in the front door, put thumbs up to the Stop, Drop and Roll sign and sat at their favorite booth. Weed and Mateo ordered a couple of beers.

"Sorry sweetie, no beer until one o'clock on Sunday, you know that," Tina said, who was the sweetest waitress ever and an absolute eye candy, winking at Weed and Mateo, looking for a big tip.

"Now," Sam asked Weed, "Who was that sucker in the red truck?"

"Well, this is the whole nine yards, Sam," Weed said, being a little nervous.

"I'll bet!"

"That man was my brother-in-law, Briccio Cadmen Donovan, he's married to my (*ten year*) older sister, Cleopatra Fernando Donovan, from Fairmont, West Virginia, and who is the baddest motherfucker that's ever existed. The sad part is that if you go after him, he will find some way to legally kill you. He is shaved bald and as strong as an ox, and has mean tats all over his body. He belongs to the Aryan Brotherhood which was founded by two white supremacists, Mills and Bingham in 1964 at the San Quentin state prison. Anyhow, the gang's founding fathers were Irish-American bikers who adopted a three-leaf clover as their official symbol. I believe he deals drugs or protects the one's that do (*partners*). The talent is in the choices, man. I wouldn't mess with him. Have your insurance fix your vehicle and forget about it. Unknown driver, get it."

"But that asshole tried to kill me," Sam said. "He should pay for my van, but I sure don't want anything to do with those skinheads."

"He does things without thinking, he's nuts, give it a rest and put it to bed, please, Sam."

"I will, thank you, Weed, now where are those toads, Deacon and Zack? They were supposed to be here, come on."

As Mateo had begun getting comfortably settled in the booth with his legs crossed, Penny Rose Daiquiri walked in through the door, did a thumbs up to the sign, Stop, Drop and Roll, and walked into the Sports Bar. She carried herself like someone who was completely in charge and she certainly had people's attention. She looked at Sam with her palms up as if to say, "What are you doing with my friends?"

"Ooooh, boy," Sam said, "Wuz sappening, Penny. I would guess that you want to know what the hell is going on, am I right?"

"That would probably be my next question."

"Well, to begin with, my van got trashed out on I-68 west, someone ran me off the road, Weed and Mateo came along and rescued me from the State Police, on their Harley's. My van was towed to Rockefeller wrecking by Liam Hercules, and Zack and Deacon are picking up my things out of the van. What else do you need to know?"

"Is your van totaled?"

"Don't know yet, we're waiting for Zack and Deacon to come back," Sam answered, winking at Penny.

"You have something in your eye, Sam. Why are you winking at me?"

"Just a reaction I guess. Thought you needed a wink."

"That is hilarious, I'm just messing with you, Sam, I totally love all you guys. So what happens if your van is a total, I think it's time to change the name of the band anyway, how do you see it, Sam?"

"Change it to what?" Sam asked with a question mark on his face.

"I'm thinking, something like 'No Two Ways', under that, 'Rock 'n Roll Band'."

"You mean 'No Two Ways… About It'?"

"No, just 'No Two Ways', period."

"How about we wait for Zack and Deacon, and then vote on it?" Sam bargained.

"Okay," Penny agreed.

Zack and Deacon soon walked in through the door, gave the thumbs up to the Stop, Drop and Roll sign, and walked over

"I guess we're all here now," Deacon said, scratching his head.

"Are we all having a meeting?" Zack asked, looking at Sam, and then Penny.

"Yes," Said Penny, "Sam wants to vote on something."

"Wasn't exactly my idea, Penny," Sam thought, and then said, "We might change the name of the band. What did Liam say about the van, Deacon?"

"Total," said Deacon, crossing himself,

"Trashed everything underneath…Complete total, Liam already contacted your insurance. You'll have to deal with them," Zack said.

"All they give you is Blue Book value if you're a total. My van is ten years old and the value is zilch," Sam said. "My question is, how are we going to haul our equipment?"

"I have the solution for everything, if you let me have the new name painted on the sides of the new van I can provide, we'll have a deal." Penny said.

"That's not fair, it sounds like blackmail to me," Zack said.

"What name are we proposing? I'm in agreement about the van, Penny?"

"No Two Ways," Sam replied, "And the more I hear it, the better I like it."

"Let's take a vote on the name of the band, and the new van. Just say aye or nay. I say aye."

"Zack?"

"Aye."

"Deacon?"

"Nay." Deacon said. "We should think about it, it might be a bad move."

"Weed?"

"Aye."

"Mateo?"

"Aye."

"Penny?"

"Aye."

"The ayes have it," Sam called out. "We are now the 'No Two Ways', 'Rock 'n Roll Band'."

"Sam, just come over at my place, it's a 2010 Mercedes Cargo Van, we can change the title and registration tomorrow at the Three A's, we'll put it in your name, Sam. Okay?!"

"Fine by me, Penny," Sam said.

"I'm crazy about it," Zack said. "What a feeling, what a rush, I'm ecstatic and overwhelmingly happy."

"Why don't you say what you mean, Zack," Deacon said. "I'm happy too."

Sam told Penny that he, Zack and Deacon, would stop at her house at about 6pm to see the van and talk about how they were going to handle things.

They all hi-fived each other and went in different directions. Sam called Deacon and Zack over for a private talk.

"Did you two pick up the leather Duffle out of my van, Deacon?" Sam asked.

"What leather duffle?" Deacon asked.

"We grabbed your things out of the glove compartment when Liam said the van was a total, is that what you mean?" Zack questioned.

"You two better be freakin' kidding me!" Sam yelled.

CHAPTER 11

Growing up on Bounds Circle in Westover, West Virginia was a Gods-send for Samuel and Anna Trainer. They rode their bikes everywhere, completely safe because of the very little traffic. Their house became the playground of the neighborhood because it had a huge backyard. Michael, their father, had built and installed a large sand box with a canvas tarp overhead to protect them from the sun, a swing set and had brought an assortment of yard games. He made an outdoor chalkboard, which was a fun outdoor activity for the kids! It was a complete collection of weather-proof materials!

"Our family has certainly grown since we rented this house, Erica," Mike said, as he swept his arm across the back yard to indicate the number of kids.

"I look at it like this," Erica replied, "We now buy the Super Giant box of Popsicles and tons of snacks constantly. It's a good thing we do our shopping at Sam's Club. We save a huge amount of money buying everything in gross amounts. You fix everything, including their bikes and whatever else breaks. I can tell that you love all of those kids and it seems that you are in a much more settled mood since you have obtained your state license for surveying, and you never complain about your carpentry work anymore. You're a good man, Michael Desmond Trainer."

"Anna is the sweetest thing," Mike said. "She's six years old and starting first grade and very brilliant. She pretty much privy's herself to be in charge of all of these kids. Sort of in control, and the best part, they all love her."

"Our children get only one childhood, Mike," Erica said. "Anna is fine."

"Well, I've learned to pay off our Visa credit card every month, sometimes it's quite a stretch to cover everything," Mike cried, wiping his eyes as if he were crying.

"It's okay to get angry with God, Michael," Erica laughed. "He can take it. Everything can change in the blink of an eye, we are doing better than most of our friends. There's nothing to worry about."

"I certainly frame every so-called disaster with these collective words," Mike barked, as he flipped a lit cigarette over the fence. "Five years from now, will this matter?"

"You better start putting those ciggies out, Mike, you're going to set something on fire someday," Erica said, as she mocked him throwing a butt and saying. "Poof!"

Mike busted out laughing and said, "You are a comedian. That just isn't going to happen."

"When it comes to you, Mike, resistance is futile, just put those cigarettes out before you get yourself in trouble. It hasn't rained in a month and a single spark in that dry grass could end up burning down someone's house." Erica said, leaving for the kitchen.

"You better not be saying things under your breath, Michael," Erica yelled through the screen door in the kitchen. "You're jumping on my last nerve!"

Mike thought to himself: "She must think I was born yesterday. I was born at night, but not last night! I'm new but I'm not brand new! That's what my father-in-law, Thurston Beltow, would say. As a matter of fact, Thurston and I need to get busy teaching Samuel golf. Samuel is in the third grade now and bringing home excellent grades. Indeed!"

"Erica, come out here, I want to tell you something funny that Samuel was telling me."

“This ought to be good,” Erica said, as she came out and sat on the porch to listen.

“He told me that his teacher, Mrs. Wilkins, was telling the class that the topic for that day would be ‘well-known facts’.”

Samuel said the kids were coming up with things like: “The Nile River is the longest river in the world”, and like, “Dolphins are mammals, and although they live in water, they breathe air.”

Well, Samuel came up with this: “The best way to stop a vampire is to stake it in the heart.”

The teacher looked at him like she had worms crawling out of her ears.

“Whaaaat?” **Everyone** knows that!” Samuel replied.

“It’s enough to make a cat bark,” Mrs. Wilkins said, and busted out laughing. “I’m sorry, Samuel, I didn’t mean to laugh. But that was just too funny.”

Samuel finished by telling his Dad, “Teachers are strange, sometimes they don’t know what they want!”

“And you thought that was funny?” Erica asked, as she went back to the kitchen without laughing.

“I actually laughed for two days,” Mike said, as he busted out laughing again.

“You are sick, Michael.”

CHAPTER 12

"Wow, take it easy, Sam." Deacon said. "We put the leather bag in Zack's trunk. Why the hell was it in your van anyhow? We thought it was in the crawlspace back at your place."

"What would you think the worst thing that could happen? I almost crapped my pants when I looked inside and the duffle bag was gone. That completely knocked my socks off. Just then my iPhone began going off. It was my father telling me that he had found the duffle bag in the crawlspace when he was in the process of checking a pipe. He didn't open it and look inside. He thought it was mine and pulled it out of the crawlspace and dragged it to the toolshed. I was panicked and my thought was that we had to find another place to hide it; I dragged it to the driveway in the front and threw it in the back of my van. I was on my way here to Fritz's when Weed and Mateo passed me on their Harley's and waved. Then some asshole in a red dump truck ran me off the road. Weed and Mateo saw what happened and came back."

"Who the hell ran you off the road, Sam?" Deacon asked in a rather concerned tone.

"We'll hunt them down and beat their asses, how does that sound?" Zack said angrily.

"Weed told me that the man in the dump truck was his brother-in-law, Whatdyacallem? Something Donovan? He said he was the scariest sum-bitch that ever existed. Married to Weed's older sister, I think her name is Cleopatra. Weed said Donovan's head is shaved; he has a lot of tattoo designs, and belongs to some Aryan Brotherhood which was founded by two white supremacists at the San Quentin state prison. I am not messing with any skinheads, Zack. Weed said that his brother-in-law would kill me in a minute, just deal with the insurance."

"That sucks," Zack exclaimed. "He can't just kill you."

"I wouldn't bet on it," Deacon said. "I've heard of Briccio Cadmen Donovan. He is one of those untouchable drug lords."

"This may sound stupid," Sam said, looking seriously at Zack and Deacon, "I think we should let Penny in on everything that has happened, about the money and all. She may be able to help us. Growing old certainly beats the alternative of dying young. If we continue messing with these corrupt law enforcement officers and these completely insane drug dealers, we are positively going to die."

"That's crazy," Deacon replied. "Seems to me the way things are developing, absolutely no one knows we have that money, you know, finders…keepers."

"Things can change in the blink of an eye, Deacon," Zack said. "We better go with what Sam is saying. Penny or her father could probably come up with something sensible. Besides, we can't turn that money over to the police or the drug dealers without being executed on the spot."

They all got into Zack's 57' Chevy convertible and drove over to Penny's house. They pulled up to the six-car garage on the Daiquiri Estate at the end of Anchor Avenue.

Penny came out of the house and greeted them and said, "I know the drinking age is 21 and above, but do you guys want a beer or something?" Penny asked. "I'm sure all of you drink beer."

"I'll have one," Zack said, wiping his lip. "That would taste good right now."

"Ditto," Deacon said. "Thought you would never ask."

"Don't forget me, I actually have to go to school tomorrow, but piss on that. Damn right. I'll take one. I hate turning down beer."

Sam said, as he grabbed a Coors Light out of the twelve pack, and thought: *"I'm not letting Penny think that I'm a wimp."*

Sam informed Penny that Zack and Deacon were going to attend WVU in the fall. "Both of them were going into the School of Law, with the hopes of becoming Attorneys."

"I will certainly see you both there because that is where I am going too," Penny replied. She was eighteen years old. She was very brilliant. "What about you, Sam?

"I'm thinking Attorney, but my father is fighting me. He wants me as a Civil Engineer.

"That's terrible," said Penny, as she moved into the garages and invited the three of them in. She grabbed the remaining Coors Lights and handed three more of them to the guys and popped one open for herself.

"I suppose you guys want to see the van I was talking about; it's a Mercedes-Benz Sprinter 2500 Luxury Mobile Office."

The three of them followed her down about three doors. Holy crap! They were looking at a 2010 Mercedes-Benz Sprinter Cargo Van, with a high roof and it looked like it was a six passenger with plenty of cargo space.

"This is out of control," Zack yelled. "Jet black, and look at those wheels. This is really dynamite."

"You aren't kidding us, are you, Penny?" Deacon asked, smiling and his eyes were wide open.

"I'm having 'No Two Ways…Rock 'n Roll Band' painted on both sides tomorrow, probably on those tinted windows. Sam and I are going to the three A's after school tomorrow and take care of the license and registration. I'm just as excited about all of this as you three, I am totally elated. I'm thinking that our band is going to go to the top. We can all work on some of our own music and lyrics. We can all do our studying at the 'WVU Collage of Law' and keep up with our band activities. No problem! All our parents will be happy, we will get our educations and at the same time do some gigs. Sam will be finished at University High School in a matter of time and then he can join us at the WVU School of Law."

"We'll see," Sam said. "You are a complete genius, Penny. Listen! Zack, Deacon and I need to bring up something that is a major concern to the three of us and we believe that you may be able to help us, Penny. Yesterday, the three of us were golfing at the Pines Country Club,"

"My favorite," Penny replied. "I'm sure that you three didn't know that I am an excellent golfer."

"Beats the crap out of me," Zack said. "You are just full of surprises."

"Go on, Sam," Penny said.

"Well, on the third hole, Deacon, on his second shot, hooked his ball into the woods and thinking he could probably hit his ball out of there, we went to look for it. Zack was looking next to the 'Butt-Hole Road' and he spotted something going on in the woods. Oh, I'm sorry, Penny, I meant the Barrowby Road."

"We call it 'Butt-Hole Road'. I didn't know that road had an actual name. We thought that it was just an old logging road; go on with your story."

"Anyhow, the three of us went to investigate, and these three dudes ran and jumped into a black pick-up and left there like a bat out of hell. On a closer look, those three thugs had shot a man who was digging a hole to bury something. There was a huge leather duffle bag that Zack looked into, and the sum-bitch was full of money, a shit pot full of money. Go figure. Deacon grabbed the bag and looked and started to panic saying, "Okay, leave everything and let's get the hell out of here!" There was also a Cadillac SUV on the road where the black pick-up peeled out and roared away. There was a trail from the SUV where the man dragged the leather money bag."

"We figured that we couldn't leave the money, because our finger prints were all over it, and hoped that those thugs hadn't gotten a good look at us. We carried the leather bag so we wouldn't leave a trail. We got back to the clubhouse, threw our clubs in Deacon's dad's car, the leather bag in the back seat, and just got the hell out of there, and headed for Fritz's."

"Were you going to turn it over to the police?" Penny asked.

"That's not the end to the story, Penny. On the way to Fritz's, the Black pick-up picked up our trail and began following us, actually wanting to kill us so as to take the money. Deacon, in an attempt to lose those suckers, zoomed over and went on the ramp for I-79 south.

"And the pick-up continued following you?"

"Tailgating, I mean tailgating, he was right up our ass. Deacon cut off on I-68 east and was driving about eighty or eighty five mph, just before the Cheat Lake exit and the pick-up pulled up like it was going to pass, but the passenger window rolled down and Deacon was looking at a double–barreled shotgun. In a panic, I told Deacon to slam on the break, which he jumped on it and started total havoc behind us. The black pick-up, probably because of the driver's shock, veered off to the left across the grass median and somehow crashed and burned."

"I heard about that crash and traffic tie-up," Penny said in disbelief, "So what else happened?"

"We were thankfully unhurt and I told Deacon to continue, get off at Coopers Rock exit, and go to my parent's house."

"You didn't wait for the police?" Penny asked.

"Hell no," yelled Sam. "We were scared shitless and how would we explain the duffle bag full of money?"

"Quite an experience, what did you think I could do to help?"

"That is not the end of the story either; our lives are still in danger."

"How's that, Sam?"

"We have reason to believe that the Morgantown Police Department is involved in these drug dealings, at least the top crust, Chief Anton Calabrese, Chief Investigator George Oliver and Sparrow Alexander. The man that was digging on Barrowby Road to bury the leather bag, Sgt. Earnest Maxwell, was also a police officer. They said he was digging a shallow grave to bury a body, and the body turned up missing. We believe that the police made up that story. We believe that Sgt. Maxwell was a bagman picking up the corrupt law enforcement protection payoff and got greedy. Probably was looking for a nice retirement. How do you see it, Penny?"

"Getting interesting, my father says that he suspects that there is some hanky-panky is going on because there are no convictions for drug distribution, trafficking and manufacturing in all of Monongalia County, targeting corrupt law enforcement dealings."

"And that is just the tip of the iceberg, Penny," Deacon stated, giving a sign of someone slashing their throats. "There is a lot more than that involved."

"So, tell me more, Deacon."

"Not only are the police involved, but Sam just had a run-in with that totally unforgiving piece of crap, Briccio Cadmen Donovan, who lives and owns almost everything in Fairmont, West Virginia. He is married to weed's older sister, Cleopatra. He is the worst sum-bitch that ever existed. The sad part is that if you go after him, he will find some way to legally kill you. He is shaved bald and as strong as an ox, and has meaningful Tattoo designs. He belongs to the Aryan Brotherhood which was founded by two white supremacists, Mills and Bingham in 1964 at the San Quentin state prison."

Well, this is the way I see it," Penny replied, "My gut feeling is that you three of you have found yourselves in a dangerous situation. Thanks for letting me in on this action.

At that exact moment, Sam received an anonymous text on his iPhone. It read: "I know what you punks did…you know what I want, punks…I'm coming to see…sooner or later."

CHAPTER 13

"What the hell does he mean by sooner or later? This is unbelievable. We just brought up about that character Donovan; he's already tried to kill me. I think there is more to this. I truly believe that Donovan is one of the drug lords in charge of the drug cartel stretching from Pittsburgh, Pennsylvania to Charleston, West Virginia, with the I-79 corridor as their avenue of delivering drug paraphernalia.

A drug cartel is any criminal organization that operates with the intention of supplying drug trafficking operations. They range from loosely managed agreements among various drug traffickers to formalized commercial enterprises. The term was applied when the largest trafficking organizations reached an agreement to coordinate the production and distribution of cocaine. Since that agreement was broken up, drug cartels are no longer cartels, but the term stuck and it is now popularly used to refer to any criminal organization that is related to narcotics.

The basic structure of a drug cartel is as follows:

Falcons (Spanish: *Halcones*): Considered the "eyes and ears" of the streets.

Hitman (Spanish: *Sicarios*): The armed group of the drug cartel.

Lieutenants (Spanish: *Lugartenientes*): The second highest position in the drug cartel.

Drug Lords (Spanish: *Capos*): The highest position in any drug cartel.

It is worth noting that there are other operating groups within the drug cartels. For example, the drug producers and suppliers, although not considered in the basic structure, are critical operators of any drug cartel, along with the financiers and the money launderers. In addition, the arms suppliers operate in a completely different circle, and are not considered parts of the cartel's logistics.

"What the hell, Sam, I didn't realized that Donovan was involved with your hit and run on I-68 west, you say he was driving the dump truck?" Penny asked, trying to calm Sam down.

"That's what Weed told me, Donovan is Weed's brother-in-law, and all of this is eerie. That's what we were trying to catch you up with. I had the huge duffle Bag in my van when I was forced off the road; I convinced the State police officer that the bag contained my gym clothes and equipment. Luckily, he believed me. I texted Deacon and Zack and they picked it up at Liam Hercules's place. The bag is now in Zack's trunk outside. We're trying to think of a place where we can hide it."

"No problem, we can hide it in my gun safe that holds all of my shotguns and rifles, I'll give all of you the combination. That gun case weighs half a ton, no one can move it."

"Sounds good, Penny," Zack replied, as they all went out and carried the duffle to a storage room in the garage and lifted it into the huge steel safe.

"I'll just give you three keys to the safe, the keys work to open the safe without the combination," Penny said, as she handed them the keys. "Sam, I will pick you up tomorrow after school. Give me a time?"

"Two thirty, I'll be in the parking lot. Text me if you don't see me. Here's my number", said Sam, as he handed her a card with the name of the band.

"You'll have to change the name of the band on your cards, Sam," Penny laughed.

"Yup," Sam agreed.

"I'll think about the mess you guys got yourselves into. I'll come up with something. Bye."

They heard a couple of motor cycles outside the garage, it sounded like big Harley Davidson's, for sure. They stepped outside and saw Weed and Mateo, Weed turned his bike's roar down and Mateo followed. As Weed put his kickstand down, he motioned for Sam to come over and said, "I have something important to tell you guys."

"What's happening, Weed?" Sam asked, waiting for the two of them to dismount.

"Let's go inside. You aren't going to believe this, I was talking to my sister, Cleopatra, after Mateo and I left Fritz's, and she said that her husband, Donovan, was really upset. She told me about Anton Calabrese being involved in the payoffs for police protection on the drug dealings that were going down and that The Chief was trying to stiff him. The corrupt group including him, Oliver and Alexander wanted some more payoff money, like double the amount. She said Donovan agreed but told her that he was going to get that son of a bitch, and he meant destroy him."

"Why do I believe, without a shred of doubt, that he would kill the Chief of Police of Morgantown, West Virginia?" Zack asked, holding his palms out.

"I would guarantee that, Zack." Deacon said. "He would kill him within a minute."

"What else?" Sam asked.

"Cleo said that she was in the office of one of the business buildings that Donovan owned in Fairmont, West Virginia, away from the front door when Officer Sgt. Earnest Maxwell came for the collective payoff for the police protection. He brought his sex-kitten younger wife, Tracy, who probably screws anything that walks. She was flirting and being, how would you say, *promiscuous*, having sexual relations with a number of partners. Anyway, she said Lucas Martini, one of Donovan's drug cartel lieutenants, was going to have his way with her. Tracy was drunk and out of control, jerked away from Lucas, fell and cracked her head hard on the sharp edge of a table. Cleopatra heard Lucas say, 'She's dead'. And then she also heard Sgt. Maxwell say, 'You killed her, you bastard'."

"Go on," Sam said, listening very intently.

"Meanwhile, Sgt. Maxwell pulled out his concealed weapon and held it on Lucas and his two hitmen, Rocco and Derrick, who he told to remove their weapons and throw them in the corner, as he removed Lucas's Glock 43 pistol and tossed it with the others. There was a huge leather transport bag, apparently filled with money, and he ordered them to drag it out front and put it in his Cadillac. He then told them to lie on their stomachs. He ran out the door and left. Cleo said she was curious about all the commotion, came out of the back office, and as she stepped into the front room, she ask, 'What the fuck is going on?' Lucas lied and said, 'That son of a bitch took all that money that we were transporting, and killed his wife; she's on the floor, over there. Cleo told them they better find him, kill him and get that money back there. She also told them, 'Get that piece of shit whore out of here. Dump her somewhere.' She told them that the three of them were making her sick and that Donovan would probably kick their asses."

"This is unbelievably crazy," Sam said, shaking his head.

"This is awful," Penny said. "My dad never trusted that upper crust in the Morgantown police department. Now we know he was right. Go ahead, Weed!"

"Lucas and the two hitmen grabbed their Glock 43's off the floor and threw Tracy in the truck with them. Rocco stuck a tracking device under Sgt. Maxwell's SUV and they could follow him with his iPhone. They followed him to the top of Log Cabin Road where they found him trying to bury the huge leather bag, Shot him numerous times, heard someone coming and apparently took off without the money transport bag. That is when they wrecked on I-68 east. Apparently, everything was destroyed."

"We heard about that accident on I-68 east," Penny sighed.

"Cleo said that Donovan still thinks that somehow Chief

Calabrese took the money and made up that story about Sgt. Maxwell digging a shallow grave and someone took the body. And guess what, his wife's body was found in the, crash and burned, black pick-up on I-68 east. Donovan doesn't believe the money was in the truck since the end of the bag found there was too small. The large leather transport bag contained two and a half million dollars."

"Holy crap," Sam exclaimed. "Two and a half million dollars?!"

"That's right," Weed said. "Cleo also stated that her husband, Donovan, received a text from an anonymous person saying that there may be others involved in this big money chase. Golfers!"

CHAPTER 14

It was May 23, 2018. George Oliver, the Chief Investigator for the Morgantown Police Department, had asserted that the Morgantown police officers were definitely keeping their town safe. Not to say that bad things never happened in Morgantown, West Virginia...for plenty of things did happen every day, since it was a college town. Morgantown was no Mayberry. Believe it...there are no more Mayberry's in West Virginia. Drugs bring on violent crime because of the need for a fix. The pushers have no care and the drugs for a short period of time are free, until users are addicted. Parents were watching TV channels involving food, golf, basketball, football, baseball or whatever they were into, such as, sitcoms, reality shows and reruns, but when it comes to the needs of their kids in a town full of addicted citizens, they have their heads completely up their ass. Now the constant attack on police officers makes everyone sick, but what is the bottom line in Morgantown? The upper crust may be unconditionally corrupt starting with the Chief of Police, Anton Calabrese, Chief Investigator, George Oliver, and Sparrow Alexander, assistant investigator.

George Oliver had served some time for illegal dealings before he became a Morgantown police officer and seemed grateful that he was promoted to Chief Investigator. He once gave an inspiring speech at a city council function, which was attended by about three hundred people. The speech read:

Mayor Conway, councilman, fellow police officers, and those

attending… I'm concerned about all the verbal attacks on the Morgantown Police Department and on the police officers that are serving this city. Look out of your houses' windows and tell me what you see! Do you see chaos? No you don't! Why is that? I'll tell you why. It's because of the men and women that get out of bed and put on the uniform that may not allow them to come home. They swore to protect and to serve their community. They are Law Enforcement Officers. Hey, listen, I haven't always been on the right side of the law. Other police officers despise me for some of the dumbass things I've done. And to be honest, there are a select few officers that I personally do not like. But I respect them enough that anytime I have had a bad dealing with them I have manned up and apologized for my part of any wrong doing. I look at what is happening in our country and it truly hurts my heart and brings me to admire the local law enforcement that much more. To the Morgantown Police Department, I thank you and I salute you for protecting the rights, freedoms, and lives of not only myself, but my family and friends, and the communities that they serve! Kudos to the University Police Department, which maintains law and order on the West Virginia University campuses by working round the clock to prevent crime and apprehend the perpetrators when crimes occur. God Bless all of you!

After a speech like that, it makes you wonder what turns a policeman corrupt. I would guess that is just going with the flow and do as you are told by your superiors. Corrupt law enforcement officers are taught to look the other way when it comes to drug dealings. There are rewards for keeping your eyes and ears closed.

There is a schedule that is followed for drug prosecutions.

Schedule I, II, III and IV drugs:

Schedule I comprises of the drugs with the highest likelihood of abuse, such as LSD, marijuana, heroin, and methaqualone.

Schedule II includes controlled substances, such as methadone, meperidine (Demerol), oxycodone (Percocet and OxyContin), morphine, opium and codeine.

Schedule III includes a combination of products with less than 15 milligrams of hydrocodone per dosage unit (Vicodin).

Schedule IV drugs have relatively low potential for abuse and include Valium and Xanax.

Penalties for possession, distribution, trafficking and manufacture can be the most severe. For example, if they are convicted of distributing a Schedule I or II drug, they may face penitentiary imprisonment for one to four years and/or a fine of up to $30,000. It is a felony.

However, if they are convicted for first-time marijuana possession of less than 15 grams, they are guilty of a misdemeanor. They face jail time of 90 days to six months and/or a fine of up to $1,000. However, marijuana laws both at the state and the federal levels can carry severe penalties. Drug crime convictions could also impact your immigration status.

What constitutes?

Drug distribution — Delivering (not including administering or dispensing) a controlled substance or a listed chemical.

Drug trafficking — the production, transport and distribution of one or more illicit substances through large-scale, highly controlled means.

Drug manufacturing — the production, preparation or processing of a controlled substance.

What constitutes a problem?

Morgantown Law Offices, such as, Rockefeller and Rockefeller, has successfully defended West Virginians from facing serious drug charges at the state and federal levels. They carefully probe law enforcement procedures to ensure that proper protocol is followed, including stopping and searching their vehicle and searching their home. They examine all the evidence against them. They challenge the assumptions and actions that lead the police to investigate them. And they expose any informants who may have testified against them.

Most of the drug distributers, traffickers and manufacturers go free with the help of corrupt law enforcement.

Another small article in the Monday Dominion Post paper about the investigation into a shooting of an off duty police officer, Sgt. Earnest Maxwell, who was found shot on Barrowby Road Saturday. His wife, Tracy Maxwell (15 years younger than Sgt. Maxwell) was found in the burnt pick-up truck that was involved in the 10 car pile-up accident on I-68 east on Saturday, May 21st. The police investigation report shows that Tracy may have been dead before the accident, which coincided with the shooting incident on Barrowby Road where a body was removed from the scene. There were handguns found on the three men found in that vehicle. All four bodies were burned beyond recognition.

The Truck was registered to a Briccio Cadmen Donovan of Fairmont, West Virginia, whom had stated, "You stay outta my business, I'll stay outta yours." The three unidentified men all worked for Donovan and he was keeping it private, until after the investigation. The weapons that they carried were registered and legal, including the shotgun that was found on the scene of the collision. Autopsies were done on all four bodies. The names of the three men were withheld. Tracy Maxwell died of a head injury. The investigation will continue under the Morgantown police, the State Police, with a major involvement of the *Federal Bureau of Investigation as well.*

The United States' Congressional Research Service acknowledges that there is not a broadly accepted *definition*, and defines a "public *mass shooting*" as one in which four or more people selected indiscriminately, not including the perpetrator, are killed, echoing the *FBI definition of* the term "*mass*-murder".

CHAPTER 15

Zack texted Deacon: "Did you see the Dominion Post...LMAO… Sgt. Maxwell's wife was in that black pick-up that crashed… Wow… did we already know that… or what?"

Deacon texted back: "You did say that things can change in the blink of an eye…that truck was registered to Weed's brother-in-law, Donovan, of Fairmont, WV…go figure. Weed said those three thugs in the black pick-up, worked for Donovan…we can finally see how Maxwell's wife got into the picture…we'll have to talk about it."

Zack was quite comfortable with his home life. His father, Gregory Taylor, was Supervisor at Mylan Pharmaceuticals. His father had the "average guy" thing about him. He often preferred duck hunting to attending the opera. To Zack, his dad was a total genius. Zack's father, in his opinion, was a total genius. He was able to come up with insights or eureka moments more than the average dad, Zack felt sure. He had infinite intelligence. Or maybe he just had a tremendous admiration for his father. At the very least, he was proud of the height that he shared with his dad. Six feet.

Zack's mother, Janice, was a nurse at the J.W. *Ruby Memorial Hospital*, the largest facility in the WVU Medicine, he was proud of his family, which also provided the most advanced level of care available to the citizens of West Virginia.

Sam texted Zack and Deacon: "I will meet you at Fritz's at six o'clock… Penny is picking me up at the high school at two thirty… We are going to the triple AAA to change the title and registration on the van… We are ordering a designer license plate with 'NO2WAYS' on it… That's my idea… Penny is bringing all the paperwork to do the transaction… She is having Liam Hercules pick up the van to have our new band name painted on the tinted windows and to have the van totally detailed… see you at six."

Deacon texted: "K"

Zack texted: "K"

When Penny and Sam arrived at Fritz's, they had already picked up the Mercedes-Benz Sprinter 2500 Luxury Mobile Office which was shining like a diamond ring, black with French lettering on the rear tinted windows, perfectly placed and reading: "No Two Ways", under that read, "Rock 'n' Roll Band", on both sides of the vehicle. Sam was overwhelmed. He had already changed his insurance over to the van.

They walked into Fritz's, gave the thumbs up to the Stop, Drop and Roll sign, and continued back to their favorite booth where Zack and Deacon were sitting.

"You should see that Mercedes van in the parking lot," Sam said. "Priceless. Penny really did the job on it."

"Pretty nice," Penny agreed. "Weed and Mateo said they will be here by seven."

They all got up and went out to see the van; Deacon motioned to his dad to come out.

"Holy Shit. This is giving me life, man," Zack exclaimed. "That is one beautiful ride."

"You absolutely have no chill, Zack," Sam laughed.

"Daaamn," Deacon said. "All we have to do now is play some music. We are looking good. We definitely need to reevaluate our lives."

Sam said, "You certainly got that right, Deacon, I cannot express in collective words how elated I am. You hit the nail on the head.

"That is certainly a show-stopper. Kudos to all of you. I'm thinking that you have a good thing going. Looking good," replied Francisco, Deacon's dad, as he applauded and went back into the bar.

They looked the Mercedes over for a while and decided to go back into the bar when they heard motorcycles approaching. It was Weed and Mateo. They pulled next to Penny's Jeep Cherokee and dismounted. Then all of them admired the Mercedes a while longer and then returned into Fritz's, giving thumbs up to the Stop, Drop and Roll sign and continued to their booth and ordered some food and beverages.

"Did you happen to see the article in the Dominion Post, Penny?" Mateo asked, as he pulled the paper out of his back pocket.

"Yes I did, Mateo," Penny answered. "I'm sure glad Weed filled us in last night, about what really was going down."

"This would all be a mystery if Cleo wouldn't have told me about Lucas and the two hitmen. That certainly let the cat out of the bag for us. The Morgantown Police Department is still scratching its heads," Weed remarked, as he was twirling his finger around his ear, "This is all crazy."

"You said that right, Weed," Zack said. "What worries me is what Cleo said about the anonymous text that Donovan received, about the golfers."

"We need to be careful. I mean we have to have some chill. That crazy, demented Donovan character is scary. He's certainly not playing with a full deck," Deacon replied.

"You think maybe Donovan's lieutenant Lucas contacted him while his hitmen were chasing us in the black pick-up, telling him about golfers taking the leather duffle bag, Penny?" Sam asked, thinking the worst. "Or am I barking up the wrong tree?"

"Your guess is as good as mine, Sam, but I don't think so," Penny said. "From what Weed said, Donovan still suspects the Chief of Police, Calabrese. He thinks he is lying and that he took the money. He's unpredictable. He may do something drastic, like assassinating Chief Anton Calabrese, or going after George Oliver and Sparrow Alexander. They would be absolutely petrified. The one's who should be scared are those two ass wipes. Anyway Sam, there was no mention of golfers until Donovan got the anonymous text."

All of a sudden the entire place got quiet. A tall, muscular man, in his high twenties with short black hair except for the back, where it hung over his collar, mullet style, walked in. Oscar Dunn wore casual slacks and an expensive crisp shirt and a loose jacket, probably packing heat. He was followed by Briccio Cadmen Donovan, with his shaved, bald head, a white oversized T-shirt and mean tattoos (Tattoos are useful indicators to identify individuals who are members of a gang or a criminal organization. It is important to note that an image may have several different, occasionally innocuous, meanings, depending on the interpretation of the individual or gangs using it.) Solo pants, saggy denim black, worn low, dragging on the ground. He also had a thick, black leather belt with an initial "D" on the chrome belt buckle. He came off as arrogant, pretentious and condescending. Definitely patronizing. Everyone felt scared of him.

Cleo had an exaggerated use of mousse, a dark jacket with Old English style lettering. Baggy, long pants dragging on the ground, Heavy make-up, dark excessive eye shadow, shaved eyebrows, dark lipstick and dark fingernail polish, a revealing blouse, Stretch belt with the initial "C" on her chrome belt buckle.

The three of them somehow asserted their authority and sense of superiority. The muscular dark-haired man led them to a table almost in the center of the dining area. They all sat down. Francisco Fritz came over immediately to greet them.

"Good evening, Mr. and Mrs. Donovan, Oscar. I hope you are enjoying your evening. Someone will be here to take your order soon. Thank you for stopping by."

"We could all use a few cold ones right now," Donovan said, as he rearranged his place setting, "Three Coors Light."

Francisco reacted right away and had a waitress respond to the order.

"And have my brother-in-law, Roberto Fernandez, with that group over in that booth, come and see me."

Francisco walked over to the booth where his son was sitting.

"What's up, dad?" Deacon asked with his palms up.

"Donovan wants to talk to Roberto. Which one of you is Roberto?"

"It's me," Weed replied, "I'll go over and talk with them."

Weed stood up and walked to Donovan's table with Deacon's dad.

"Sit down, Roberto," Donovan ordered. "Now, no beating around the bush, which one of your friends did I force off the road?"

"It was Sam."

"Go get Sam and bring him over."

Weed returned to the booth and told Sam that Donovan wanted to speak to him.

"Oh shit," Sam said, thinking the worst. Golfers!"

"I don't know, Sam. He wanted to know who he had run off the road."

Sam stood and joined Weed and they walked to Donovan's table, pulled over an extra chair and sat down.

"This is Sam," Weed said. "And this is my sister, Cleopatra, and that's Oscar Dunn."

"Nice to meet you."

"Thanks for taking Roberto and Mario into your band," Cleopatra said, shaking Sam's hand.

"Oh no," Sam answered. "Both of them are great musicians."

"Sam, I want to apologize for running you off the road that day on I-68 west. Roberto and Mario were in front of me when we came off the Cheat Lake ramp. I watched them pass you and I thought you were giving them a hard time because you were signaling back and forth. I thought you were being nasty and that's when I got upset and ran you off the road."

"I remember," Sam replied, thinking that this was a blessing in disguise.

"Anyway. I didn't realize that you were friends with Roberto and Mario and I want to make it right."

"The van was totaled," Sam said.

"Why don't you find out what the insurance will give you for your van and I will double that amount, does that sound fair?"

"More than fair, Mr. Donovan."

"OK, Roberto will let me know. You two can go back to whatever you were doing." Donovan said, shaking Sam's hand, as he motioned for the waitress to come and take their order. "How about one of those steaks that we keep hearing so much about, Cleo?"

"That sounds good to me. What do you say, Oscar?"

"Right on!"

Sam and Weed went back to their booth.

"Oh my God, What did he want, Sam?" Zack asked, overwhelmed about what was happening.

"He wanted to pay for my van. I'm in total shock."

"I guess every cloud has a silver lining," Penny said, with a huge smile. "Everything is coming together."

"Yup," Sam laughed, as everyone's attention went to the big screen TV's that were located in strategic places all over the Sport's Bar. They were announcing the tragic death of the Chief Investigator of the Morgantown Police Department, George Oliver.

CHAPTER 16

Young Samuel Earl Trainer had his heart set on playing a certain instrument - the trumpet. A number of students over the years had looked at the trumpet and said, "I want to play that. It only has three keys, so it should be easy." They hadn't realized that having just three keys doesn't make it easier to play; it makes it harder. Notes are produced on brass instruments by a combination of lip tension and key combination (keys on brass instruments are referred to as "valves"). So a student has to manipulate those valves while tightening and loosening his or her lips to produce the notes. Samuel bought his trumpet a*t Fawleys Music Store* in *Morgantown, rather than purchasing a poor quality instrument.* You pay more, but in the long run he would be happier, the instrument would last longer and need fewer repairs, and it would be easier to play also.

Samuel played his trumpet at the Mountaineer Middle School for Three years, the band did concerts, attended football games, marched in parades and once a year they even participated in the Buckwheat festival Parade in Kingwood, West Virginia, which was a huge event with carnival rides, entertainment and a lot of buckwheat pancakes.

Samuel developed another interest in playing the guitar. One summer, while visiting his grandparents, his grandfather Thurston Beltow III, bought him a hollow bodied guitar at the local pawn shop. They had it restrung and tuned and Samuel was planning to take some guitar lessons. His dad later bought him a Fender

American Standard Stratocaster guitar, which he learned to play like a professional performing artist.

Samuel idealized his cousin, Riley Giuseppe Van Lorne, who lived in Bartow, Florida, and later in Malibu, California. Rie Guy had a rocking garage band in which he played guitar and sang. The band played small gigs in Lakeland and Daytona Beach, Florida. Samuel had dreams of having his own band in the future.

Samuel's sister Anna was spending her time cheerleading and doing dance routines with a local dancing group.

Michael's uncle, Robert Covington, whom he was living with before he hooked up with Erica, had already passed away. His uncle Bob was never married and had no children, so his house and all of his belongings were left to his brother in Michigan and his sister in Maui, Hawaii, who was Mike's mother. Mike was interested in purchasing his uncles house and wanted to apply for a loan to pay his mother and his Michigan uncle. The value of the home was around one hundred and fifty thousand dollars and he would try to get a loan for that amount and pay his mother and uncle for their shares. Mike was unable to get a loan for that amount, so Mike's mother said that he could use her share of Uncle Robert's house as collateral and borrow only enough to pay off the uncle in Michigan. It worked and they bought the house.

The house was a three-bedroom Brick split level that sat majestically above the Laurel Drive, with a long-paved driveway and a concrete parking area for three or four cars. A one-car garage. It was located in Coopers Rock State Forest less than a mile from the Coopers Rock overlook.

Coopers Rock State Forest is a 12,747 acre state forest in Monongalia and Preston counties in the State of West Virginia. Its southern edge abuts Cheat Lake and the canyon section of Cheat River. It is roughly bisected by Interstate 68. The northern portion of the forest was managed by a forestry program at West Virginia University and was lesser developed. The southern part was jointly managed by the West Virginia Division of Natural Resources and

West Virginia Division of Forestry. It was more developed than some of the other state forests as it functions as a major recreation destination for the Morgantown area.

The house was in Preston County but Samuel and Anna were permitted to finish their education in Monongalia County because they were already in the school systems.

Samuel became friends, through the band, with George Deacon Fritz who played percussion drums in the band; they would jam together at Deacon's house on Downwood Drive, in Downwood Manor, where Deacon had a set of drums. Deacon was an "A" student and planned to become a lawyer. Samuel was an above average student and wanted to get into Engineering or become an attorney as well.

CHAPTER 17

Police officers put their lives at risk every day in the line of duty. When a police officer dies, we feel a collective sense of loss as we recall their bravery and their commitment towards keeping our communities safe.

While mourning the *death* of the Morgantown Police Department's well-respected Chief Investigator, George Oliver, who was slain in the police departments parking garage, the Chief of Police Anton Calabrese said that the *investigation* was in the early stages, and it was the *chief's* decision to involve the FBI in the investigation.

George was a former Marine, and had entered the police academy in 1977. He loved law enforcement and liked interacting with the community. George was perfectly suited for law enforcement, was never able to sit perfectly still, always eager for something exciting, and relating to other people in a down-to-earth, sincere way.

George was raised in Anaheim, California, and on one of his first few jobs, worked at Disneyland. He attended the Clara Barton Elementary School and Loara High School. He played water polo and was also on the high school swim team. Just before his senior year, his family moved to Morgantown, West Virginia where George graduated from the University High School. He loved the move to West Virginia, being able to ride a dirt bike daily in the hills behind his family home. After graduation, George worked a series of jobs, mostly in the auto mechanics field. He loved working on cars and raced his cars a few times at the Greater Pittsburgh Raceway.

George was hired as a corrections officer with the Monongalia County Sheriff's Office in the December of 1978 and one year later, he was hired by the Morgantown Police Department. George earned a bachelor's degree from the West Virginia University by taking two classes a semester while working full-time to support his family. His degree was in Sociology with a Criminal Justice certificate.

George was survived by his wife, Madison, and his two daughters, Matilda and Meredith.

"What the hell do you think happened here, Chief Calabrese?" Sparrow Alexander asked, his voice low, almost breathless. "Do you think Donovan had had any part of this?"

"You know it was him," Calabrese answered, as his cheeks puffed out and he blew out some air. "He has a perfect account of his whereabouts when George was shot; he was at Fritz's with plenty of witnesses, the perfect alibi. You can bet your last dollar that son of a bitch killed George, even if he didn't pull the trigger. I'm trying to get it straight in my mind about what happened with that piece of shit Sgt. Maxwell. He was supposed to be picking up our law enforcement protection payoff from Donovan and he ends up on Butt Hole Road digging a shallow grave to apparently bury his wife. Go figure. The body ends up missing and shows up in a burnt pick-up on I-68 east in a vehicle belonging to Donovan. What the fuck."

"You think that's why he had George Oliver done in?" Sparrow asked. "He is definitely pissed about something."

"I have got to talk to Donovan. Maybe he can clear some of this up. Drastic times call for drastic measures, Sparrow."

"Why don't you call him now?"

"I can't. I have to wait and call at noon. That's our agreement."

Chief of Police Anton Calabrese waited until noon to punch in the number to connect with Donovan.

"Chief Calabrese calling, Mr. Donovan."

"Yo, partner."

"Hello, Donovan, this is the chief. We need to talk. Our Chief Investigator, George Oliver, was shot and killed last night and people are pointing their fingers toward your direction, they have reasons to believe that you had something to do with the shooting."

"It's funny how the people that know the least about you, always have the most to say about you. I'm afraid you're barkin' up the wrong tree, Chief Calabrese. I had absolutely nothing to do with that killing. People are going to talk no matter what you do, Chief Calabrese. You're gonna talk about me, because you know me, right? You think you know me so well. You think you know everything about me; my influences, my choices, what hurts me, what helps me, what haunts me, all my fears…you know it all, right? You know what I've been through, going through and will eventually go through, don't you? You know all my choices and the reasons to why I made them, right? Listen, Calabrese, your man Sgt. Maxwell ran off with a transport bag full of my money, two and a half million dollars, and I know that you have that money and that you will return it. If you're gonna act like you don't know shit, you're gonna get your ass kicked. What happened to your man George Oliver is nothing compared to what's coming your way. I was born a sweet little baby, but those mean New York streets raised me up fuckin' crazy, man."

"What are you saying, Donovan? I have no knowledge of any transport bag. Sgt. Maxwell was dead when we came on the scene. There was no transport bag," Calabrese begged. "Why don't you fill me in on what is actually happening here."

"You're fuckin' lying, Calabrese, there is no other explanation, you and your police investigator buddies were the first on the scene and you confiscated that money. I know you fuckin' have it. I'm going to make you an offer, Calabrese, either you come up with that money or your ass is going to be splattered all over that fuckin' police station."

"How did Sgt. Maxwell come up with that money transport bag anyway? Did he steal it, or what? We did find our zippered payoff bag on Maxwell with thirty thousand dollars in it, which we did confiscate, because naturally, that was ours, right? Except these things, I'm completely in the dark. There was no other transfer bag."

"The payoff money bag you found on Maxwell **was** yours."

"Someone shot Sgt. Maxwell, repetitively, who we believe was digging a grave to bury his wife Tracy, and then the authorities find Tracy burnt up in a vehicle with three other men, and the pick-up truck was registered in your name. They also said that the girl was already dead before the accident. Are you sure those three men didn't take your money, Donovan. There was no bag on the crime scene. I swear to you."

"Cleopatra said that Maxwell's wife, Tracy, came with him to pick up the payoff money and she fell and hit her head on a table. The fall was fatal for her. Maxwell got pissed and ordered our man, Lucas Martini, and two others to put the transfer bag in his Caddy SUV, which was sitting outside. They also put a tracking device on Maxwell's vehicle. Cleopatra ordered them to take the girl, dump her and find Sgt. Maxwell, kill him and bring that money back. I have no idea how they wrecked on I-68 east."

"Was there anyone else involved, Donovan?" Calabrese asked, looking for an answer.

"I had an anonymous text saying that there were some golfers involved. What the fuck was that all about?"

"Hold on," Chief Calabrese replied. "I can get a list of the golfers who played on the May 21st at the Pines Country Club and maybe figure something out."

"Just do fucking whatever you want. I'm not playing around, Calabrese, you fucking piece of shit. I'm giving you one week to come up with my money; otherwise, I will have enough conviction to put you in the ground."

CHAPTER 18

It was Tuesday morning and Sam was at University High School. He only had until the end of the week to finish his senior year. Penny, Deacon, Zack and Weed were planning a day of golf at the Pines Country Club. Mateo had to be at work at the airport.

"I was reading the Dominion Post this morning and they said the George Oliver was shot in the Morgantown Police Station parking garage, he was shot execution-style," Weed said.

"What does that mean, Weed?" Penny asked.

Weed had come on his motorcycle and met Penny at her house, where he had kept his golf clubs. Now, they were driving to the Pines Country Club to meet Deacon and Zack.

"Execution-style killing is a shot to the head, and victims are killed while kneeling," Weed answered, as he posed with his hands clasped as if he were shooting.

Execution-style killing is an act of criminal murder where the perpetrator kills at a conscious victim at point blank. The victim is under complete physical control of the assailant and is left with no course of resistance or escape. In this respect, an "execution-style murder" is similar to the usual meaning of execution, which is taking life by the due process of law.

"The type of killing that is used by the Aryan Brotherhood of white supremacists. I'm sure my brother-in-law, Donovan, killed George Oliver, even though he didn't fire the bullet. You better freakin' believe that shit. This has brought on a troubled time for law enforcement in the city. Many people now think that certain police officers of the Morgantown Police Department sold their badges by taking payoffs from drug dealers that they should have been arresting. They not only betrayed the citizens they were sworn to protect, but also betrayed the thousands of honest, hard-working law enforcement officers who risk their lives every day to keep us safe."

"My father said that federal agents are now working with local law enforcement partners to pursue that corruption, wherever it lies," Penny replied, "That is horrible, what you said about execution-style killings. Donovan certainly secured an alibi being at Fritz's last night."

They pulled into a parking space next to Zack and Deacon.

"I wonder what Chief Calabrese is doing in the Pro-Shop?" Deacon asked, as he pointed to the unmarked black car with a spot light on the driver's side. "That's his car parked in front."

"I hate that sum-bitch, Calabrese," said Zack.

"OK," Penny said. "I have to go in the Pro-Shop to sign us up. When I'm in there, I'll find out what Calabrese is up to."

Zack and Weed went to the cart barn and brought back two golf carts, loading the golf clubs. Zack was talking to Weed about how the federal agents were investigating the Morgantown Police Department, and how his Dad told him that the locker-room talk is that Chief of Police Anton Calabrese has earned the reputation of being the most corrupt cop in the city.

"I will guarantee you that George Oliver was killed to pressurize Chief Calabrese. Cleopatra said that Donovan still believes that Calabrese stole his money," Weed responded, as he did a fist bump with Zack.

Penny returned and said that Chief Calabrese was getting a list of all the people that golfed on the May 21st and that he wanted to talk to some of the groundskeepers to see if they noticed anything strange that day.

"Christ's sake," Deacon exclaimed, "What if one of those groundskeepers saw something. I told you and Sam to just leave everything the way we found it and get the hell out of there. Those dudes saw us when they took off in that black pick-up with the heavily tinted windows. We were on the course for only about an hour."

"Remember what Weed's sister said about Donovan's anonymous text about some golfers being involved. Maybe Donovan and Calabrese talked and that is why Calabrese is checking it out," responded Zack. "We may have screwed up in a dramatic and ignominious fashion!"

"Why are they so concerned about people who golfed here on the May 21st?" Weed asked, with a puzzled look.

"Maybe you should fill Weed in on what went down that day, Deacon," Penny said, as she teed up her golf ball and hit a drive.

"Nice hit, Penny," Weed yelled. "Yeah, fill me in, Deacon."

"Well, maybe Zack can help me with this," Deacon said, "On that day we were going to interview Penny, we decided that we could get in eighteen holes that morning. All was well until I hooked a ball on my second shot in the woods on the third hole. We went to look for it and on the other side of Butt-Hole Road, Zack saw something going on and we went closer to investigate. There was a man lying face down in the dirt that he was digging. He was shot many times in the back. There was a large leather duffle bag full of money. A whole shitload of money. These three dudes saw us and took off. We decided to take the money and leave, and later turn it in to the police."

"So you turned it in to the police?" Weed asked.

"Hell no," Zack replied. "We got the duffle bag to the car and decided to go to Fritz's to figure out what to do with it, but on the way we got followed by the black pick-up. Sam told Deacon to get to I-79 south and we could lose them, the truck stayed close. Deacon cut off on I-68 east and the truck was right on our bumper and before we got to the Cheat Lake exit, the truck started passing and the passenger side window went down and a double barreled shot gun was pointing at Deacon. Deacon slammed on the break and the truck veered off to the left, hit a manhole and exploded. That's when we decided and stashed the money at Sam's, and came back at Fritz's."

"So where did you stash the money?" Weed asked.

"We put it in a crawl space under Sam's mom and dad's house," Zack answered.

They finished their round and texted Sam, telling him to meet them at "The Clubhouse Grille" when he was done with the classes. Penny wanted everyone to have a steak dinner with double-baked potato and salad, the club specialty. She ordered an extra meal for Sam.

"This was quite an interesting day," Penny said. "We all shot pretty well and I enjoyed the conversation. I really didn't like hearing about the execution-style killing though. That seems so cruel. I would rather they just shoot them, why make them kneel in their final moments?"

"Is Mateo going to be able to practice with us today?" Deacon asked. "I believe Sam has all of our equipment in the van, we're going to practice at Penny's. We have a gig on Saturday at the Community Center."

"Mateo will be at Penny's at five thirty sharp," Weed said.

Sam got there about the same time that the dinners came and they were ready to eat.

"We have a couple of things to tell you, Sam," Deacon said. "Chief Calabrese was snooping in the neighborhood."

"What the hell did he want now?"

"He seemed to be very interested in who played golf here on May 21st and wants to question some of the greenkeepers and groundskeepers to see if they saw anything strange going on that day. Go figure! We also filled Weed in on what went down that day."

"Well," Sam replied, "Let's hope those groundskeepers didn't see anything."

"That blows my mind when I think how much money is in that duffle bag that we confiscated, two and a half million dollars,"

Deacon said, taking a big bite of his steak. "How do those druggies come up with that much damn money?"

"That's pretty damn easy, Deacon," Zack replied. "I've been reading about it. Drug trafficking generally refers to the sale and distribution of illegal drugs. Smuggling is to contraband drugs from one country to another illegally and secretly. Illegal drugs in the United States create a huge black market industry, an estimated two hundred to seven hundred billion dollars a year in size, with the current decade seeing the largest per person drug usage per year in American history."

"I know this much," Weed continued. "I read a lot also and I've also learned a lot from my family, Zack. Most of the illicit drugs come into the United States across the vast 2,000-mile land border between the United States and Mexico; it's called the Southwestern border or SWB. Drug cartels in Mexico utilize drug mules, tunnels, boats, vehicles, trains, aircraft, and couriers to smuggle illegal drugs into America."

"I guess there is a method to their madness, seven billion dollars," Deacon said. "That is quite a payday."

"Tell them about the money laundering and about Turks and Caicos Island, Zack," Sam said, as he put more butter on his potato and took a bite.

"The money that we are holding in that duffle bag is what the drug lords call dirty money," Zack said, "Money laundering is the process of transforming the proceeds of crime and corruption into ostensible legitimate assets, so as to avoid taxation or confiscation. The concept of money laundering goes back to ancient times and is intertwined with the development of money and banking. The Nassau and Turks and Caicos Islands are in that mix, big time."

Turks and Caicos Islands are being used as a critical transit point for drug trafficking between countries such as Haiti, the Dominican Republic and the Bahamas. Small sport fishing vessels and pleasure crafts move cocaine from the Bahamas to Florida by blending them with legitimate traffic that transits these areas. Penalties for federal drug trafficking convictions vary according to the quantity of the controlled substance involved in the transaction. A drug trafficking conviction may also lead to denial of federal benefits and further, forfeiture of personal property and real estate.

"Well, I've certainly learned enough about the drug world for one day," Penny said, as she called for and signed the check. "Why don't we finish up here and go over to my place."

Sam was getting another anonymous text on his iPhone: "I'll be coming after my money…and you three punks are going to die."

"This sucks, you can't respond and it shows no return number," Sam yelled, holding his iPhone up for everyone to see.

"You've got to be shitting me," Zack exclaimed. "Whoever is sending those messages is using one of those throwaway phones. It's one of those that you can buy at a 7-Eleven, or wherever, use it for a short period of time, then pitch it."

"I guess we can all guess where those texts are coming from," Weed suggested, "Donovan is a snake in the grass. I think he means every word he's saying about killing people."

"That is scary," Deacon said, as he signaled to Zack to get into his truck. They got in Deacon's truck, backed out of the parking space and spun the wheel, heading out of Country Club Drive towards Penny's house.

Penny and Weed got into Penny's Jeep, took off, and Sam followed in the Mercedes. Sam backed the Mercedes van up to the door of the utility building attached to the garages at Penny's house.

CHAPTER 19

Deacon was setting up his drum set. The base drum had "No Two Ways" printed in designer letters diagonally across the face. It looked terrific. He brought in the soundboard and all the lighting system that lit up the band, Weed brought in his keyboard and assembled it, guitars and guitar stands, amplifiers and giant speakers. They connected all of the wires and had everything pretty well set up. Deacon went out to the van for a pair of pliers and a police cruiser pulled into a space next to the Mercedes Benz van. The new Chief Inspector, Sparrow Alexander, stepped out of the cruiser, brushed his dirty blond hair back with his hand, and as he was approaching Deacon, he pulled out his weapon and told Deacon to freeze and keep his mouth shut. He held his revolver with a silencer attached to it, pointing it towards Deacon's back and ordered him back into the utility building door. When they entered through the door, Weed walked over toward Deacon and saw that Sparrow was holding a revolver to Deacon's back.

"What the hell is going on, Sparrow?" Weed asked.

Sparrow swung the weapon and caught Weed on the side of his head and sent him sprawling to the floor, knocking him out.

"Alright," Sparrow yelled. "We can make this easy, or we can make this hard. I want everyone to stand over by that wall."

Zack and Penny stood still, wondering what Sparrow was up to.

"What's this all about, Sparrow, Did we do something wrong?" Sam asked, moving close to the wall.

"Just shut the fuck up, and do as you're told," Sparrow screamed, getting out a roll of duct tape and throwing it over to Sam and pointing at Weed, who had frozen in his place. "Take that duct tape and wrap it around that Hispanics arms and legs and put a strip over his mouth. Roll him on his stomach and tape his hands and feet together."

He looked back to Zack and Penny and said to Sam, "Pull those two chairs over here, sit those two down and tape their arms and legs," Sparrow shouted, and waited for him to finish. "Now wrap the tape around them and those chairs."

"Can I ask what it is you're doing, are we under arrest or what?" Penny asked, trying to pull free of the tape. "This is crazy."

"I suggest all of you shut the fuck up, girl! I'll let you know what I'm doing."

Sparrow scooted another chair over and told Sam to do the same with Deacon, now holding the revolver at Deacon's head, "Don't try anything cute, or I'll blow his fucking head off."

Sam did as he was told, as Sparrow kept his revolver pressed against Deacon's temple.

"Are you the one who has been sending me those anonymous texts? What is it that you want, Sparrow?" Sam asked wrapping the duct tape around Deacon and the chair.

"One more remark out of you, punk, and I'm going to shoot **your** fucking ass," Sparrow yelled, "Here it is…I'm confiscating that leather transport bag you and your buddies brought in here yesterday. I've been doing a little investigating myself, and guess what? I followed that 57' Chevy convertible here and witnessed you three taking it out of the trunk."

"How the hell did you find out about that transport bag, anyhow? Is Chief Calabrese in on this?" Deacon asked, "What if we don't give it up?"

"Oh you'll give it up, Deacon Fritz, because people are going to die here, starting with this Hispanic dude, followed by you."

Sparrow snarled. He handed Sam the duct tape, and ordered, "Tape Deacon's mouth shut."

"Now for your information," Sparrow shouted. "I am personal friends with Liam Hercules, the Manager of Rockefeller Towing, and he just happened to give me a call and said that he towed in a wrecked van, and that there was a huge leather bag of money left in it. I told him not to do anything, and that I would be right over. By the time I got there the bag was gone and he told me that two dudes in a 57' Chevy convertible had picked it up. I spotted the 57' Chevy at Fritz's and followed you here. Now, this is the way I'm seeing it. We will be loading that transport bag into that cruiser and Sparrow Alexander and his Sweetie are making off to the islands, where we will have that money laundered and live happily ever after. How do you guys see it?"

"That's enough," Penny screamed, as she spotted Mateo through the window in the back. "I'll show you where the damn transport bag is. It's in my gun safe. Don't have a cow, Sparrow!"

Mateo had spotted the police cruiser as he made the turn on Anchor and decided to park his Harley and walk over and see what was happening. He went around the back of the two sets of garages to the back of the utility building. He peeped in and saw what was happening. He tried the back door and it was unlocked. In a dilemma about what to do, he was clear on the fact that he had to do something fast. He thought: *When in doubt, take the next step* He opened the back door; there was a wall that hid him when he entered.

"Alright, bitch, how do we get into the safe?" Sparrow demanded.

"Undo this tape, I know the combination."

Sparrow ordered Sam to get her loose. He made them stay close together as they approached the safe, "OK, open it up, sister, and that bag better be in there."

Mateo moved along the inside wall, on a shelf was a set of nonchucks. He picked them up and made a decision that he had to do something.

Penny put in the combination, pulled the handle and the safe swung open, and there was the transport bag.

In the heat of the moment, Mateo appeared from behind the wall and Sparrow spotted him and shot off a round. Mateo screamed and swung the nonchuck as hard as he could on Sparrow's head. It sounded like an egg cracking as Sparrow dropped to the floor. His head was cleft, bleeding profusely.

"Mateo,' Penny yelled. "Are you alright?"

"It nicked my left shoulder, but I think it's OK, the bullet didn't go in," Mateo answered, crossing himself, "Is he dead?"

Penny turned around and kicked Sparrows gun away and kicked him hard, "That's for calling me a bitch!" Penny shouted.

"I doubt if he felt that Penny, he's wasted, he's not breathing," Sam replied, as he unfastened Deacon and Zack. Mateo and Penny ran over to undo Weed.

"Isn't that a shocker? That son of a bitch was going to kill us. I guess that will be the end of those anonymous texts, Sam," Deacon said, letting out a sigh of relief as he helped get the duct tape off of himself and Zack. "I'm getting tired of having to live with the shit scared out of me all the time. What are we going to do with the Sparrow's corpse?"

"We sure as hell can't call the police," Zack replied. "We just have to get rid of the body. Any suggestions?"

"We take him and leave him at the police station, behind the wheel of his police cruiser. That's what we do with him, and that's all she wrote," Weed exclaimed.

"What the fuck?" Deacon agreed. "Let's do it."

"We've got to wear some rubber gloves before touching him or his vehicle, Penny said, "and we have to clean up that blood too. My father has a solution in the garage that is used to clean up crime scenes. Forensics can't pick it up blood stains with their magic dust and lights. Here is a box of rubber gloves, everyone put them on."

They all put on the rubber gloves, wrapped a towel around Sparrow's head and grabbed his arms and legs and carried him out to the police cruiser and loaded him into the passenger's side. Weed said that he would drive the car.

"We'll have to wait until it gets dark before we pull this off," Deacon said. "For the time being, we'll have to clean up inside and get rid of all that blood."

Weed and Deacon leaned Sparrow down into the seat so no one could see him and covered him with a blanket and went back inside.

"Who wants a beer?" Zack yelled. "My damn nerves are shot."

Everyone responded and Zack retrieved a crate from the fridge and passed it around.

"You think the police will put me behind bars for killing Sparrow, Penny?" Mateo asked, looking for some support.

"Not to worry, Mateo, It's alright. That piece of crap Sparrow needed to be stopped. And you stopped him. Nothing is illegal unless you get caught. Am I right?" Penny asked. "Some people just suck the life right out of you, and that man was an evil sucker. Don't get it twisted, if you did anything, you saved our lives."

"Absolutely, Mateo, what doesn't kill us, makes us stronger," Sam said, as he started to clean up the blood that was all over the floor. "Now where is the solution you were talking about, Penny?"

"I'll get it," Penny said, as she went into the garage.

"So how did the transport bag get in Penny's safe anyway?" Weed questioned. "I thought you stashed it in the crawl space at Sam's mom and dad's, Zack?"

"We had to move it before Sam's dad found it. It's a long story," Zack answered.

They got the blood cleaned off the floor and gathered all the loose duct tape into a garbage trash bag and it was getting dark.

"We've got to get this job done with Sparrow before they miss him. He hasn't called in and they may start looking for him soon," Sam said, "Weed, jump in the police cruiser and keep those rubber gloves on, and don't stop for anything or anyone. Deacon and I will follow you downtown. Go in the alley behind the city building and we'll stash the car there. Zack, you hang around here with Penny and Mateo." Weed grabbed his hooded sweatshirt.

"Don't take any chances. Just dump him and the cruiser and get back here, "Zack shouted as he gave them a take it easy jester. It had begun drizzling.

Sam thought: "My God, rain, this crap really doesn't faze me anymore. Not one person can say or do anything that would surprise me. What else could possibly happen?"

By the time they were on the drive downtown, there was a total cloud burst and it began raining cats and dogs. Weed could barely see out of the windshield. Another vehicle coming from the opposite direction rammed into Weed's ride, head on. The rain was pouring down strong and hard. The rear end of the other car slid into a gutter on its passenger side.

Push him out of your way Weed told himself. *Push him into the damn gutter* Weed was definitely in a painful and unpleasant situation but he stepped on the gas and pushed the other car backwards into the gutter and continued driving.

"That would be regarded as a narrow escape from a disaster, Sam," Deacon shouted, as they continued following Weed in the blinding rain. "That was a piece of work."

"You can say that again," Sam said, expressing a wholehearted agreement. "That man in the other car seemed alright. The accident was that man's fault anyway. Weed just moved him out the way, that's all."

Weed continued in the pouring rain on Van Voorhis Road as they passed two police cars, with their lights flashing, going in the opposite direction, probably to the scene of the wreck. All of a sudden, one of the cars turned around.

"One of those cop cars is turning around. He must have spotted Weed in the wrecked cruiser. I have to call Weed and tell him that there is a change of plans," Sam yelled, but before he could punch Weed's number, Weed had turned on the flashers on the cruiser and was speeding away. A few seconds later the other police car was zooming past them with its flashers on, Weed continued driving on Van Voorhis and was squealing the tires and racing the cruiser for all it was worth, he made a snap left turn onto University Avenue. Weed suddenly turned off all the lights on the cruiser and made a right turn on Riverview Drive, went two blocks and turned right again on Rawley Avenue. He zigzagged on Evansdale Drive and back onto Rawley, with only one headlight; it was extremely hard to see. He tried ditching the cruiser behind the Subway, pulled the hood up on his sweatshirt, but when he got out, he heard someone yelling.

"Hey, amigo, you can't leave that car there. Why are you driving that police car anyhow?"

The man, who was taking out garbage to a dumpster at Subway, spotted a body in the front seat and immediately called 911, and was yelling for Weed to stop.

Weed was removing the rubber gloves from his hands, stuffed them in his pocket. He pushed the hood off his head, cut through the Kroger parking lot and across Patterson Drive. He entered Eat'n Park and dialed up Sam and told him where he was.

"Stay there, Weed," Sam said. "We'll pick you up in two minutes."

Deacon swung his truck into the parking lot at Eat'n Park and Weed jumped in. There were now three police cars with their flashers on across the street at Subway and the Kroger parking lot. Weed was soaked and it was still raining.

"Damn it! Someone saw me when I ditched the car behind the Subway. He must have known I was Hispanic because he used the word amigo while addressing me. I had the hood up on my sweatshirt so he couldn't have seen much. Let's get the fuck out of here before they start searching the area," shouted Weed.

"You didn't touch anything in the cruiser, did you?" Deacon asked, circling around in the parking lot and out on Patterson Drive and headed back towards Penny's. "We'll go back another way to avoid where you crashed, Weed."

"No, I had the rubber gloves on the whole time. I took them off in the Kroger parking lot and put them in my pocket." Weed said.

"I doubt anyone would even recognize you, Weed. Not with a hoodie! You guys all look alike!" Deacon laughed, as he did a high five with Weed. "It was dark."

"No shit Weed," Sam said, as he threw him a towel in the back seat. "We have to get you dried off."

"No fear, but I wonder why he called me amigo? Maybe he was Hispanic." Weed replied, as he was drying his face and hair with a towel.

"There you go, Weed, you answered that one yourself. He was Hispanic. No shit," Sam repeated. "You're as clean as a whistle."

When they got back to Penny's, Zack was elated and asked if everything went alright. Everyone was spooked and not chilled when they told about their encounter with the cops that they had just been through. Penny brought out a set of her dad's jogging clothes for Weed to put on. They all went for some music, put a couple of songs together and decided to call it a night.

"Maybe we can try this again tomorrow," Penny said, giving everyone a hug. "Everyone's okay with that idea? I can't wait to read the morning papers."

They all agreed. Deacon and Zack got into Deacon's truck and took off. Mateo and Weed cranked up their motorcycles, put on their helmets, and roared away. Penny got in the van on the passenger side with Sam.

"I need to talk, Sam...You may not know this, but I've had a crush on you from the first moment I saw you playing and singing in your band. That smile on your face had just blown me away. I know we have just met and we're just friends, but I wanna be your girl, Sam. You know what I mean, your girlfriend! How do you see it, Sam?" Penny asked, swinging over and pressing her sweet lips to his. She paused and pushed away, but Sam pulled her closer and continued kissing her.

"That's the way I see it, Penny," Sam replied, being elated, his heart almost pounding out of his chest, "I've always had a thing for you. I just didn't know that you had a thing for me also. I'm crazy about it, and yes, you can certainly be my girl."

"I want you to be sure now," Penny teased, as she kissed him again, long and hard this time. "I have something that I want to bring up and I need an answer from you, Zack and Deacon. You only have till Friday to finish at University High School and I need for you three to tell me if this can happen."

"What is it, Penny?"

"Well, as you know, my grandfather, Benjamin Franklin Daiquiri, who lives in London, is friends with your grandfather, Thurston Beltow, who is visiting at the present time in London, along with your grandmother, Judith."

"My mom was just telling me about that this morning. Unreal. It's hard to believe what a small world this is," Sam exclaimed, shrugging his shoulders.

"When is your graduation, Sam?"

"June 10th, about two weeks from now, on a Friday."

"Alright, think about this, and let me know. My mother and father want all of us, you and me, Zack and Deacon, to go on vacation with them to London. We leave on Saturday. All expenses paid by my father. My father also has a six passenger helicopter that he flies to and from the Pittsburgh International Airport and his own landing pad in the rear of our house. No problem there."

CHAPTER 20

Roberto "Weed" Fernandez and Mateo Martinez were inseparable cousins. Their parents were legal immigrants from Mexico who had settled in Morgantown a few years before Roberto and Mateo were born in 1997.

Mateo's mother, Martina, was married to Miguel Martinez and a sister to Juan Fernandez and Roberto's mother, Nicole, was married to Juan Fernandez and a sister to Miguel Martinez. Siblings married to siblings. What an advantage for Weed and Mateo. They had the best of both worlds. They had two other relatives that lived close. Weed's mom had two more sisters, aunt Camila, and Aunt Luciana. Weed and Mateo's mothers and the two aunts worked as maids at the Euro-Suites hotel on Chestnut Ridge Road. They all lived at the Country Squire Mobile home & Park located just before a neighborhood called "The Crossing", in exclusive mobile homes. Roberto reached about six foot, one inch, and Mateo was a little shorter, around five foot, eleven inches. Roberto's father always said that, "Roberto is growing like a weed", thus the name "Weed". Roberto & Mateo were both twenty one years old, and were still living at home. They both had girlfriends at different times, but ditched them because they were too busy riding their bikes. Their only vehicles, besides the family cars and SUV's were their Harley Davidson Sportsters and off road vehicles (quads and trail bikes). They both worked at the local airport, Morgantown Municipal, which paid pretty damn well for part time. One thousand dollars a week, apiece, thirty two hours per week, four days, eight hours a day. Roberto had acquired a valid pilot's license to fly light propeller aircraft, after taking flight training while working at the airport.

Mateo's mother always had a beautiful attitude, spoke English very well, but spoke Spanish with her sister-in-law, Nicole, and Nicole's two sisters, Camila & Luciana, whenever they worked together. She would always tell Mateo, "If we all threw our problems in a pile and saw everyone else's…we'd grab ours back."

"Yeah, right, mom." Mateo moaned and repeated. "Grab ours back."

Roberto's mother was a little feistier, a unique person to say the least. She would tell Roberto, "Envy is a waste of time, accept what you have, and not what you need."

"OK, mom," Roberto remarked. "Whatever?"

Mateo's father, Miguel Martinez, was a postmaster at the United States Postal Office on High Street in Morgantown, WV, and Roberto's father, Juan Fernandez, was a postman delivering the mail.

Mateo was an only child, but Roberto had an older sister, Cleopatra, who was ten years senior to him. Cleopatra got herself hooked up with a character that Roberto wasn't crazy about, Briccio Cadmen Donovan. Donovan was born and came up in New York City, NY, and was hardened by the New York City Streets. He had been caught many times for drug trafficking and a couple of arrests. Donovan was moved to Chicago, IL, for his affiliations with drug cartels, where he met two brothers, Diego & Santiago, who ran with a gang and developed ties to a wide network of Hispanic and black dealers across the Midwest and east coast. The cartel's scope is definitely staggering. About half of the estimated $65 billion worth of illegal cocaine, heroin, and other narcotic that Americans buy each year enters the U.S. via Mexico. (*Cartel: an association of manufacturers or suppliers with the purpose of maintaining prices at a high level and restricting competition*) The failure is as much Chicago's as is the nation's. That city has replaced Miami as the primary U.S. distribution point for illegal narcotics, mainly cocaine, heroin, marijuana, and methamphetamine…imported from Mexico. The U.S. Department of justice named the Chicago metro area the #1 destination in the United States for heroin shipments, the #2 for marijuana and cocaine, and the #5 for methamphetamine. Chicago is the only U.S. city to rank in the top five for all four major categories.

West Virginia was a prime target for drug dealers from outside the state; gangs in Detroit have divided the state in territories. They're in the sect of the bloods, known as the Seven Mile Bloods from Detroit, the connection between Detroit and Charleston is drugs. Selling pills, heroin, and cocaine. Criminals like Briccio Cadmen Donovan, with major gang affiliations retreat to the mountain state to hide from charges they face in the big cities. Donovan was moved to Fairmont, West Virginia as a Drug Lord. His gang included a mercenary, Arthur Mariano, an assassin, Oscar Wilde, a fighter, Arnold Cress, an interrogator, Roscoe Dashon and an assaulter, Marco Anthony. Donovan was shaved bald and was as strong as an ox, and has meaningful tattoo designs. He belonged to the Aryan Brotherhood which was founded by two white supremacists. He was, unconditionally, meaner than a junkyard dog.

Donovan had purchased a trucking company that became "Donovan Trucking", which was located in Fairmont, West Virginia, and served as a perfect front for his illegal drug dealings. His territory was one of the biggest and took in a small part of Pennsylvania.

The Donovan complex is located on Opekosko Road in Fairmont, West Virginia. The brick and stucco home was situated on 3.8 acres of level land, just 20 minutes south of Morgantown. The 6,248 square foot, English Tudor-style mansion was fenced completely with a double security guarded gate. There were eight bedrooms, seven full baths and housed his entire gang. Donovan's favorite feature of the house is a door on the first floor by the Dining Room that looks like an old wooden "Speak Easy" door that leads down to the basement where there is a pub and a game room, which really is the ultimate man cave. The house had sprawling grounds that made you feel like you were on the English countryside, with big, old trees, a nice yard and a pool. The market price was 2.8 million dollars. And of course there were eight garages.

Different strokes for different folks. Donovan was perceptive about the right way to motivate people and he used the right method with the right people. He would use fear to motivate some people (*Chief of Police Anton Calabrese*), he was very respectful of some people (*Diego & Santiago*), and he gave others a swift kick in the pants (*Cleopatra, his wife*, whom he loved very dearly). He always listened carefully and did not do too much talking. He'd occasionally ask for clarification, but he never interrupted. There was a large warehouse on the back of the complex where the drug paraphernalia was stored.

CHAPTER 21

Sam was up early, looking for the daily paper. He needed to know about the occurrences that had taken place the previous night. He looked outside and found it in the paper slot below the mailbox. He glanced quickly at the front page of The Dominion Post and saw the article right away. It read:

Newly assigned Chief Investigator murdered

The Morgantown Police Department is investigating the brutal murder of their newly assigned Chief Investigator Sparrow Alexander, who was reportedly on duty last evening, and was cruising in a marked police vehicle post which he was somehow overtaken and killed. He took a severe blow to the head and was transported to the Kroger parking lot, where he was found. A Subway hoagie shop employee, Carlos Domingo, stated that a man jumped out of the police car, with a hoodie covering his head, and ran. Domingo could not identify anything about the man. He alerted the police, who showed up immediately. The police could not find the suspect. The front driver's side fender on the police cruiser had crashed in, which was connected to a hit and run accident that had occurred previously on the Van Voorhis Road. Chief Calabrese stated that an ongoing investigation will continue until the perpetrator is found. This was the second Chief Investigator killed within a week. Chief Investigator George Oliver was killed earlier in the week.

Sam was elated and thought: *Oh my God!* The Subway employee was Hispanic. Holy crap. That was amazing, and they wouldn't find any finger prints or any sort of evidence pointing toward Weed. Alright. Sam decided to text everyone and have them meet at Fritz's Place later and return to Penny's house for some practice. He went ahead and texted everyone. He decided to have some Cheerio's for breakfast.

"Good morning, you big dummy," his two year younger sister Anna said. "Mom is upset with you for staying out so late. You have to go to school, you know."

"Shut it up girl before I kick your butt," Sam replied.

"Mom," Anna yelled. "Sam's being mean to me."

"Little Brat," Sam whispered. "Tattletale, The devil's gonna get you."

"Mom," Anna repeated. "Sam's being mean to me."

"Just settle down you two," Erica said, as she walked into the kitchen. "Why were you out so late last night, Sam?"

"Got me a girlfriend, mom," Sam replied. "Yup, and I am crazy about her."

"I'll bet it's that pretty little guitarist, Penny, whom your band picked up?" Erica grinned. "I wanted to let you two know what your cousin, Riley G. Van Lorne, who lives in Los Angeles, has accomplished. He has graduated from the Georgetown University, Magna-cum-laude, and has received a Bachelor of Science in Foreign Service (B.S.) degree. He has also won the prestigious Rhodes scholarship to study for two years at University College, Oxford, in the United Kingdom, where he will study Philosophy, politics, and world economics.

"What is "Magnetcomelotta" and where is Georgetown, mom?" Anna asked.

"It's Magna-M-a-g-n-a….cum-c-u-m….laude-l-a-u-d-e, Anna. It is Latin Honors used to indicate the level of distinction with which an academic degree is earned," Erica replied.

"How do you get that?" Anna asked.

"Well, let's see, I believe that you are required to achieve a specific grade point average, and I think you are also required to submit an honors thesis for evaluation, to be part of the program."

"That is sooo boring!" Anna yelled. "Where is that Georgetown University?"

Erica grabbed a letter from the counter and looked it over, "It's in Washington, D.C."

"So boring! Not at all interesting." Anna wailed, sitting at the table with her chin propped on her hands.

"Not really," Erica said, "You two should take some inspiration from your cousin, Riley. Since Aunt Cathy and Uncle Jon moved to Malibu along with your grandparents, Riley has excelled in his studies. He became the valedictorian of his class at the Malibu High School."

"Enough about Rie! By the way, mom, I've made straight A's for my final two years," Sam said, "Now, what did you decide on Penny's parents wanting to take Zack, Deacon and I to London on vacation with them. What do you think about that?"

"I don't know, Sam. You have to have passports and everything! Did you run that past your father? I don't know if he wants to be bothered with passports at the moment."

"No problem there, mom. Mr. Daiquiri said he would take care of all of that, not to worry."

"I wanna go," Anna exclaimed.

"Sorry, Anna, not this time, maybe some time in the future. Still love you!" Sam replied, as he threw her a kiss.

"Talk to your father, Sam, I brought it up to him, anyway, I have to get going to work," Erica said, as she grabbed her keys, kissed them both and headed for the door.

"Be careful, mom," Anna yelled. "It's a jungle out there."

Michael Trainer came down the steps of the split level home and appeared in the kitchen, "Good morning," he whispered, as he put two slices of bread in the toaster. "How are my rocker and my cheerleader doing this morning?"

"Dad, do you know how to spell mountaineer?" Anna asked, doing a couple of cheerleading moves.

"I don't know, how?"

"WVU," Anna yelled, with a big smile. "Get it, isn't that funny?"

"Yup, that West Virginia Mountaineer Football team has been outstanding. I hope they continue. Samuel will be going there this year, and will be studying to be a Civil Engineer."

"We need to talk about that, dad. You know my thoughts about becoming an attorney. Anyway, Zack, Deacon and I have been invited by Penny's parents, to go on vacation with them to England. Penny's father is Ben Daiquiri. He is the son of Grandpa Thurston's lawyer friend in England, Benjamin Franklin Daiquiri. They called him, 'Daiq', for short, remember? What a small world. He said he would take care of the passports or whatever is needed to get us there. He has an itinerary set up with transportation, hotels, golf, a tour of the Beatles in Liverpool and golf at the Royal Liverpool Golf Club. We even have a couple of days in St. Andrews, Scotland. What about playing at the Royal and Ancient Golf Club at St. Andrews? How do you see it dad?" Sam questioned, as he made a gesture as if he were praying, and crossing himself.

"Oh yes, your mother mentioned all of that to me, and as a matter of fact, your grandparents are visiting Daiq in London as we speak. Daiq has a beautiful multimillion dollar luxury home there in Richmond, and your grandfather is seriously thinking about moving to England in the future. I think it would be alright if you three go," Mike said, with a big smile.

"Thanks, dad!" Sam replied, crossing himself again. "You, mom and Anna will get to go sometime, I'm sure. Love you."

"Oh, by the way, "Mike continued. "I need to talk to you two about the opioid abuse that is going on in the Tri-State area; Ohio, Pennsylvania and West Virginia have had an abundant amount of heroin overdose deaths lately. Ohio has an average of about five deaths per day. Pennsylvania and West Virginia aren't any behind either. Prescription opioid drugs are part of the drug problem also, and funding for detox centers is next to impossible. Insurances will not cover opioid abusers and the detox centers are full (*no more room at the inn*). Thirty-seven million dollars are spent on short term detox centers a year, with constant repeaters. It is like beating a dead horse, trying to keep up with long term recovery. I have told you two about the consequences. If your take drugs, you will die, that is a consequence. So please make wise choices. I love you guys."

"They're spreading it around school that marijuana is safe and alright. Hail Mary Jane," Anna responded, with a puzzled look.

"Marijuana is a come on, Anna, don't be taken in, stay away from it," Samuel warned.

"That's right, alright get going you two, it's time to get to school," Mike said.

They both grabbed their book bags and ran out the door.

CHAPTER 22

At two-thirty, Sam busted out of the door at the school. It was Wednesday, and the summer vacation was just one day away. He had no school Friday, and was getting anxious about the trip that all of them were going on to London. All these magnificent things that are going down lately are the sort of things that only happen once in a lifetime. Everyone was meeting at Fritz's at 3 pm. He ran across the grassy area to the parking area designated to the seniors to park, threw his book bag in the back seat of Mercedes Van, and climbed into the driver's seat. He couldn't wait to tell Weed that the man working at the Subway hoagie shop could not identify him with the hoodie, and that he was Hispanic. That explained the "amigo"! He slammed the door, cranked up the engine, and took off. He made his way to Fritz's in about fifteen minutes. It was quarter till three. Sam got out of the Mercedes and walked into Fritz's, giving thumbs up to the Stop, Drop and Roll sign. Everyone was there as he gave Penny a huge hug and high fived the others.

"Hey, Weed, I guess every cloud has a silver lining. You are clean as a whistle," exclaimed Sam, as he threw his arms around Weed. "That Hispanic guy at Subway couldn't figure out whether you were black or white, let alone Hispanic."

"Cool it, Sam," Penny warned, motioning towards the bar. "There's an elephant in the room."

Sam looked towards the bar and standing there was a slight man in a suit, which looked like it was two sizes too big for him. One could probably stick two fingers between his neck and his buttoned shirt. His tie was all askew, and it was pretty early in the day for anyone to look so unkempt.

Sam thought: "That's the guy that got sand kicked in his face on the back page of the comic books when we were kids."

The man walked over to where Sam was standing and shifted his cigar from one side of his mouth to the other.

"Is there something I can help you with?" Sam asked, trying to figure out what was on a lapel pin on his suit. It looked like a duck.

"Are you Sam Trainer?" the man asked. He stood at a distance much closer to Sam than that Sam was comfortable with.

"Yeah," Sam answered, gently pushing him back a little, thinking that he must be some kind of private dick, whatever. "And who might you be?" he asked.

"Detective Hunter McClain, I'm an investigator for the prosecutor's office, the Chief of Police Calabrese wanted me to look into a few things. Which one of you is Deacon Fritz?"

"That would be me," Deacon replied. "My father owns this place."

"Okay, Deacon," Hunter said, writing in his notebook, and calling the three of them aside. "I need to ask you a couple of questions. On the morning of May 21st, you signed yourself, Sam Trainer, and Zack Taylor up at the Pines Country Club, to play 18 holes of golf. Is this information correct?"

"Yes, that is correct."

"And did the three of you finish those eighteen holes of golf?" Hunter asked.

Deacon thought: *Oh, crap, I can't tell him we finished, he definitely knows something*

Deacon replied, "No, we didn't finish. Zack was feeling a bit under the weather, so we decided to stop the game midway and returned to the clubhouse."

"Alright, that checks out. The man attending the cart barn said that the three of you turned the golf carts in early," Hunter said, and made a note in his book, muttering under his breath. "Quit golf early."

"Why are you so concerned about when we finished golfing?" Sam asked. "What was going on that day?"

"We are investigating the disappearance of a leather transport bag that went missing that day," Hunter replied. "One of the groundskeepers said that when the three of you came off the course, there was a huge bag fitting that description. It was loaded on one of your golf carts, and was put into the back seat of a Nissan Altima. Chief Calabrese asked me to question the three of you and possibly make you a deal."

"What kind of deal?" Zack asked, thinking: "This should be good."

"If you quietly turn that transport bag over to him, in private, there may be a reward of $30,000 dollars for its return. That would be ten thousand tax free dollars, apiece. How does that sound to you?" Hunter asked, "No questions asked, and the three of you would be off the hook. Possibly stay alive. Otherwise, he will contact Mr. Donovan and let him know the whereabouts of the transport bag."

"Gotcha," Deacon said. "A little bit of a payoff to keep our mouths shut."

"Let's say it would be a security blanket, which would help you stay alive," Hunter warned. "You guys don't realize how dangerously you're living. I would advise you to take the deal, and walk away as quietly as possible."

"Here is what we'll do. We are all going on vacation for about a week. We will be leaving this Saturday. Once we return, we will definitely make the deal. Run that past the chief, see if he agrees," Sam bargained. "And then let us know."

The detective got up to leave and said, "You three are completely fucked. You are playing with dynamite."

"What was that all about?" Penny asked. "Are you three in trouble? Who was that spooky character?"

"He's a private detective; he was here on the behalf of Chief

Calabrese. They actually know that we have the money. Chief Calabrese wants to make a deal," Sam answered.

"What kind of deal?" Penny asked,

"Calabrese wants to reward the three of us with $30,000 tax free dollars in return for that leather duffle bag in your safe," Deacon shouted, searching his pockets, "By the way, where are my truck's keys? Has anyone seen my truck keys?

"Nope," everyone said, looking around on tables and all over the floor.

"Did you leave them in your truck, Deacon," Zack asked, shrugging his shoulders.

Deacon pulled Penny aside and said, "The key to your safe was on that key ring."

"Not to worry, Deacon," Penny replied. "I'll give you a new one."

"I'll have to call my dad and tell him to bring my other set of keys," Deacon said, as he ran out to his truck for a quick check.

"So what did you tell the detective? Are you accepting the deal? If it was me, I would take the reward!" Penny shouted, giving thumbs up. "That way, you won't have to worry about Donovan chopping your heads off."

"I told him to tell Chief Calabrese that we would make the deal when we all returned from the United Kingdom," Sam said. "How do you see it?"

"I think you're just pissing off the chief. You're playing the Devil's advocate. He'll probably just kill the three of you, that's the easier way."

"I really don't think so, Penny," Sam countered. "Calabrese needs to know where that money is located. Besides that, we'll be away for a week."

Weed and Mateo were sitting and drinking Coors and listening to what was transpiring when Weed said, "This is the way I see it. Donovan is a very impatient man and I believe Calabrese and Donovan are in this thing together. If Calabrese turns the leather duffle bag over to Donovan, everything will be cool. It will be business as usual. I think we are adding insult to injury. I mean, furthering Donovan's loss, with mockery or indignity; it is like actually worsening his miserable situation."

"I just want to see Chief Calabrese squirm a little. Both Calabrese and Donovan are at our mercy. So that's the deal. If Chief Calabrese accepts our deal, and we give him the benefit of the doubt, it will be the best thing that happens since sliced bread. But let's think about that later team. We have to get to Penny's house for practice."

"By the way," Zack said. "My parents said that it would be alright for me to go to the United Kingdom. They think it would be a terrific experience."

"Ditto!" Deacon exclaimed. "My mom and dad are cool with it as well."

"Good," Penny said. "My father will have your passports done tomorrow! I wish that Weed and Mario were going, but my father said that we are at our unconditional limit. We will be flying out at nine thirty Saturday morning. We'll all meet at my house 7am. My father will fly us out in his helicopter to the Pittsburgh International Airport. Are you guys excited?"

"Absolutely," Zack screamed. "We can't wait. Actually, I can't wait to get to Liverpool. You guys know that the Beatles were always my favorite group, and that is on our itinerary when we get to England. I think we are scheduled to stay at the Liverpool Hilton City Centre on our third day. We have a private Beatles tour booked there, in a Limousine to boot. Sum-bitch! I sure wish we were around when the Beatles had first started. They certainly left their mark in the history of Rock 'n Roll. The Royal Liverpool Golf Club in Hoylake which hosted The British Open Championship in 2006 is also pretty damn close to Liverpool. We will also be staying at the Hoylake Holiday Inn Express, and will play golf there, according to the schedule."

"Yup, we are all crazy about the Beatles. Before they arrived in the United States, Elvis Presley was the most famous singer in the world, along with Little Richard, and Chuck Berry, who made the guitar the lead instrument in Rock 'n Roll," Deacon remarked.

"Chuck Berry was the man; his distinctive guitar playing has been imitated by almost every guitar player in the world. His songs were so popular and so well known that he could play with any local band and be sure that they would know his music. The Beatles played many of his songs in their early days. They put, 'Rock and Roll Music' and 'Roll over Beethoven', on their early albums. The three most influential musicians of the 1950's and early 60's were Little Richard, Chuck Berry, and Elvis Presley," Sam added.

"I still believe that Buddy Holly was the real father of Rock 'n Roll, it's too bad that his life ended at the height of his career. In my opinion, he would have been the greatest," Penny stated, as she kissed her hand and blew it in the air.

"You are probably right, Penny, I believe there would be millions of Rock 'n Roll music lovers to agree with you about Buddy Holly," Sam agreed. "Alright let's get going over to your place, Penny, we have to get something put together for tomorrow's gig."

Deacon had to wait at Fritz's until his father arrived with his keys. He went out to the parking lot, unlocked his truck and slid into the driver's seat. His radio was having a special report on a local station before he switched over to his Sirius XM Satellite Radio. The special report was saying that a horrendous explosion and fire had occurred earlier in the day at the home of Briccio Cadmen Donovan of Fairmont, West Virginia. Donovan and his wife Cleopatra had fallen victims to the fire along with three others who were apparently living there.

"What the Hell?" Deacon yelled. "You've got to be kidding me."

CHAPTER 23

The Chief-of-Police Anton Calabrese was born in Manhattan on July 7, 1965. He had graduated from Cardinal Hayes High School, which was a Catholic High School for boys in the Concourse Village neighborhood of the Bronx, New York City. He attended New York University, which is a private nonprofit research university, where he studied Criminal Law. During that period of time, he met Sandra Renee Bailey from Albany, New York. Sandra and Anton got married at the All Saints Catholic Church in Albany on July 18, 1986. They honeymooned at the Niagara Falls, New York, at a popular spot for getting wowed or soaked amid natural splendor. Anton joined the New York City Police Department through a training class in 1986. Over the course of his twenty year career with the NYPD, he'd risen to the rank of deputy chief, with notable stops as first-grade detective and executive officer with the chief of detectives. During this period, he sold his badge a couple of times for big money payoffs from the big hitters of the drug world, to look the other way. These deals sometimes involved Briccio Cadmen Donovan, whose business was all under the table and no-one knew. Anton wanted to get away from the hustle and bustle of the big city, for it meant a lot of activity and work for him and that too in noisy surroundings. He totally enjoyed taking his family on annual vacations, especially to Myrtle Beach. His plan was to relocate, simply put, "I want a life with fewer distractions and more opportunities to dig deep into the things most important to me, and I also want a life with a lower cost of living and a lower need to earn a mountain of money. A rural provides all of these things."

In 2006, Anton had seen an ad for a job as Chief of Police of Morgantown, West Virginia, and the prospect had immediately grabbed his attention. He trusted his gut instinct; going with an idea that had just come to him was usually a better plan than the one he had carefully thought environment over for months and months. He was offered the job and he graciously accepted the offer. Anton and Sandra, along with their two daughters, Cindy, 18, and, Cathy, 16, moved to Morgantown, West Virginia in August of 2006. They purchased a home near Cheat Lake on Shadyside Lane, a Greystone home with a spectacular addition that was perfect for entertainment. Further there were two family great rooms, two kitchens with granite & solid surface countertops, bar, new stainless top of the line appliances, two gas fireplaces, four bedrooms, two GFA furnaces and central air, extensive decking and patio space, high bronze ornamental aluminum fencing, a low maintenance Viking in ground swimming pool, and a three-car garage.

Anton Calabrese was sworn in as the Chief of Police by Morgantown's honorable Mayor Harold Conway, and was introduced to the members of the city council, the city manager and many other dignitaries attending the ceremony. Chief Calabrese became familiar with his new surroundings and was meeting with few of his new staff, including George Oliver, the Chief Investigator, Sparrow Alexander, Assistant Investigator, a lieutenant, Bernard King and Sgt. Earnest Maxwell.

"Chief Calabrese," George Oliver said, "Because of the protection from some of our law enforcement officers in our Morgantown Police Department, there are very few convictions for drug distribution, trafficking and manufacturing in all of the Monongalia County, targeting corrupt dealings. The four of us, Sparrow, Bernie, Gary and me have been in contact with a gentleman, Briccio Cadmen Donovan, who says that he can make our lives a little more comfortable, if we keep it that way. How do you see it?"

"I've had dealings with Mr. Donovan before when I worked as a detective for the New York Police Department," Chief Calabrese replied. "The way I see it, you are dealing with a hot potato. Corrupt law enforcement is an issue that many people are talking about and which is usually highly disputed. This would not be the first time that I have received money under the table. How much is Mr. Donovan willing to pay for this protection?"

"Thirty thousand dollars a month," George answered, "the four of us would each receive five thousand a month and that would leave you ten thousand tax free dollars per month, Chief Calabrese."

"Sounds like a no-brainer to me, we will meet with Mr. Donovan and work out all the details," Chief Calabrese responded, as he shook all of their hands

George Oliver also explained that their dealings were completely separate from Donovan's dealings with the Morgantown Law Offices, such as, Rockefeller and Rockefeller, who have successfully defended West Virginians facing serious drug charges at state and federal levels. They carefully probe law enforcement procedures to make sure proper protocol is followed, including stopping and searching your vehicle and searching their homes. They examine all the evidence against them. They challenge the assumptions and actions that lead the police to investigate them. And they expose any informants who may have testified against them.

"Most of the drug distributers, traffickers and manufacturers go free with the help of corrupt law enforcement."

CHAPTER 24

Deacon cranked up his truck, put it in gear and drove directly to Penny's house, busting at the seams, anxious to deliver the news about Donovan. When he arrived at Penny's and rushed into the utility building, he saw that all of them were already watching a special report about a horrendous explosion and fire at the Donovan complex. The home was completely destroyed and the bodies of Briccio Cadmen Donovan and his wife Cleopatra had been found, along with three other bodies of persons, who were supposedly living at the complex. All five of the victims were supposedly shot in the head, execution style, before the explosion and fire. The report said that the explosives were detonated off site after the killings were done early this morning. Lieutenant Frank Harrison of the West Virginia state police said that an ongoing investigation has been going on involving the gang-related illegal drug operation run by kingpin Briccio Cadmen Donovan. The local and state police were working closely with the FBI, the Criminal Investigation Division of the IRS and other federal agencies. Meth, marijuana, cocaine and heroin were found in what the state police and FBI were calling the biggest drug bust in department history…an estimated twenty to thirty million dollars in drugs and drug paraphernalia was confiscated from a warehouse on the property, which also included money, weapons, and vehicles.

"What do you think happened there?" Sam asked. "Do you think the cartel did this? Maybe a rival gang?"

"Your guess is as good as mine. Maybe that freakin' Chief Calabrese had something to do with blowing Donovan away. What do you think?" Zack blurted out.

"I don't think so, Zack," Deacon replied, "He had no reason and besides, he was already getting a payoff from Donovan."

"I can't believe they executed your sister Cleopatra, Weed," Mateo said.

"Doesn't surprise me in the least about Cleo," Weed said. "I just can't believe that a drug cartel gang would do a killing like that. They would privately eliminate Donovan and replace him. Mass killings are relatively rare and basically stupid ideas. All this will do is generate relentless pressure from federal authorities and give them open access to the Donovan complex. Whoever pulled this off was intending to shut down the entire multi-million dollar operation. It was definitely a set-up to make it look like it was gang related."

"From what I've heard, that had to be a rival gang from another part of the state, or from another area such as Pittsburgh or Columbus, to completely shut Donovan's operation down. Donovan's people handle millions and millions of dollars a year and I don't think they would do anything to disturb their own operation. Like Weed said, if they had a problem with Donovan, they wound have taken him away and killed him and just replaced him," Penny replied.

"Oh, yes," Weed said. "This will be very crippling to the whole operation, especially with all the drug paraphernalia that they confiscated; they will now have to completely reorganize. Possibly with the law enforcement holding tight, they may not be able to resurface. Donovan had a huge three-state operation going, and the drug shut down could easily spread to Chicago to New York City."

"What about Chief Calabrese and the deal that he wants to quietly pull off with the $30,000 reward?" Deacon asked with outstretched arms.

"I'm thinking that he plans to keep all that money for himself. There is no way of tracking that money in the leather duffle bag and

I really don't think that Chief Calabrese would hesitate killing us for it," Zack remarked.

"There have certainly been a whole lot of people killed this last week, all because of that leather bag. Sgt. Maxwell, the three thugs and Maxwell's wife in the exploding black Pick-up, Chief Inspector George Oliver, Chief Inspector Sparrow Alexander, and now Donovan, Cleopatra, and three of their gang members. I don't think that Chief Calabrese would be too liberal about not killing three more; definitely not if it means getting his hands on that money," Mateo replied, gesturing slicing his throat with a knife.

"Amazing, and it's all because of greed, and how people will kill for it." Sam said. "We'll have to handle Chief Calabrese. We will have to be ready when the time comes. Now that Donovan is out of the way, you can bet your last dollar that Calabrese will be over-anxious to get his grubby hands on that money. Like Mateo said, we are history if Calabrese finds out where that money is. You can also bet that the piece of shit detective, Hunter McClain will be coming around again with another deal. We may have to let this all cool down. You know, like put it all on the back burner until we return from the holiday."

"Do you think Hunter McClain knows what is in that bag?" Deacon asked.

"I doubt it. I think Chief Calabrese would want to keep that a secret, I don't think he wants anyone to find out what is in that bag." Sam responded. "We don't even know if Calabrese is in on this by himself. There may be others involved. Right now, we have to focus on getting the band set up to play some good songs. Penny has a song that she wrote that she and I are trying to put together. It sounds a whole lot like something Bob Dylan would have put together. Mateo and Weed know the sound and we can all blend in until we get it. It's a mix of different things. Its face-melting guitar rock chopped and sautéed with heart-wrenching keyboard sounds, and elegantly garnished with awesome lyrics. The name of the song is 'No Two Ways' and this song just may be a hit."

After practice, everyone had packed up the equipment, said their goodbyes, and was heading out. Penny reminded them that they were meeting at Fritz's, 2 PM tomorrow, before we all head to the Community Center for the gig.

Sam hung around after the practice, wanting to spend some time with Penny alone, still humming the music of the song that Penny had written and trying to remember the words.

"That part of the song where the man was the teacher and the girl was the student," Sam asked, giving her a little smile. "Was that about you and me?"

"If I wrote the song about you and me, I would have written this," she said and went on to sing, "I see myself as your student… and you as the teacher so wise…my mind is wide open…and not to mention my thighs. Oh, no, I meant my eyes."

"Whoa," Sam laughed, covering his mouth.

"Isn't that funny?" Penny laughed and kept cleaning up and stashing empty beer bottles in a trash bag, and wiping off the top of the bar, while Sam walked up behind and wrapped his arms around her.

"Are you trying to turn me on?" Penny asked, as she turned and was facing Sam, their faces were close, he felt the warmth of her cheeks, and it was the kind of thing that could never happen in another hundred nights, but this night it was possible. The conversation, the booze, the song.

They grabbed each other, Sam was pushing her up against the bar for better leverage. Penny breathed out heavily at that moment, which only made Sam more insistent on touching her, touching everything at once. And her, letting him.

She pulled away from him, her breathing hurried, "Come with me in the van, Sam."

Sam paused.

"Come with me in the van," she said again. "I want to be with you."

They spent some time in the Mercedes van, kissing, then returned to the utility building.

"Let's be good," Penny whispered. "I am so much in love with you, some day, my teacher. I'll teach you a thing or two."

"I couldn't love you more, Penny," Sam replied, giving her a huge hug.

They finished cleaning up, took all the garbage bags out to the trash, and decided to call it a night.

"I can't wait to read the paper in the morning to see how everything is developing with the drug bust," Sam said.

"I just wish that you guys would settle up with Chief Calabrese."

"I'm thinking Calabrese may not want to leave any witnesses to say something in the future. He may just trash the three of us if we give up that leather bag. We may be able to give it over to the proper authorities if we wait and see what happens with what is going down now."

"Okay then, I'll be seeing you tomorrow Sam."

They kissed a few times before Sam jumped in the Mercedes and went home.

CHAPTER 25

In the morning edition of The Dominion Post, the headlines were all about the huge drug bust and the destruction of the Donovan complex in Fairmont, West Virginia that took the lives of Briccio Cadmen Donovan and his wife. The news article read:

Huge Drug Operation Taken Down

A horrendous explosion and fire occurred at the Briccio Cadmen Donovan complex on Thursday, as the home was completely destroyed and the bodies of Donovan and his wife, Cleopatra, were found, along with three other bodies of persons believed to be living at the complex. The other three bodies were identified as Arnold Cress, Roscoe Dashon, and Marco Anthony. All five victims were supposedly shot in the head, execution style, right before the explosion and fire broke out. The report said that the explosives were detonated off site after the killings were done early this morning.

Lieutenant Frank Harrison of the West Virginia state police reported that an ongoing investigation has been going on involving the gang-related illegal drug operation run by Briccio Cadmen Donovan. The local and state police were working closely with the FBI, the Criminal Investigation Division of the IRS and other federal agencies.

Meth, marijuana, cocaine and heroin were found in what the state police and FBI have called the biggest drug bust in department history… an estimated twenty to thirty million dollars of drugs also included money, weapons, vehicles, and an entire trucking operation, including trucking vehicles and buildings that were all purchased with ill-gotten gains. (Obtained in an evil manner or by dishonest means)

Many arrests are being made today at undercover locations throughout the states of West Virginia, Pennsylvania and Ohio. The presence of Meth Labs continues rising in all the counties and townships. These Meth Labs have been identified in suburban houses, hotel rooms, department store bathrooms, college dorms, and in the run-down shacks. The local and federal law enforcement authorities are not only shutting down the clandestine Methamphetamine Laboratories, but they are also busting all known drug trafficking operations that they have been watching for over a year. Arrests may be in the thousands.

While reading the article Sam thought: *Oh my God!* Chief Calabrese was really going to be anxious about getting his hands on that drug money now, so he could make his escape. He would surely be found out. All of his law enforcement corruption had caught up.

Sam texted Penny: "The crap is coming down in the drug bust; did you see the morning papers?"

Penny texted: "My dad is reading it right now, but I saw it earlier, what about Chief Calabrese? This is honestly getting scary, Sam."

Sam texted: "I agree… scary… we will probably hear from him today…see you at The Fritz at 2."

This really sucks! Sam thought, as he ran through the mudroom to the half bath to take a shower, while also thinking how wonderful it was that he didn't have school today. As a matter of fact, he was finished going to University High School forever. Now he had the entire summer to convince his father to nuke the idea of him studying to become a Civil Engineer. He had his heart set on getting a law degree. He had secretly submitted an application to the Yale Law School. He had achieved the specific grade point average required, and had also submitted an honors thesis for evaluation, hoping to receive some kind of scholarship. He actually thought that he was spinning his wheels. Gads, expelling a whole lot of effort with little or no return from his dad. A scholarship from Yale University would probably do the trick, if only he could get chosen. Damn it, he looked at the itinerary of the United Kingdom that Penny had given him, which he had folded carefully and stuffed in his pocket, and thought: Oh my God, look at this, two days in London sightseeing, two days in Liverpool, Beatle tour and golf, and two days in St, Andrews, with golf at The Old Course. Seems surreal! He folded it jammed it back in his pocket, shot upstairs and into the kitchen.

"Where's the paper, Samuel?" Michael asked.

"I left it in the mudroom, I'll get it," Sam said.

"You know your father likes to read the paper before he goes to work," Erica yelled while trying to get Anna ready for school.

"I got it! I got it!" Sam yelled.

He returned and handed the paper to his father.

"Oh, you have to go to school today, Anna?" Sam teased.

"Yes, I can't stand it, we have another week," Anna said. "Stop making fun."

"Stop teasing your sister, Sam. What time are you supposed to leave tomorrow morning?

"I want to be there at six thirty." Sam answered.

"Well I see that they're finally cracking down on the drugs in Morgantown and Fairmont. That is some kind of huge operation they had going on. That Donovan character and his wife were both killed in that explosion and fire," Mike said.

"Where was that?" Erica asked, coming over to take a look.

"That Donovan's house was South of Morgantown in Southern Fairmont." Mike said. "It says that Donovan, his wife and three others living there were shot in the back of their heads before the explosion and fire. Execution style. I'm thinking it was gang related."

"Probably right, dad. Looks like the proper authorities are

kicking some butt. They are sure shutting down all the trafficking joints and Meth labs. They are arresting hundreds as we speak, Mom.

"I wanna go," Anna cried, as she stuck out her lower lip.

"Sorry, girl, you have to go to school. Remember!" Sam teased, sticking his lower lip out at Anna.

"Stop it, you two, oh, by the way Mike, I still smell gas in the back of the house. You better get someone to look at that." Erica suggested. "Did you hear me, Mike. We don't want an explosion here, like that one in the paper."

"Yeah, I heard you. There must have been a leak in that crawl space. I got the Gas Company coming tomorrow or the next day. Not to worry," Mike replied.

"Anna, don't forget your lunch, I put it next to your book bag," Erica said, as she gave them all a kiss. "I have to get going."

"Be careful, mom" Anna said. "It's a jungle out there."

"Okay, honey. I'll be careful."

"Hey, dad, that Briccio Cadmen Donovan was the jerk that ran me off the road in my old van. He is married to Roberto Fernandez's sister, Roberto is one of the new guys in our band, and Donovan was one mean sum-bitch. Believe me, he thought that I was harassing Roberto and Mateo out on I-68 East and that's why he cut me off. After Roberto explained what happened, he actually apologized for wrecking my van and paid me the same amount of money that I received from the Auto Insurance Company. I am just using Penny's van until I can find something else. Maybe when I become an attorney, I'll be able to afford something nicer. How do you see it, Dad?" Sam asked, subtly throwing a hint.

"First of all, watch that language around your sister, and second, Howard and I have big plans for you in the construction business as a Civil Engineer. You may end up owning and operating the business eventually. Listen, incoming freshmen are automatically considered for merit-based scholarships at the time they submit their application to WVU Engineering. Therefore, early applications are strongly encouraged," Mike said.

"Alright, dad," Sam replied. And then he thought: *What the hell am I even saying?* Was Sam beating a dead horse here? He wanted to be a lawyer. Was he dwelling on something that is well beyond its point of solution?

"Oh, dad," Sam said, throwing another hint. "Don't you sometimes need an attorney around the business to take care of deeds and settling disputes?"

"Forget it, Sam," Mike replied. "I know what you're aiming at, you becoming a lawyer. It just isn't going to happen. We cannot afford it; anyway, I have to get to work now."

"Be careful, dad," Anna said. "It's a freakin' jungle out there."

"I'm fighting a losing battle," Mike laughed. "Make sure Anna gets to the school bus, Sam."

"Yeah, right!" Sam yelled distastefully.

Sam texted Penny: "I'm getting nowhere with my dad about wanting to be a lawyer… can't crack the shell."

Penny texted: "Things will work out… did you look at the itemized itinerary for our trip?"

Sam texted: "Are you kidding me? Hour by hour, what a layout… I have it opened up on the table right now… I am so excited to go."

Penny texted: "My grandparents have eight bedrooms in their house. Darn it."

Sam texted: "Be good… I can't wait to see my grandparents… Mimi and Fuge… and my cousin Rie Guy."

Penny texted: "It's going to be a blast, look over the itinerary and I'll see you at Fritz's at two."

Sam Looked at the Itinerary, It read:

Sat. 7:15 am…	Leaving in a six-passenger helicopter to the Pittsburgh International Airport.
Sat. 9:30 am…	Departure from Pittsburgh International Airport.
Sat. 10:30 pm…	Arrive at Heathrow International Airport, London.

Tue. 8:30 am… Departure from Heathrow International Airport, London.

Tue. 9:30 am… Arrive at Liverpool John Lennon International Airport, Liverpool.

Thu. 8:00 am… Departure from Liverpool John Lennon International Airport, Liverpool.

Thu. 8:30 am… Arrive at Dundee Airport, Dundee, Scotland.

Sat. 8:00 am… Departure from Dundee Airport, Scotland.

Sat. 9:00 am… Arrive at Heathrow International airport, London,

Sun. 10:00 am… Departure from Heathrow International airport, London.

Sun. 1:00 pm… Arrival at Pittsburgh International Airport.

Sam folded the itinerary again and stuck it back in his pocket. He turned on the golf channel as he thought: *You're right Penny; we are really going to have a blast*

At 1:30 pm, Sam jumped into the Mercedes, revved up the engine and was just beginning to leave for Fritz's, when he got an unidentified text from someone. He brought it up and it was from none other than Hunter McClain.

McClain had texted: "Mr. Trainer, I need to have another talk with the three of you. Let me know when and where. It is of utmost importance."

Sam texted Hunter McClain back: "The three of us will be at Fritz's after two o'clock today; we will talk to you… but don't waste our time."

McClain texted: "See you there, boss!"

CHAPTER 26

While driving to Fritz's, Sam thought: *That little weasel* Hunter McClain knew more than he is letting on. There is no longer the thought that Chief Calabrese needed that bag of money to give it back to Donovan, to save his own neck. Now, his intent is clearly very selfish. He needed escape money to go away to another country or to the islands, like Sparrow Alexander envisioned, as an alternative for jail time. Sam certainly needed to talk to Deacon and Zack before we meet again with Hunter. He didn't want them slipping up and saying something about the amount of money they are dealing with. They would be there early anyway.

Sam swung the Mercedes into the parking lot at Fritz's, jumped out, locked the door and proceeded to the entrance. He walked in, gave thumbs up to the Stop, Drop and Roll sign and spotted Deacon right away. He was helping his dad move something to a storage room in the back of the bar.

"How you doing, Mr. Fritz," Sam said. "Wuz sup, Deacon."

"Sup," Deacon replied. "We're just stashing the money Francisco brought in last night."

You could tell that Francisco and Deacon definitely had some black DNA in their family tree, because of their wiry hair, which they kept clean shaven, and their skin tone.

"I wish," Francisco uttered. "We're barely keeping our heads above water. Deacon was telling me that your band is playing tonight. What was that new name again?"

"I told you dad, 'No Two Ways', it's pretty cool, we look good."

"It's something Penny thought up, and we voted on it," Sam said, rolling his eyes. "Penny won, of course."

"I love that Penny who comes in here with the band." Francisco smiled. "She's very pretty. I see you have six musicians now. Thank you for the help Sam."

"We have a good thing going, Mr. Fritz," Sam said. "You should come and hear us sometime."

"I will hear you eventually."

Everyone showed up and everyone did their hugs and high fives. They all ordered burgers and cokes, Weed and Mateo each had a beer.

"I got some news for you guys," Sam said. "Guess who's coming to see us this afternoon? Mr. Hunter McClain. We have to be very careful about what we say to that toad. No shit about it. We can't say anything about the amount of money in that leather bag. He said he needed to talk to the three of us. It is something of utmost importance."

Just then, the entrance door opened and a man in an ill-fitting suit stepped in. Just as unkempt as before, his suit was a wrinkled mess, his tie was a little more askew. He let his eyes adjust to the inside and walked directly through to the outside wharf side patio that overlooked the river and motioned Sam to follow. Sam, Deacon and Zack followed Hunter McClain and as he sat at one of the wooden tables, and invited them to sit down. He took out his tattered notebook and a Samsung Galaxy smart-phone.

"Alright, first of all, I am here to collect information for Chief Calabrese. So, don't shoot the Messenger. Chief Calabrese is paying me, a whole lot of money, as a private investigator. To prove to you that this is not pure and utter bullshit, without evidence, I have a video and a sworn statement from one of the groundskeepers at the Pines Country Club who witnessed the three of you carrying and driving off with a large leather bag. You can go to jail for just concealing evidence. Chief Calabrese is making a final offer to you to turn over that bag, privately to him. Ignoring him is not an option. If you do not respond or refuse to accept his offer, there will definitely be consequences."

"Why do you work for that asshole?" Deacon asked. "He is nothing but a greedy freakin' corrupt cop."

Hunter wrote a couple of things in his notebook.

"Why would you say that?" Hunter replied. "You must know something that I don't know, ya think?"

"He just wants to get his mitts on those two and a half million dollars, that's what I'm talkin' about," Deacon yelled, being totally pissed.

"Deacon, Stop!" Sam and Zack yelled simultaneously.

"Get a grip, man," Sam said, his face turning completely red.

"Wow, this is bigger than I ever dreamed. No need to get your shorts in a knot. I haven't told you what the deal is yet. You might like it."

"Yeah, well, I suppose this will be his final offer, before he starts killing us off one-by-one," Deacon replied, trying to calm himself down.

"The offer is this: Chief Calabrese is willing to make this deal, fifty thousand dollars of tax free money for each of you, that's one-hundred and fifty thousand dollars. He will pay the money up front with the agreement that the drug money will be at a designated point. Another policeman will pick up the money and the transaction will be complete. Chief Calabrese will resign and disappear. I would suggest that you take the offer," Hunter said, as he slid the smartphone back into his pocket. "There's no need for this."

"You tell Chief Calabrese that the deal is the same on our part," Sam bargained. "The transaction will go down when we return from our vacation."

"If you don't hear from me, we'll see you in a week." Hunter said. "Oh, Deacon, you ask how I work for that asshole, Calabrese. Do you know how many people would have jobs if they refused to work for assholes? The whole world would be unemployed."

"You are a piece of crap, McClain," Deacon spat out.

"Don't bother showing me out," Hunter replied, as he headed back to the door he came in.

The three of them returned to the table where Penny, Weed and Mateo were sitting.

"Well," Penny said. "Let's hear it."

"Here's my suggestion. We grab that asshole Calabrese late at night, give him a pistol whippin', break his collarbone, chain a couple of cinderblocks to his ankles, and throw him over the back railing in this place into the river."

"Why don't you say what you mean, Deacon," Zack laughed.

"You're the one that let the cat out of the bag about the money, you screwball!" Sam laughed, as he reached over like he was going to smack him in the head. "What the hell were you thinking?"

Deacon braced himself for the verbal assault. Sam was such a control freak. Deacon just kept silent.

Sam accepted that Deacon's intentions were honorable, gave him a high five, and not to mention a huge hug, "You're cool, Deacon," Sam laughed, as he looked at Penny and winked.

"I had a brain fart, that's all. Kill me," Deacon said, pointing his finger at his head like he was going to shoot himself.

"Why are you chaining cinderblocks to the Chief's feet, Deacon?" Penny asked, laughing at what Deacon had said. "We don't want him around, do we?"

"Oh, the cinderblocks are for the weight, Penny," Deacon chuckled. "The current will keep him moving, we don't want him popping up out of the water between here and Pittsburgh."

"You guys are hilarious," Weed interrupted, waving to stop what was happening. "Now what happened with the weasel?"

"Picture this," Sam replied. "Chief Calabrese wants us to turn over the money to him in exchange for one-hundred and fifty thousand, tax free dollars. We leave it at a designated area for another policeman to pick up. When he gets a message that everything is cool, he hands over our money. He says there are no options. They hold a video and a sworn statement from a groundskeeper that witnessed us putting the money in Deacon's car that day. Now, if we didn't respond or refuse the offer, there would be consequences. He will have us arrested and institute legal proceedings against us for concealing evidence, and then we would definitely go to jail.

"When do you want to grab Calabrese, Deacon?" Mateo responded, holding his arms above his head. "I'll do the pistol whipping."

"Alright, let's get serious people, we have a situation here, we have until after our vacation to think about this, and come up with a solution. Maybe we could get Hunter McClain to throw Calabrese under the bus, and come over to our side. Calabrese is actually blackmailing us," Sam barked, as he was holding his chin and thinking. "Let's try to get hold of Hunter after the gig. He may just laugh, but then again, maybe not. We'll text him."

The gig went over like gangbusters. They drew quite a crowd, standing room only, and turned many fans away, who stood and waited outside. They actually did a couple of songs by the "Beatles", thinking about their trip to the United Kingdom. The crowd couldn't stop cheering and screaming, when they announced and played Penny's new song. It was definitely a show-stopper. Everyone was still singing and dancing on their way out.

"That song is going to be a hit," Sam exclaimed, as he was hugging Penny and high fiving everyone. "We have to record a video, for sure."

When everything calmed down, Sam texted Hunter McClain: "Hunter, I'm sure you know that Chief Calabrese is blackmailing us and that he is running a corrupt organization, how would you like to help us clean up this city's mess? We can't pay you a lot of money, but maybe you'll be able to sleep a little better at night if we stop Calabrese's scheme. How do you see it? Please respond tonight if you can, we are leaving on our vacation in the morning."

"That's all you can do, Sam," Penny said. "Let's hope he responds.

Well, Mateo, Weed, I'm so sorry that you two aren't going with us tomorrow morning. We'll bring you some cool stuff."

Penny hugged and kissed them both on the cheek and thanked them for doing such a wonderful job playing in the band and told them that they were all going to be famous someday. Sam, Zack and Deacon also hugged them and thanked them.

"We will see you in a week, we love you to death," Penny said, wiping away a tear. "Be good."

"Yup, see you later," Weed yelled.

"Ciao, Adios, Amigos," Mateo screamed, as they both cranked up there motorcycles and left. The sound was loud and deafening.

"Who wants to get a burger and some fries?" Penny asked.

"I'm heading home," Zack replied. "I still have to take Deacon home, see you in the morning."

"Yup, sorry about my big mouth guys. That Hunter McClain was getting on my nerves. See you in the morning."

"Don't fret about it, Deacon, just get a good night's sleep, my friend," Sam said.

"I'll take a Tylenol PM and sleep like a baby. Bye."

"See you in the morning," Zack yelled, waving. "Sleep tight… Don't let the…You know the rest. Bye."

"Yup," Penny and Sam answered and laughed.

"How about you, big boy, how about a burger and fries?" Penny repeated, grinning like a hog eating coal.

"Oh, hell yes, I'm not going to sleep anyway, I just want that Hunter to respond," Sam moaned, rubbing his eyes.

Penny texted her mom and told her that she was going to be late and not to worry.

Penny's mom texted: "7 AM, sweetie."

Penny and Sam found an all-night, 24/7, restaurant and ordered a couple of burgers and some drinks.

"What do you think, Sam. those kids really liked my song?"

"I think they are all still dancing. That song is going to make it to the top. I believe it is what the kids of today want to hear. They're crazy about it."

Sam's phone beeped and was vibrating.

"That's him. That's Hunter. Come on Hunter, come over with us and bust that freakin' Calabrese."

Sam opened up his phone to the Messenger. The text from Hunter McClain read: "Hello my friend, I have no idea what you are talking about concerning Chief Calabrese. Are you crazy, I mean really, are you on drugs. You want me to believe that Chief Calabrese is mixed up some kind of corrupt law enforcement? How dare you! Chief Calabrese is an honorable man. I would advise you to do as you are told, Sam, see you in a week. Have a nice vacation, boss."

"You got to be shittin' me, they are in this together, Penny. Believe me, him and Chief Calabrese have us completely handcuffed. We have no other alternative but to go along with them. How do you see it, Penny?"

"Yup," Penny sighed.

"This sucks big time."

"I don't know. It may be a God send, Sam. You were looking for something to happen. There's your college money, Sam. That's the way I see it. You can go wherever you want to go, sweetie."

"My God, I never thought of it that way. You are a genius, Penny. What the hell was I thinking? Hell yeah, that is the answer, you sweet thing, wow, it does the same for Deacon and Zack to pay for their educations. Let's ride over to my mom and dad's house, pick up my vacation stuff. I'll just stay at your place tonight. Oh my God. I'm going to Yale Law School at Yale University in New Haven, Connecticut," Sam said, grinning from ear to ear and crossing himself. *Forgive me, sweet Jesus*

CHAPTER 27

Sam heard some people clambering around, moving, talking and getting in and out of things. He looked at the clock on the nightstand; it said 5:15 AM. He looked out the window and there was a helicopter out back being loaded with suitcases. Sam realized where he was. He stretched and went into the adjoining bath. He splashed water on his face and on his hair and combed it straight back. He took a quick shower, dried and put on some clean clothes for his trip to England. He yawned and went out to the hallway.

"Good morning, Sam," Ben Daiquiri said. "Are you ready for an exciting day? We are packing the chopper. When you get your clothes on, we'll pack your suitcase and carry-ons in there, okay? You can call me Ben."

"Yes, I'll throw on my clothes and take my stuff out," Sam said, shaking Ben's hand.

"Your friends will be here early?" Ben asked.

"Yup, they will be here. They are quite excited, Mr. Daiq..., I mean Ben."

"That's more like it. I'll see you in a while, Sam," Ben replied, as he went back down the hall.

"Okay."

"You two seem to be hitting it off, alright, you look like you haven't had any sleep," Penny chuckled, as she gave Sam a big hug and kiss. "You can sleep on the plane. The flight is like, eight hours long."

"Thank God for that, what time do we land in England?"

"Ten thirty, at night!"

"What?"

"England is five hours ahead of us."

"Damn, it'll be time to go to bed," Sam replied, as he was scratching his head. "Go figure."

"I'm going for some breakfast, hurry up and join me, sleepyhead," Penny said, as she walked down the hall.

"Yup," Sam said.

Deacon and Zack showed up at 6:45 am, and were astonished to see the chopper. They got out and grabbed their suitcases and their backpack carry-ons. Ben met them and helped get their things loaded in the chopper.

"I'm impressed, Mr. Daiquiri," Zack yelled, with his arms outstretched. "I'm crazy about this. I have never flown in anything quite that amazing."

"You'll like it, anyway, you two can refer to me as Ben, and refer to my lovely wife as Mary Ann. We like to be called Mary Ann and Ben."

"Okay Ben, we have no problem with that. This makes things more comfortable. What time are we leaving?" Deacon replied, giving Ben thumbs up.

"Around 7:00 AM."

They all boarded the helicopter at 7:05 am, fastened all of their safety belts, tested the flotation devices, secured and locked the doors, and we ready for the uplift. The giant propeller began to turn slowly and gradually picked up speed. When the indicator light came on, they began rising. What a rush, everyone was gripping tightly and hanging on for dear life. Once they cleared the trees and were mid-air, everyone relaxed. Sam was sitting between Penny and Deacon. Penny had finally released her death grip on Sam's hand and his blood began to circulate a little.

"Thanks Penny, my hand was turning blue," Sam stammered,

rubbing his hand. "Have you been pumping iron or something? That's quite a powerful grip."

"You talking to me?" Penny grinned, as she really pissed in his cornflakes. "Why the crocodile tears, big boy? I thought you were so muscle bound?"

Everyone burst out laughing.

"You asked for it, Sam, quit your belly aching," Deacon exclaimed.

"You're just saying that because you know I fear you, look at those finger nails. That would be worse than a mad lioness attacking." Sam laughed, as he made a move like Kung Fu. "I'm not stupid. Give me a break."

"I would not think so, Sam," Penny echoed, with laughter.

"Penny does hold a black belt from the Tae Kwon Do Academy in New York, but she's harmless. Too much love in that girl, but if I were you, I wouldn't try to throw her under a bus. You might be the one going under, Samuel," Mary Ann stated, shaking her finger at Sam. "I'm sorry, you prefer to be called Sam, don't you?

"It's okay, but I do prefer Sam, it's only my parents that call me Samuel!"

"Sam it is," Ben yelled from the cockpit. "I don't want you guys to worry. Mary Ann can fly this chopper as well as me, probably better."

"Knowingly better, babe," Mary Ann spouted. "Like shooting fish in a barrel, just performing a simple task. We're going to let Deacon fly the chopper a while, is that alright Deacon?"

"Oh, hell no," Deacon screamed. "Get out of here. I'm not going near those controls."

"How about you Zack? You ever wanted to fly a chopper?"

"No way. I like it just where I'm sitting," Zack said, hanging on to his seat.

"You toads are all chicken. I'll fly this baby, mom," Penny squealed, undoing her seat belt and laughing.

"No way! This is where we draw the line; you would do anything for a song and a dance," Sam said nervously pulling her back in her seat.

"She's an excellent pilot, Sam. Not much this girl can't do, is there, babe?" Mary Ann boasted.

"Nope," Penny said, flexing her muscles.

Ben maneuvered the helicopter perfectly into position to land where he was being directed. The six of them exited the helicopter and the sky cap attendees removed their luggage and handed their carry-ons and back packs to them. The luggage was transported over to the large Boeing 747, and was placed on a conveyor belt leading to the storage area of the private executive jumbo jet. The six of them were escorted to an exclusive waiting area where they were served coffee, fountain drinks, and water.

At 9 am, the attendant alerted them that it was time to board.

"I am so excited," Penny said, as she did a small clap. "I can't wait to get in the air and on our way. They have a large collection of recent movie videos that we can watch on-board. It's an eight hour trip, you know."

"I plan on catching some shut eye, Penny," Sam yawned. "I think Deacon and Zack probably feel the same, what do you say guys?"

"Yup, that's the way I see it, Sam," Deacon agreed. "How do you see it, Zack?"

"Ditto, I'm bushed."

"Good deal, you three can sack out in the back section, no problem," Ben stated. "Mary Ann and I have had our hearts set to watch one of the new feature videos. Everything is cool."

Ben had borrowed the private (Boeing 747) flying mansion from a mystery billionaire. The unknown billionaire's Boeing 747 was recently disclosed and as expected, it was nothing short of absolute extravagance. Private air buses such as the Bombardier Global Series were the epitome of luxury air travel. These are converted airliners into private flying palaces. The inner flying mansion exudes luxury, filled with the finer things in life, which bring pleasures so freely and easily that one could say without a hint of sarcasm that the mystery billionaire is the kind that views living without luxury as enduring a day without sunshine.

Their Daiquiri party boarded the exclusive airliner and was greeted by Captain Simon McArthur, and his assistant co-pilot, Stephen Gregory, who made them feel very welcome. The stairs were removed and the Captain guided them to the facilities, introduced them to their Flight attendant, Jaqueline Fernandez, and informed them that they will be taxying out very shortly and to enjoy the eight hour flight. Jackie, as she preferred to be called, instructed them to take six of the eight seats and fasten their safety belts until the plane was in the air and levels off. Everyone was super stoked. Ben released Jackie so that she could get belted in herself, along with two others in her crew.

When the airliner leveled, they were told that they could maneuver around and do what they pleased. They were all fascinated with the entire luxury. Not a thing missing. Sam, Deacon, and Zack found a private room with a huge television that they claimed as sleeping quarters, and retired from the Daiquiri's. Penny said, "Forget it. I'm coming with you three!"

Ben said that him and Mary Ann were going to catch up on some movies and went into the small theater. "See you later," Ben said, waving them goodbye.

"What a bust," Zack said. "And you live like this all the time, Penny?"

"I'm at a loss for words," Penny answered. "Basically, yeah, my father has huge money, Zack."

"Cool," Sam said, giving Zack a small punch. "You don't have a spark of decency, asking her that, Zack."

"Sorry."

"Would you two give it a rest? I thought you were going to sleep on this flight," Penny responded.

"I'm wide awake now, too damn excited to sleep," Sam yawned and stretched, as he was being alerted to a text, he pulled out his phone, swiped and pressed the view button on messages. It was from

Hunter McClain, it read: "You people are pissing Chief Calabrese off. He said if you don't do as you are told, people are going to start disappearing, and probably put in jeopardy. Have a nice vacation, boss."

"What the hell," Sam whispered under his breath. "Hunter said that people are going to start disappearing. I have to text Mateo and Weed right now. I have to tell them to keep an eye out for that sort of trouble."

Sam texted Weed: "Be careful... Calabrese and Hunter McClain are talking about grabbing people."

Weed texted back: "No problem, Sam. Mateo and I are packing heat... we'll blow their balls off."

Sam texted Weed: "Okay...this is probably our last text message...no skip land messaging..."

"You don't think those toads will hurt Mateo and Weed?" Penny asked, with a bundle of nerves.

"Those two have no fear, Penny, I would fear for the chief and Hunter, and whoever else is involved in this whole corrupt mess." Sam clarified, pointing his fingers like guns.

"Do you know what I'm thinking, Deacon?" Sam asked.

"Wus that Sam."

"At your dad's place, on the back deck where we had our meeting with Hunter, did I see a surveillance camera pointing almost at our table...Could we possibly view some surveillance footage and maybe screw over that asshole Hunter?"

"Not gonna happen, Sam," Deacon answered. "Those cameras are only in operation at night. There is a huge light on that deck after dark. Good thought though, Sam."

"Damn it," Sam said, looking a little disgusted.

"Hey, Deacon, What was that bullshit that you were laying down, about slamming someone?" Zack asked.

"No Zack, that isn't it. Recently, many people have been saying 'shots fired'. And this is the way I see it. When someone gives you a witty remark or a serious burn, you know! If you ever find yourself on the receiving end of one of those burns, you can say 'shots received'. Get it."

"I don't get it," Zack frowned, shrugging his shoulders.

"Ahhh, if I say to you, Zack, 'Your birth certificate is just an apology from the condom factory', something like that."

Everyone burst out laughing.

"You would say, 'Ouch, Shots received'. See?"

"You're an asshole, Deacon," Zack screamed. "You can't argue that point."

"See there, Ouch, shots received." Deacon laughed. "That is a taste of your own medicine, Zack, remember you telling me, that opinions are like assholes, everyone has one. Ouch. Shots received."

Everyone laughed again.

"You guys are nuts," Penny replied, twirling her finger on her ear.

"Hey, what do you say we play and listen to some of these video's that are in this wall unit? This is some kind of fabulous, big screen, TV-stereo system they have here, and all these couches have reclining seats with earphones. There is even a Beatles series of videos," Sam suggested. "Let's just relax for a while and wait for lunch."

Lunch was served, indeed, and later on the trip, a dinner was prepared.

Ben and Mary Ann got engrossed in a new release video, which was produced and directed by J. J. Abrams, from a book written by a promising star author. Jeffrey Jacob Abrams had films such as, Star Trek, Star Trek-Into Darkness, Mission Impossible-Ghost Protocol, and Super Eight under his belt.

At 10:15 pm, they began circling the Heathrow Airport in England and were preparing to land the huge 747 Luxury Flying Mansion and taxi the massive airliner to the private executive section of the airport, where they would unload and be escorted to a waiting area where a stretch limousine would pick them up. The limo driver was instructed to then proceed to Richmond, England, where Benjamin Franklin Daiquiri and his wife Elizabeth resided.

Daiq & Liz's three-story, six million-dollar home, was within a short walk of Richmond Park, and was approached via electric gates with a generous driveway providing ample space for off street parking and leading to the garage. The ground floor accommodation provided an entrance hall, cloakroom, a magnificent drawing room, and a dining room, a family room with delightful views over the rear garden, a recently remodeled kitchen and breakfast room with a range of integrated appliances. The first floor offered an impressive principal suite with large en suite bathroom and dressing room, guest suite, two further bedrooms and a family room. The second floor was ideal, and was generally used as a guest area or annex and provided a large media room with central light rotunda, doors open to a Juliet balcony and there were more stunning views over the large rear garden with further views overlooking Palewell Common which adjoins Richmond Park. Two further bedrooms on this floor share a magnificent bathroom with a feature central island bath. A detached log cabin style chalet can be found towards the rear of the garden which was ideal for entertaining.

As the limo approached Daiq's street, Ben called ahead so that the electric gates would be open when they arrived. As they pulled into the parking area, they saw Riley G. Van Lorne waiting outside impatiently. He couldn't wait to see his cousin, Samuel, and all of his friends. He also wanted to meet Daiq's son and his wife. It was dark.

CHAPTER 28

Everyone was excited to see each other, they introduced everyone to everyone. Sam and Rie Guy were absolutely elated. It was a perfect gathering place for all of them. The bags were all taken out of the limo by a couple of Daiq's employees. They were put near the designated bedrooms that Liz was assigning for her guests. Every one met in the family room until everyone was comfortable, and Rie suggested that the younger group meet in a detached log cabin style chalet, which they found towards the rear of the garden, and where they could chew the fat and get to know each other better. Daiq, Liz and the others retired to the kitchen to get beverages and a bite to eat.

"What up, guys?" Rie asked, as they bumped fists, high-fived and hugged.

"What up with you, Rie?" Sam replied. "This is Penny. She wants to be my girl. What do you think? Those other two characters are my forever band sidekicks, Deacon and Zack. We also picked up two of Penny's friends in the band, Roberto and Mateo, they're cool."

"Well, let her be your girl, Sam. How are we doing, guys?" Rie asked, holding out his hand to be slapped.

"Sup?" Deacon replied, slapping Riley's hand.

"We have heard a lot about you, Rie. Sam tells us that you are into Rock "n Roll. That is what we are into, also. This is all so fascinating, I actually can't wait to go to the 'Beatles my Story

Magical Tour', in Liverpool," Zack exclaimed, also slapping Riley's hand.

"No crap, Zack, you have not let that rest since we saw the itinerary for this trip. Put a lid on it." Deacon said, giving Zack a cool burn.

"Ouch, shots received, Deacon." Zack yelled, pretending to be hurt.

"Hey, do you people do that, shots fired and shots received?" Rie asked, being amazed.

"Ever since we were on the airplane," Penny laughed, pointing at Deacon and Zack. "Those two are hilarious with their burns."

"I took a look at your itinerary, looks like one hell of a good time, wish I were going. I have to get back to Washington. I am working on some top secret negotiations with some of the president's key people."

"We heard it on the grapevine that you were hanging around Washington, DC, lately, after your graduation from Georgetown," Sam remarked, putting his thumbs under his armpits.

"Ouch, shots received, Sam, take it easy on me. I'm only visiting England to take a look at the University College, in Oxford with Grandfather Fuge and Daiq. They still have some plans for me here in England. They are pushing for me to be a candidate for the Ambassador to England from the United States, Some unbelievable crap, huh?"

"Big position, Rie, maybe we should be asking for your autograph now, before all the shit goes down," Deacon expressed with sincerity. "My God, you are going to be famous, my man."

"I also saw on your itinerary, that you are going to Scotland, at St. Andrews. Remind me to tell you about Fuge and his ties to Saint Andrew," Rie said.

One of Daiq's servants, Edbert, came to check what everyone wanted to eat or drink. They all gave their orders; Rie ordered a six pack of beer and some chips and dip.

"You know that it's on the schedule for us to go to church in the morning, Rie," Sam said. "To St. Patrick, no less, maybe we shouldn't be drinking too much then?"

"When did you turn into a holy roller, Sam?" Deacon asked.

"Suck it up, Sam," Rie whispered. "We're on vacation, remember. Oh, Edbert, make that a twelve-pack of beer."

"No problem, Rie," Sam and all of them said, simultaneously.

"You have made us curious now, Rie," Penny insisted. "Why don't you tell us about Fuge now?"

"Okay, now remember, you asked for it. Our grandfather, Fuge, became a Catholic convert in the later years of his years. He always teased that he received the 'Triple Crown', after taking instructions, being baptized, confirmed and received his first communion on the same day. Fuge chose Saint Andrew for his Patron Saint, and became Andrew within the church, who was the Patron Saint of Social Networking, fishing and Golf. At that time, Mimi let Fuge know that Andrew was God's name, also."

"Really?" Zack questioned, shrugging his shoulders.

"That is so cool, Rie," Sam said. "Did Fuge fill you in on all of that?"

"Yes he did, anyway, having Saint Andrew as Scotland's Patron Saint gave that country several advantages: Because he was the brother of Simon, whom Jesus would call Saint Peter, founder of the church, the Scot's were able to appeal to the Pope. The Declaration of Arbroath protected them against the attempts of English Kings to conquer the Scots."

"I am totally amazed, Rie, how do you know all of that? Penny asked. "It's certainly a good thing to know, because we are going to Scotland, at St. Andrews. What else have you got?"

"Remember, you asked, Scotland needed a national symbol to rally round and motivate their country. Saint Andrew was the inspired choice and the early Scots modeled themselves on Saint Andrew and on one of his strong supporters, the Roman Emperor Constantine the Great, who became Christian and went on to make Christianity the religion of the Roman Empire. The Saltire Cross of

Saint Andrew became the heraldic arms that every Scot could fly and wear. Saint Andrew was crucified by the Romans on an X-shaped cross at Patras in Greece. This happened in 69 AD. He probably did not feel worthy to be crucified on a cross like Christ was."

"My God, Rie," Zack exclaimed. "That is an amazing story that will be stuck in my brain forever."

"I have to agree, Rie," Deacon Said. "You certainly got my attention. I am honestly touched by that story, and your Grandfather Fuge had one hell of a choice for his Patron Saint, especially Patron Saint of Golf."

"I suppose you want to know why Mimi told Fuge that Andrew was actually God's name. Is anyone curious?" Rie questioned.

"Yes, how would your Grandmother Mimi know that?" Zack said, throwing his arms out at his sides, with his hands up.

"Well," Riley replied, "Fuge asked Mimi what she was talking about. God's name wasn't Andy, and Mimi proceeded to tell Fuge that it says so in the words of a popular Christian song. Now Fuge, who was getting frustrated asked, 'What Christian song?' Wait for it… Mimi sang, 'Andy walks with me, Andy talks with me, and he tells me, I am…' Fuge screamed, 'that's not the words... His name isn't Andy. That's ridiculously funny.'"

"That is the funniest thing I've ever heard," Penny squealed. "You are going to make me pee myself. That was hilarious."

They all had a good and hearty laugh.

"You know, Fuge and Daiq are two amazing men," Rie stated. "They are really inspired and elated about the outcome of the presidential election last year in the United States of America, although actions speak loader then words. I am elated also."

"Why is that, Rie?" Sam asked. "A lot of people are upset with the result. Ignorance is bliss."

"The country certainly needed to go in another direction, especially with all the drug influx into a couple of our major cities, and some agencies of the government letting it happen. The new president is making some good moves in the right direction. He's actually building a wall. I am crazy about it."

"I can't believe what Riley just eluded Sam," Penny stated, putting her hands on her hips. "Our three genius's, Sam, Zack and Deacon, are totally involved with the drug cartels and the corrupt Morgantown, WV, law enforcement, Riley. Sam will have to fill you in on that mess."

"We'll talk about that sometime later, Rie, tell me what is going on with your mom and dad, Aunt Cathy and Uncle Jon, and what is going on with their younger sister, Aunt Vicky?" Sam asked, not wanting to talk about what was going on at home.

"Mom and Dad are actually running the two greenhouses that they purchased in Malibu, California, which are bringing in a lot of cash. They supply, at least six or seven retail operations that sell Shrubbery, plants and flowers. They have employed around 20 people who work at their greenhouses and they live in a beautiful home on Malibu Beach, facing the Pacific Ocean," Rie answered, twisting the cap off of a bottle of Coors Light. "Aunt Vicky, who lives with her friend, Jill, in an exclusive apartment in Los Angeles, is still a Title One Reading Specialist, and Jill is a very successful fashion model. Aunt Vicky teaches at Nora Sterry Elementary School, which is about18 miles from Malibu Beach, in the city of Santa Monica, and she and Jill live relatively close to the school. It is about a 30-minute drive to Mimi and Fuge's home in Malibu, CA. Vicky is dating a rising and promising film producer that has absolutely, piles of money. He buys her anything she wants and takes her everywhere. Go figure."

"Looks as if everyone is pretty much squared away, your Aunt Erica and Uncle Michael are still living on Laurel Road in Morgantown, Anna is a spoiled cheerleader at University High School, from where I just graduated."

"Congratulations, cuz, you are the man."

"Would you tell Sam that he needs to go to law school like the rest of us," Deacon declared, looking at Rie. "His dad wants him to become a Civil Engineer."

"I am fighting a losing battle with my father, you know that, Deacon. I have done everything except kissing his feet. He wants me in the construction business with him and Howard."

"Piss on Howard, They can continue running that business without you," Zack said.

"Something will happen, Sam," Penny cheered. "You are destined to be an attorney. We need to finish our beers and get to bed, what you say. It's 12:30 now."

"Yup. I really miss you guys, my life is pretty well laid out. Daiq has some instruments in the music room. Guitars and Drums. Before I leave, we'll have to jam a little. After all, I am the 'Musician of Destiny'." Riley boasted.

"You certainly are, Riley G. Van Lorne," Sam said, as they all got up to say goodnight.

CHAPTER 29

Everyone was up early and the breakfast was quite a layout. It was 6 am, and anything that you could possibly want for your breakfast was tabled, buffet-style. There were two servers, a male and a female, Adele and Edbert, who replenished all the delicious choice food, gourmet breakfast food, specialties, and an Australian delicacy treat as well. They would refill, top up and freshen everything, made them full and complete, and naturally, replenished their glasses and cups with beverages, coffee or flavored tea. It was total luxury.

Riley was just bubbling over with excitement as he sat next to Penny, who was between him and Sam, while both Zack and Deacon were busy filling up their plates from the huge layout of breakfast. Ben, Daiq and Fuge were in a deep conversation as they were filling their bellies full of all of the delicious food, and the women were eating lightly and enjoying the flavored tea.

"Oh, Rie Guy," Fuge said, getting everyone's attention. "We would not be able to go to Oxford University tomorrow evening. We had to move the time up to 10 AM tomorrow morning. That way, they can have someone escort us and explain everything."

"No problem, I would rather go early anyway," Riley responded. "We'll miss the vintage tour but you, Daiq, Mimi & Liz, have been on those tours many times before. I'll catch it some other time. I'll be living here for two years."

"We'll still have six people for the London Vintage tour tomorrow, that should be exciting." Sam said patting Mimi on the shoulder. "It would be more fun if you were along, Rie. Wish you were going."

"We're sort of anxious to see the Oxford University, we are so happy and proud of Riley, he has worked hard and is very deserving," Mimi stated. "Daiq and Fuge are busting at the seams about Riley's progress. They have pretty big plans for him."

"The boys of the rising generation are to be the men of the next, and the sole guardians of the principles we deliver over to them, Mimi," Fuge blurted out, quoting Thomas Jefferson.

"Would you stop with the quotes, Fuge," Mimi growled. "Would you just put a lid on that, they must have run out of brains when they got to you, and they gave you that nice wooden one instead."

"Different strokes for different folks, Mimi, get it, I say tomato..."

"You say tomato...I say shut up!" Mimi replied, giving him a big, wide smile.

"Oh, my," Sam laughed, "Shots received, Fuge."

"I take it all with a grain of salt, I'm new, but I'm not brand new," Thurston exclaimed. "I wasn't born yesterday, you know."

"You could have fooled me," Mimi laughed, putting her arms around her husband.

"Let's check out the music room," Rie suggested. "We still have some time before we leave for church."

"Cool," Deacon said, "I need to beat on some drums, I'm missing the feels."

"Yeah, let's do it," Zack agreed.

"You have to hear the song that Penny recently wrote, it will touch you and yet, is untouchably precious, Rie." Sam said. "It's called 'No Two Ways' and it sounds great."

"I'll sit this one out," Riley said. "Sing it, Penny."

They all grabbed their instruments, turned on the sound, tuned up and then played. It was deafening, but Penny and Sam cranked it out and it was fabulous.

"Awesome, you guys, that will climb the charts pretty damn quick, great sound. Your band needs to cut a video and get it out there. I hear you like Buddy Holly, let's play a little of 'That'll be the Day', then we'll have to get dressed for the church."

The Stretch Limousine was waiting outside and they all jumped in and were going to head for St. Patrick Roman Catholic Church at the Soho Square for the 9:00 o'clock mass. Daig, Fuge, Mimi and Liz were traveling in Daiq's private vehicle and would meet them at the St. Patrick parking lot. After mass, they were returning to Daiq's place to enjoy the day there, while the others were going to take a tour of the Buckingham Palace and take a flight on the London Eye, the giant observation Ferris wheel.

"Believe me," Fuge stated. "You could never get Mimi on that monstrous illuminated tambourine, not with her fear of heights."

"I'm not crazy about that, myself," Daiq added, waving all of that off. "I would much rather do whatever sightseeing I have to do from the ground level."

"Same here," both Mimi and Liz responded.

"It's hard enough, just getting me on an airplane," Mimi complained. "That is scary enough, I'd much rather do my traveling on the ground also, Daiq."

"Alright, we'll catch you later," Ben said, as the rest of them loaded into the limousine that was heading for the Buckingham Palace; the heat of the moment had overwhelmed everyone, this was going to be one hell of a day. They were scheduled for the Buckingham Palace tour at 11:00 am.

Buckingham Palace is the London residence and administrative headquarters of the reigning monarch of the United Kingdom, located in the city of Westminster, and the palace is often at the center of state occasions as well as royal hospitality. It has been the focal point for the British people at times of national rejoicing and mourning. It was originally known as Buckingham House.

It took around 35 minutes for the limo to get to the Buckingham palace. A private guide met them outside the palace and started their tour by posing for photographs by the gates. After hearing the history of the royal landmark, they strolled to the nearby St James'

Palace to see the Changing of the Guards ceremony that takes place daily. They strolled through St James' Park with their guide to admire the manicured lawns and the flowerbeds. The beauty of having a private guide was that any commentary was tailored to their interests. They exited St James' Park near a cluster of the top London attractions; they walked past the Houses of Parliament, took photos in the backdrop of the Big Ben and learned about the wedding of Prince William and Kate Middleton outside of the Westminster Abbey. They gazed over the Thames to see the London Eye, the 443 feet high Ferris wheel. They took an insider tip from their tour guide for the best place to eat lunch. They met back up with the guide heading south of the river by walking across the Millennium Bridge, one of the filming locations that was used in *Harry Potter and the Half-Blood Prince*, and headed into the Shakespeare's Globe Theater. They also visited St Paul's Cathedral, took a taxi bus to the Tower of London, the formidable 11th-century tower that was built to act as a fortress, palace and a prison. They saw the Beefeater guards with their black ravens, the Crown Jewels, and also clicked photos by the famous White Tower.

There are 775 rooms in Buckingham Palace, including 19 State Rooms and 78 bathrooms. The Royal Wedding Reception (William & Kate) was held in one of the State Rooms. These State Rooms are awash with sparkling candelabra, damask wallpaper, fine furniture, sculpture and works of art. Further, the Grand Staircase, the Throne Room and the Garden top it off.

"My God," Mary Ann exclaimed, leaning back in the limousine, as they were on their way toward the Westminster Bridge on their way to the London Eye. "No one should ever miss that tour in their lifetime, for certain, that visual presentation is far more descriptive than words."

"I was totally impressed with the Changing of the Guards ceremony," Penny expressed. "Those soldiers are so well-programmed and so much into their formations."

"They repeat those movements every single day, Penny, give a monkey a banana and they could do the same thing," Sam laughed, pretending that he was marching like a soldier.

"You aren't right," Deacon yelled, laughing out loud. "Those soldiers would kick you in your ass if they heard you say that, Sam."

"That wasn't nice," Penny snickered. "But funny, the way you said it, about the monkey and the banana. You are crazy."

"Not a spark of decency, Sam," Zack laughed, pretending that he was peeling a banana.

"You guys are sick," Ben exclaimed. "What are you going to come up with for this monstrous illuminated tambourine, as Fuge called it?"

"It is certainly large, and comical to take in, it's huge," Mary Ann chuckled.

"Now they got you started, Mary Ann," Ben replied. "We're really in trouble now."

The limo dropped them off at the opening into what looked like a park. You could see the London Eye extending into the sky. They walked across the huge concrete park to the entrance and swung over to the fast-track skipping the line access to the highest paid attraction in London. The London Eye has 32 passenger capsules, there is one royal capsule that marks the 60th anniversary of Queen Elizabeth II, there is no #13 capsule since the number is considered unlucky, the capsules are numbered 1-12 and 14-33, and each capsule can hold 25 passengers.

"Are you sure you want to go on this? I'm scared, Sam. I may jump ship," Penny sighed. "I mean leave this activity. Merely standing under this monster is frightful enough."

"It's up to you to make that decision, that ball's in your court," Sam said. "I would never force you to ride."

"Piss on it," Penny sassed. "If Mary Ann's going, I'm going too."

A huge capsule continued moving while picking them up. The size of the capsule made it even scarier.

"No problem, Penny, we'll all help you," Zack said, trying to ease her fear. "Believe me, this is honestly a little spooky."

"We'll all help each other," Penny laughed, holding on to the inner railing of the capsule, saying a little prayer and crossing herself.

"Thirty minutes, Penny, you can do that standing on your head, girl," Deacon commented. "You take the cake."

Once the capsule began rising, everything became settled and the ride became enjoyable, the space inside the capsule was like a dance floor. They began to move around and they began to recognize some of the historical places below. The guide in the capsule pointed out the landmarks and told a little about them, the Big Ben, the biggest, most accurate four-faced, striking and chiming clock in the world, towering over the British parliament. They also observed the Westminster Abbey, the Buckingham Palace, the Tower of London, London Bridge and the Tower Bridge, St James' Palace and St James' Park.

"This is wonderful," Penny said, as she was tripping the light fantastic, actually dancing in the capsule. "I can't believe that I was acting like a little toddler, I was scared shitless."

"Damn, girl," Deacon yelled. "You were scaring the crap out of all of us."

"Yeahaaah!" Zack added. "Absolutely scaring the crap out of us."

"This has been quite an experience for all of us," Ben said." I'm glad you jumped on the bandwagon, Penny. This was utterly amazing."

"Let's ride it again," Mary Ann yelled.

"No way, Mary Ann," Penny and everyone else exclaimed together.

They decided to wrap it up for the day and head on back to Daiq's house to get something good to eat. They called for the limousine; it was a half-hour drive back home and they decided tell a couple of jokes.

"Did you hear about the lady in Pittsburgh that had eight boys and she named them all Leroy?" Deacon asked.

"What? Isn't that a little confusing?" Mary Ann questioned,

thinking it was ridiculous. "Why would she do that? What happens if all of them are upstairs and she wanted to call one of them down?"

"That's easy," Deacon replied, with a huge smile. "She calls them by their last names."

"What?" Mary Ann exclaimed. "Their last names?"

"Oh my God, that is absolutely hilarious, mom. Get it!" Penny shouted. "They all had different last names."

"You mean all of them were born to different fathers?" Mary Ann laughed. "That is hilarious. I got it, duh."

"Yeahaaah!" Penny screamed.

They all laughed hysterically.

"Here's one," Sam exclaimed. "Do you know where they get virgin wool?"

"No, where?" Penny asked.

"Ugly sheep."

"Now that is funny," Penny laughed, along with everyone else.

"Do you know what the blonde said when she looked into a box of Cheerios?" Zack asked.

"Alright, we don't know," Mary Ann said a little defensively, since she had beautiful blonde hair.

"Oh look, donut seeds!"

"That wasn't funny, Zack," Mary Ann said, acting as if she was insulted, and laughing.

They all laughed as they were pulling up to Daiq's gated driveway, and they all climbed out and went into the house. It was 4:30 pm by now.

Adele and Edbert were preparing a sit-down candlelight dinner for Daiq and Liz's guests, and what a luxurious dinner it was! They all had showered and cleaned up and were seated at the table. Naturally, the meal begins with the beverages - water, coffee, or flavored tea, followed with a specialty appetizer, which was served to each person. The French cuisine…followed through a shellfish course, an entrée, a sorbet, steak, salad. Then came the cheese and dessert. Adele and Edbert would refill, top up and freshen everything, made them full and complete, and naturally, replenished their glasses and cups with beverages, coffee or flavored tea. It was a total luxury once again.

After the meal, Sam suggested that the younger group should meet in a detached log cabin style chalet, towards the rear of the garden. They all excused themselves and returned to the chalet.

"What a terrific day, I believe that we are all very well entertained," Sam said. "Penny is overly curious about what you know about the drug world, Rie."

"Well, one of my theses was an argumentative thesis about crystal methamphetamine. It's a white crystalline, synthetic drug with more rapid and lasting effects than amphetamine. It is used illegally as a stimulant and as a prescription drug to treat narcolepsy and maintaining blood pressure."

"This is where the four of us are," Sam explained. "We got involved with a huge drug ring and the corrupt upper crust of the Morgantown Police Department. We're into knee-deep shit; deeper than we actually wanted to be. Here is a small scenario of what was going on. Deacon, Zack and I got our hands on a bag of money that upset the illegal drug traffickers and the corrupt police perpetrators, including the Morgantown, Chief of police, Anton Calabrese. Many people have died, a police Sgt. and his wife, two police investigators, a few drug traffickers, and now the Drug Lord, Briccio Donovan and his wife, Cleopatra, and members of their cartel were shot and burnt in their complex in Fairmont, WV. A huge drug bust followed and many arrests were made at undercover locations throughout the states of West Virginia, Pennsylvania and Ohio. The presence of meth labs has continued to rise in all the counties and townships. The local and federal law enforcement authorities are not only shutting down the clandestine methamphetamine laboratories, but they are also busting all the known drug trafficking operations that they have been watching for over a year. Arrests were made in the thousands."

"Now we are dealing with a little weasel detective and the Chief of Police," Deacon added, showing his dislike of the situation.

"Chief Calabrese was threatening and blackmailing us, because we still held that bag of drug money and he wanted it. He threatened to put us in jail for concealing the evidence," Sam continued. "He hired a private investigator named Hunter McClain to negotiate with us, offering us monies to keep our mouths shut. This all happened right before our vacation. We have put him off until we returned. Chief Calabrese passed on that there were no options, and that there would be consequences. My last text from Hunter, while we were in flight here, said that people were going to start disappearing. So, I texted Roberto and Mateo to keep them in the loop."

"So what was the deal that he was offering anyway?" Rie asked.

"The deal was that we turn over the bag of money to Chief Calabrese and the three of us would receive fifty thousand dollars apiece to keep our mouths shut and walk away unscathed, and that he would resign as the chief and disappear forever," Zack blurted out, shrugging his shoulders.

"Holy crap," Riley stammered. His eyes opened wide. "What kind of money are we talking about?"

"Two and a half million dollars," Sam said.

"Penny was right, you three are geniuses. So what is stopping Chief Calabrese from killing Hunter McClain, the three of you, and departing with all the money? That would leave no witnesses, right?"

"What should we do, Riley?" Deacon asked. "I think growing old beats the alternative of dying young, how do you see it?"

"Right on, Deacon," Rie said. "Let me get back to Washington, and maybe I can use my influence with the FBI to have that man pinched out of the system and whoever else is involved in that corruption. We can also make good use of that money to develop a few Methadone Clinics. I won't make any mention of the money that you are holding. That's the way I see it."

"Good deal. We'll see what happens with that and try to enjoy the rest of our vacation, Rie, let's hope something works out."

"You said you wrote a thesis about methamphetamine, Rie," Penny said. "I have no idea about that drug. I read somewhere that West Virginia meth doesn't come from the makeshift labs of yore but from a crude 'shake and bake' process, packing ingredients into a bottle to make a sludgy but effective product. Hundreds of meth cook sites are being uncovered; many times the meth cooks die due to mere inhalation. What happens with those cook sites, and what is methamphetamine?"

"No matter how large or small, once a cook site is busted, the state law dictates that it should be 'remediated' by a licensed company after the police determine there is no immediate threat of an explosion, then tested to see if there is enough meth residue to meet a State's standards for contamination. The average cleaning job rakes in thousands of dollars."

"Again, what is methamphetamine?" Penny asked, with her palms up and outstretched.

"Methamphetamine is an illegal drug in the same class as cocaine and other powerful street drugs. It has many nicknames, Penny, Meth, crank, chalk or speed," Riley began. "Crystal meth is used by individuals of all ages, but is usually used as a 'club drug', it is taken while partying at night clubs or in rave parties, and its street names are ice and glass. People take it by snorting, smoking it or injecting it with a needle."

"So, almost the same as cocaine," Sam remarked.

"Some people take it orally, but eventually, all users develop a strong desire to continue using it because the drug creates a false sense of happiness and well-being…a rush of confidence, hyper-activeness and energy. It is a dangerous and potent chemical and, as with all drugs, a poison that first acts as a stimulant but then begins to destroy the body. Thus it is associated with serious health conditions, including memory loss, psychotic behavior and potential heart as well as brain damage."

"Do Methadone treatment clinics help cure addiction, Rie?" Zack asked.

"Methadone maintenance treatment is the most effective treatment for opiate addiction. Abstinence-based rehab therapy for meth and cocaine work about as well as rehab for other drugs…

meaning that about one third of the users improve following treatment. There are doctor prescribed drugs used to treat narcotic addiction that contain buprenorphine, an opioid medication. Sometimes, the states will distribute opioid antidote kits, which is a lifesaving antidote that, if administered in a timely manner, can effectively reverse problems like respiratory depression caused by opiate overdose and revive the victims."

"Damn, Riley," Sam shouted. "No wonder you were on the top of all your school adventures. Fuge always said that you were like a walking encyclopedia, he was absolutely right, you are a walking miracle."

"You're just saying that because it's true, Sam. Things do come easy for me. Okay guys, who wants to go to the music room and jam some more?"

As they were returning to the music room, Sam received a text from none other than Hunter McClain. It was 5:45 pm then. That would make it, 12:45 pm, Morgantown time.

Hunter texted: "Hope you three are having a good time, the chief is getting more pissed each day. He was very displeased about you leaving the States and wanted to remind you that there would be consequences. I'm sure he has something in mind, does your sister still go to University High School? Just curious, boss,"

"That son of a bitch better not harm my sister," Sam yelled. "What the hell are we supposed to do now?"

"Sometimes they just try to scare you, Sam. I doubt that he would do something stupid like that, especially when we're still holding the aces. He needs to know where that money is, and I'm sure he wouldn't jeopardize that. He's just pulling your chain," Deacon exclaimed.

"You're right, Deacon," Sam said. "We still have the upper hand."

"We have to stay cool," Penny replied, trying to calm Sam down.

"Let's play some music," Zack suggested. "It'll take our minds off that bullshit."

CHAPTER 30

The following morning's breakfast was about the same, luxurious. Everything was picture-perfect and delicious. Adele and Edbert kept all the items on the extreme buffet refilled and the beverages, replenished. Again the breakfast was done in total luxury.

Riley was carrying his backpack in preparation for the hour and an half drive to Oxford. Daiq was alerting his personal chauffeur, Adrian, to bring the car to the front. It was 8 am, and they wanted to ensure that they had plenty of time in order to meet up with their guide at the university at 10 am. Oxford University is situated in the city of Oxford, which lies about 60 miles north-west of London. There are 38 separate colleges and six Permanent Private Halls of religious foundation at the University of Oxford. The provost and scholars of the house of the Blessed Mary the virgin of Oxford, commonly known as Oriel College, is where Riley would live throughout his scholarship program. The Rhodes scholarship, named after the British mining magnate and politician Cecil John Rhodes, is an international postgraduate award for students to study at the University of Oxford. It is considered to be one of the most prestigious scholarships in the world. It was established in 1902 under the terms and conditions of the will of Cecil John Rhodes, and funded by his legacy. Rhodes, who attended Oriel College, Oxford, chose his alma mater as the site of his great experiment because he believed its residential colleges would give breadth to their views of instruction. The Rhodes House is a part of the University of Oxford in England. It is located on South Parks Road in Central Oxford, and was built in the memory of Cecil Rhodes.

"I'm not crazy about the hour and half drive, but this will be interesting to see my new home," Riley said. "I think Fuge is more excited than I am, and so is Daiq."

"We're excited for you, Rie," Daiq remarked. "These are stepping stones to your future!"

"Daiq will have someone pick you up, when you need a break, Riley," Fuge said.

Mimi said "Maybe you'll find a true love, Rie, maybe get married to a wealthy beauty."

"I don't know," Riley said. "We'll see. What about that vintage bus tour and the Thames Cruise. Are you getting pumped, Penny?"

"I certainly am," Penny replied. "This is going to be a blast. I can't wait to grab a seat on that vintage red double-decker bus. They say the best seats are in the back of the bus."

Adrian held the door as Daiq, Liz, Mimi, Fuge and Riley were preparing to leave.

"We'll see you back here a little later today," Ben said. "We will be leaving in an hour or so."

They all waved goodbye as Daiq's personal car exited the gates.

"See you later," Riley beamed. "Have a good time."

At 9 am, Ben opened the gate for the stretch limo to enter and the six of them loaded up, Mary Ann, Ben, Penny, Sam, Zack and Deacon, heading for the Victoria Coach Station at city center. They met their friendly guide and grabbed the back seats in the vintage red double-decker bus, as they sat back to take in the fantastic views of the city awakening around them. As they rode, they heard interesting anecdotes about the passing local sites such as the Big Ben, the Houses of Parliament, St Paul's Cathedral and Westminster Abbey.

"There have been 16 Royal weddings at Winchester Abbey," Abigail the guide said. "Also, the venue for every coronation since the 11th century."

"This is the most enjoyable thing that we have done," Penny yelled with outstretched arms.

"I'm glad you picked the back of the bus, Penny," Zack shouted. "We have the best view of everything from here."

"I love the open-air ride," Mary Ann added.

"You can say that again, Mary Ann," Sam shouted, expressing his wholehearted agreement.

"This is a blast," Deacon agreed. "We couldn't have asked for anything better. I think we're going on the Thames Cruise after this."

They headed to the banks of the Thames, where they got an up-close view of the formidable Tower of London, built by William the Conqueror in the 11th century. At the Tower pier, they boarded a sightseeing boat and they could sit in the glass-encased saloon or on the open deck. They chose the open deck. They drifted in total comfort along the banks of the historic Thames and discovered London's history through live audio commentary. A relaxing ride as the boat made a loop under the London Bridge, passed the Houses of Parliament, and the London Eye. After the cruise, they hopped back on the bus and went for a traditional fish-and-chips lunch at a London Pub.

"That Tower of London has a long and stormy history," Ben replied, as they were having their lunch. "I was reading that it was once a prison and an execution site. King Henry VII executed two of his wives at that tower."

"Wasn't there something about the Beefeater Guards and the Crown Jewels that were housed in the fort? There is a lot of history there."

"Wonder why they called those guards beefeaters?" Deacon asked, shrugging his shoulders.

"The royal bodyguards used to receive chunks of beef as a part their salary until the 1800's, so they were called the beefeaters," Ben responded.

"What I heard was that King Henry VII executed two of his

wives on Tower Green at the Tower, both of these wives had strong supporters." Mary Ann replied. "Henry became extremely paranoid that he would be poisoned, so he had his Royal Bodyguards taste his food first, his meat, his beef, and they were his beef eaters."

"Where are these crown jewels, anyway?" Sam asked. "Does that mean the Queen's crown?"

"I know the answer of that one," Zack remarked, "I know it's guarded by Yeomen Warders, the jewels are kept in the Jewel House at the Tower Of London, where this precious collection has been held since the 14th century, including the Queens Crown."

"How do you know so much about those Crown Jewels, Zack?" Deacon exclaimed. "You were just jumping on the bandwagon, making us think you were so brilliant."

"I actually read it on one of the signs, Sherlock", Zack answered, laughing out loud.

Everyone laughed, hysterically.

"Shots received, Zack. You got me," Deacon replied, joining the laughter.

They returned to the bus, which took them to the Buckingham Palace for the last leg of the tour. After another long tour of Buckingham Palace, they returned to Victoria Coach Station in city center. The limousine was waiting to take them back to Daiq's place, where they would enjoy another sumptuous dinner prepared and served by Adele and Edbert.

All of them got cleaned up and Ben and Mary Ann were in the family room where they all met to reminisce about the day. They were all elated about the red double-decker bus excursion and the cruise on the Thames. The next morning, they would be flying to the John Lennon Airport in Liverpool, and check-in at the Hilton Liverpool in City Centre. Everyone was anxious to go on the Beatle's story tour.

"It's amazing how the Beatles' legacy lives on, they came to the United States 50 years ago in 1964 before any of us were even born,"

Penny stated. "Yet we know them by name and know most of the songs they sang."

"Fuge is the one that remembers them the most; he had just graduated from high school in 1961. He said that the nation was saddened by the death of President John F. Kennedy in 1963 when Rock 'n Roll was just coming alive," Sam said. "The Beatles came in 1964 and knocked everyone's socks off with their hair and hype."

"Daiq was also into the Beatles," Ben replied. "They were popular when he was attending Chancellor's University in London, which was spread all over the capital. Daiq even had his own Rock 'n Roll band."

Riley returned from his trip to Oxford University at 5:00 pm. He was totally impressed with the Oriel College where he would be spending the biggest part of his next two years as a Rhodes Scholar. They all agreed that Oxford was a beautiful city.

"I wonder if anyone does anything at Oxford but dream and remember. The place is so beautiful. You almost expect the people to sing instead of speaking. It is all like an opera," Mimi remarked.

Then, they all ate their dinner. Riley suggested that the young ones all go for a walk in the neighborhood and look around. Everyone was anxious to find out what Riley thought about going to Oxford University.

"I got to talk to a couple of students that are taking classes there and they informed me that the weekends were not for partying at Oxford. During the week, you had to attend the lectures and meet your tutors, and they said that it's easier to do those things in a hangover than to actually study. Unlike the typical American college experience, partying happens during the week at Oxford. When and why the tradition began, nobody seems to know, but it's a given: bars and nightclubs run their special parties on weekdays, and it is the rare students who go out on a Saturday night. No, the long, uninterrupted weekends are for studying after all that partying during the week.

"They certainly didn't beat around the bush about the drinking habits of the university," Deacon laughed, giving a big fist pump. "First things first."

"Sounds like a real party to me, Rie," Zack said. "I'm sure there will be a lot of good looking ladies roaming around."

"Oxford is where all of the rich people send their daughters, looking for eligible men," Riley responded, pointing his thumbs at himself.

"At least you're hearing it straight from the horse's mouth, Rie," Sam said. "I think you're going to like it at Oxford."

"Those ladies will all be chasing you, Riley," Penny added, giving him a big hug.

"Let's hope," Riley said. "I'll be leaving in the morning to go back to Washington. My lease isn't up until August and I'll be coming back here for my classes. I'm going to see what can be done with that Chief Anton Calabrese in Morgantown. I'm sure they can put a stop to that blackmailing and get him put away."

"We'll be leaving for Liverpool in the morning, also," Penny replied, clapping her hands.

They ventured around the neighborhood, taking in all of the multi-million dollar homes, and eventually made it back to Daiq's house. Everyone enjoyed the rest of the evening, and decided to hit the bed.

CHAPTER 31

Everyone was up at 5:00 am again, since the breakfast was being prepared early by Adele and Edbert, Ben's flight to Liverpool in the huge 747 Luxury Flying Mansion was departing at 8:30 am, from Heathrow Airport, and they had to be on their way in the limousine by 6:00 am, because the trip to the Heathrow airport took about 20 minutes. Ben, Mary Ann, Sam, Penny, Zack, and Deacon were loading their luggage in the limo. This time, Daiq and Fuge were going along with the kids. They were just as anxious to see the Beatles' story, and they would also make up the two golf foursomes at the Liverpool Royal Golf Club. Riley was hugging everyone and saying goodbye, as they loaded into the stretch limousine, exited out the gate and were on their way. Riley's flight back to Washington, DC, was departing at 10 pm, so Daiq's driver, Adrian, would drop him off at the Heathrow Airport about an hour later. Mimi was staying back with Elizabeth and they were going to take a day off shopping. Mimi gave Riley a couple hundred dollars for his trip to Washington, and sent him on his way in Daiq's private car. Liz gave Adele and Edbert the rest of the day off when they had cleaned up after breakfast, and told them that she and Judith would be having their evening meal at a downtown restaurant.

At the Heathrow Airport, the Daiquiri party boarded the exclusive airliner again, and were again greeted by the pilot, Captain Simon McArthur, and his assistant co-pilot, Stephen Gregory, and made to feel very welcome. The attendant Jaqueline directed them to where they would be seated for the takeoff, instructed them to fasten their seat belts, and informed them that they would be taxying out very shortly and to enjoy their one hour flight to the John Lennon Airport in Liverpool.

"This is quite an airplane, Ben," Fuge stated, as he looked around at the flying mansions luxury. "This must have cost you an arm and a leg."

"Oh, no, no, no. this surely isn't mine, I borrowed it off of one of my billionaire friends. He wasn't using it this week," Ben replied, as he reached to buckle his seat belt.

After the luxury airliner left the ground and leveled off, they were told that they could maneuver around and do whatever they pleased.

"Did you ever think what you would do or buy if you were a billionaire, guys?!" Penny exclaimed, as she began to think what she would do. "I'm just curious, what would you do or buy, Sam?"

"Good question," Sam said. "I believe that money can buy happiness, especially if you're a billionaire. Billionaires have the world at their fingertips, literally. They can do anything and everything because there are no limits. The ones that are lucky enough to be a member of this extremely wealthy club get the best of the best. I would definitely have a luxury airliner and I would travel everywhere and see everything."

"What about you, Deacon, what would you do or buy?" Penny asked.

"I would definitely dabble into the sports business, mainly by becoming the owner of a team. Whether its baseball, football, basketball, or hockey, it would be a true status symbol to be able to say, 'I own that team'."

"That was a good one, Deacon. What about you, Zack?" Penny asked.

"After purchasing all of the luxuries, such as a mansion, airplanes and yachts, I would definitely have some extra play money for building my own automobile museum, purchasing hundreds of designer vehicles. I would also have a Rock 'n Roll Guitar collection."

"This is fun," Penny said. "What about you, Fuge? What would you do?"

"I would have a staff at my beck and call and not do much on my own. Have people do things for me. Such as a personal chef, chauffeur, a cleaning staff, accountants, assistants, butler, gardeners and stylists, you know, sort of what Daiq has now," Fuge teased.

"I resemble that remark," Daiq said, putting his arm around Fuge's shoulders.

They all laughed and then got busy doing something else until it was time to land.

"How are we getting to the Hilton Hotel after we land at John Lennon Airport, dad? Is there a limo here to transport us?" Penny asked.

"No, we don't have a limo at this airport, but we have a mini bus that will take us to the Hilton Liverpool City Centre, it takes about 25 minutes," Ben said.

"How many rooms did you get at the Hilton?"

"We have seven rooms at the Hilton Hotel. That is for the one night in Liverpool, tomorrow we are staying at the Holiday Inn Express in Hoylake, which is a 35-minute drive from here." Ben answered.

"Why the Holiday Inn Express, you cheapskate?"

"It was the closest hotel to the entrance of the Royal Liverpool Golf Club, that's why," Ben answered.

They circled and landed at the John Lennon Airport in Liverpool, and their luggage was transferred to a mini-bus that was waiting for them. They all boarded the bus and were on their way to the hotel. A huge storm blew up and it began raining cats and dogs. They were planning on walking the .03 miles to the Beatle Story attraction from the Hotel Hilton, but it was pouring down heavily. They carried their baggage and everything into the hotel, and the bellboys took them to their rooms. They decided to eat their lunch at the hotel. They enjoyed a quintessentially British afternoon tea in the Cinema Supper Club restaurant at the exchange. They indulged in a selection of freshly prepared sandwiches, scones with cream and jam, and a delightful array of mint cakes and desserts. Silent black and white movies played in the background, while they sipped traditional English tea. They also enjoyed a chilled glass of champagne.

The downpour continued outside even after they were done with the lunch, so they decided to take the Hilton shuttle bus down to Albert Dock and the Beatles Story Building. They entered and purchased tickets to the Beatle's magical mystery tour where you could see how four young lads from Liverpool were propelled to dizzying heights of fame and fortune. They purchased tons of Beatle paraphernalia, shirts, hoodies and everything that they could pick up at the Cavern Club at the end of the tour. They went behind the scenes at the famous Abbey Road Studios. They took an underwater trip on the Yellow Submarine. They hung out at the Casbah Coffee House and a stunning replica of the Cavern Club. A colorful Magical Mystery Tour bus took them on a two hour tour of the places associated with the Beatles. They saw where John, Paul, George and Ringo grew up, met and formed the band that took the world by storm. They saw their childhood homes, their birthplaces and the places that inspired some of their most renowned songs, such as "Penny Lane" and "Strawberry Field". Their final destination was the infamous Cavern Club where the Beatles cut their musical teeth and played over 300 times over the course of their careers, with free admission and a souvenir postcard. They sat and ordered some drinks. They picked up all their earlier purchases, four huge bags. By now, the rain had stopped.

"I liked how they kept playing those Beatle songs in the background, 'I Want to Hold Your Hand', 'She Love You', and 'All My Lovin'," Daiq said, as he was singing some of the words. "It sure reminded me of my growing up days in England."

"I can remember like it was yesterday," Fuge reminisced. "The

British invasion of the United States had started when they appeared on The Ed Sullivan Show in 1964. Ed Sullivan introduced the Beatles, and was almost immediately drowned out by the screaming girls in the studio audience, and 'Beatlemania' had begun."

"I liked when they showed that skit of them interviewing the Beatles, when they asked Paul McCartney about where did the name Beatles come from," Penny laughed. "Paul said that they were those 'little crawly things', and everyone laughed like crazy."

"We certainly learned a lot from the tour guide about Penny Lane being an actual road in Liverpool and that Strawberry field was the name of a Salvation Army children's home just around the corner from John Lennon's childhood home," Sam remarked.

"The Beatles were undoubtedly the most influential band of the century," Zack said.

"Seeing the humble beginnings from which the Beatles came, it's hard to believe how they became so famous and how their personalities evolved with fame," Deacon commented. "Like Sam said, to see Penny Lane and see the buildings and people mentioned in the song and also Strawberry Field, where John Lennon played as a boy, was brilliant. Daiq and I sang along with most of the songs on the Beatles' tracks that were playing during the tour. Didn't we Daiq?"

"Yup," Daiq answered. "That was my most favorite part of the tour."

"I'm calling the Hilton to have the shuttle bus pick us up," Ben said. "We'll have to find someplace to eat."

"I enjoyed that Cinema Supper Club restaurant at the Hilton," Mary Ann said. "I wouldn't mind going back there."

"I agree," Penny nodded enthusiastically. "Maybe we can have a couple more bottles of that chilled champagne?"

The Hilton shuttle picked them up and they returned to the hotel. After freshening up, they returned to the Cinema Supper Club restaurant for something to eat. After the fabulous dinner and a couple bottles of chilled champagne, they returned to their rooms, and got together in Penny's room. Deacon retrieved a six-pack of beer from the room snack bar. Ben, Mary Ann, Daiq and Fuge remained at the hotel bar for a couple of drinks.

"This is what I call a party, we have three more room snack bars to raid," Penny laughed, as she opened a can of beer and handed it to Sam. "We certainly have plenty of beer, Sam."

"We are on vacation, so no problem," Sam answered, as he was receiving another skip-land text from Hunter McClain.

Hunter texted: "Hope you three are having a good time. It seems that your two Hispanic friends, Roberto Fernandez and Mateo Martinez, have come up missing. Their motorcycles were found in the parking lot of 'The Fritz' and no one has seen or heard from them. They have just disappeared. Chief Calabrese did say that there would be consequences. Enjoy the rest of your vacation, boss."

"Oh my God, what do you think happened to those two?" Penny exclaimed. "They wouldn't leave their motorcycles anywhere. Do you think Chief Calabrese has hurt them or he's maybe holding them hostage?!"

"That's all bullshit! Hunter McClain is just trying to get us upset," Deacon yelled. "There is no freakin' way that Chief Calabrese could have taken advantage of Weed and Mateo! Both of them carry guns. Hunter is making that shit up, or they went somewhere with their friends. I'm telling you, its utter bullshit."

"He's trying to pull the wool over our eyes," Zack added. "Chief Calabrese must be pressurizing him."

"That's all, we still have the upper hand," Sam said. "We'll have to see what Riley comes up with in Washington. We can try to get a hold of Weed tomorrow. But right now, let's drink some beer."

The next morning, they were all a little hung over. They had taken a limousine to Hoylake, England, and checked in at the Holiday Inn Express, had breakfast, and were preparing to play golf at the Liverpool Royal Golf Club. Six sets of golf clubs had been shipped to the Liverpool Golf Club from the United States. Daiq and Fuge had brought their clubs from London and they were all set to go.

The Liverpool Royal Golf Links can be, beautiful, uplifting, awe inspiring and, on occasion, soul-destroying. These links were created to be the toughest and most demanding tests of golf and to remain so. Players are soon lost among the dunes, the heather grass and the pine woods. There are fearsome pot bunkers and tight, narrow fairways which meant that wayward drives were heavily punished. There were 206 bunkers on the course. Two times Masters Champion, Bubba Watson, counted 17 bunkers on the closing hole. The course has hosted 12 British Open Championships on the PGA Tour and a number of professional tournaments on the European Tour.

"I feel really privileged to be playing on the same course where Tiger Woods won the British Open in 2006," Sam said, as he was putting on his golf shoes. "I can't wait to see how much trouble I can get into."

"This is going to be an exciting day, and quite an experience," Penny laughed, as she finished putting on her golf shoes. "What do you say, Deacon, are you and Zack ready to have some fun?"

"I'm always ready to play," Deacon answered. "The harder the course, the better I like it. How do you see it, Zack?"

"I'm crazy about it," Zack replied. "I can't wait to get in one of those pot bunkers."

"Some of those pot bunkers are ten feet deep, Zack," Mary Ann said. "They're pretty hard to get out of."

"I don't think any of us are expecting to have low scores," Ben exclaimed. "Maybe Daiq and Fuge. They know how to scramble."

"Yeah right," Fuge said. "Let's get going, our first tee time is at 10:45 am."

They loaded up everything, including the refreshments, on the four golf carts, and moved to the first tee box.

CHAPTER 32

Chief Calabrese was getting over-anxious and a difficult person to deal with because of all the investigations that were going on around him. All he wanted was to get his hands on those two and a half million dollars and fetch his way out. He was getting the run around from the three punks who were holding the money and he needed to set things in pace. His private investigator, Hunter McClain, needed to pressurize the boys more. He had gotten a divorce from his wife a year ago, had sold their house, and was planning an escape with his new girlfriend to the islands - never to be heard from again. All he needed was that money, and he was going to eliminate everything that got in his way, even if that meant murdering people. It was 3:00 pm on Wednesday and he was waiting for a report back from Hunter McClain, who was supposed to be hurrying this along by threatening the three punks. His phone beeped; there was an anonymous message.

It read: "Chief Calabrese, the leather bag filled with money that you are looking for, it is at the home of Michael Trainer in a crawl space in the back of the house at 1245 Laurel drive."

Calabrese had no idea who had sent the text. He texted Hunter McClain and Lieutenant Bernard King, and told them to come to his office immediately. He waited and they were both there within fifteen minutes. Hunter and Bernard were the only others who knew about the drug money.

"I don't know if I am being played," Chief Calabrese began,

"but I received a text this morning telling me where to find the drug money."

"Who was the text from?" Hunter asked.

"That's what I was going to ask you. Do you think those band punks might have sent it?" Chief Calabrese asked, looking directly at Hunter. "What did you tell them yesterday?"

"Could be, I told them that their two Hispanic buddies disappeared and that you had said that there would be consequences. They may think that you are holding their Hispanic friends hostage, and maybe they don't want to see their friends hurt."

"Where did they say the money was?" Bernie asked.

"The message said it was at a Michael Trainer's house, in a crawl space."

"That makes even more sense," Hunter said. "Michael Trainer is one of the band members' father. I'm sure that text must have come from Sam. What are you planning on doing, chief?"

"The three of us are going over there to check it out," Chief Calabrese shouted, as he walked across the room and put on his gun-belt, he was wearing his police uniform. "We'll bring that money back to my apartment, and maybe split it up. Bernie and I will get one million apiece and you'll get five hundred thousand, Hunter. How do you guys see it?"

"That sounds great to me," Hunter replied, giving him thumbs up.

"Let's do it then," Bernie agreed.

Chief Calabrese had nothing like that in his plans. Once he got his hands on that money, Hunter McClain and Lieutenant Bernard King would, with a bullet in their heads, become history, and anyone else that was around. He would make certain that there was no interference with his escape. He would just snuff out Hunter and Bernie, along with the Trainers, go pick up his girlfriend, Carrie, and head straight for the airport.

"The Trainers should be home from work by the time we get there. We won't have any problem with them."

They drove Chief Calabrese's vehicle on I-68 east and took the

Coopers Rock exit and made their way to Laurel Drive. They parked in the driveway, got out of the car and knocked the front door. Mike answered the door and greeted them.

"How are you doing officers? You look like you're on a mission. My daughter, Anna, is at her girlfriend's house, so I guess you're not here to arrest her, how can I help you?" Mike asked with a chuckle.

"I'm Chief of Police Calabrese and this is Lieutenant King and Detective McClain. We have reason to believe that a leather bag full of drug money lies in your crawl space in the back. We need to check and see and if it is actually there, we will need to confiscate it as evidence for the federal law enforcement authorities."

"Why would there be any drug money in our crawl space?" Erica asked, as she appeared out of the kitchen. "Are you trying to say that we are involved in that illegal drug operation? Are we under arrest? If so, I think you need a search warrant before you can enter and search our premises, Chief Calabrese."

"I guess I'm being forced to do this the hard way," Chief Calabrese yelled, as he pulled his revolver out of its holster. "Let me make this perfectly clear, I came here to get that money peacefully, but now, you are throwing shit in the game, honey. Now I suggest that everyone keep their fucking mouths shut, and we are all going around back and look in the crawl space."

"What kind of crap is this, I thought that you people were the law enforcement," Erica yelled. "Why are we being treated like criminals?"

"I suggest that you shut the fuck up, girl, before I blow your brains out."

"Just do as he says, Erica," Mike pleaded. "We don't know if that bag is in there or not."

Mike thought to himself: *I dragged that bag out of their and put it in the shed, it's definitely not in the crawl space*

They all went around the house to the back; the smell of gas was really strong. Mike and Erica stood back away from opening to the crawl space and so did Hunter McClain. Mike lit up one of his cigarettes because his nerves were shot. Lieutenant King unlatched the door to the crawl space and opened it, got down on his knees and was looking inside. Chief Calabrese put his head inside the door. The gas smell worsened. Erica tried to get Mike's attention, and was motioning Mike to flip his cigarette inside the crawl space. Mike, being hesitant and unsure, flipped his cigarette and it splashed inside the crawl space, as he tackled, and dove on top of Erica. A huge blast and a horrendous flash of light followed as the entire rear of the house exploded and burst into flames. Detective McClain was thrown about twenty feet from the blast. Flaming pieces of wood and debris spewed everywhere. Mike helped Erica up and they got away from the flames as fast as possible. Needless to say, Chief Calabrese and Lieutenant King were totally fried, and very obviously, dead.

Mike dialed 911 and reported a fire at his address. He requested fire fighters, police and ambulances, possibly paramedics to come soon.

"Are you two alright?" Hunter asked, as he rushed over to Mike and Erica. "That explosion knocked me for a loop. I don't think either of Chief Calabrese or Lieutenant King are going to make it. I don't know what was going on with Chief Calabrese. He was completely off his rocker. He was going to kill all of us."

"He was loose cannon alright," Mike agreed, as he brushed himself off, and watched his house burn, feeling sick. He wasn't expecting such a blast. He was terrified.

"That man was really nuts," Erica yelled. "This is horrible, I'm glad that you were here to see and witness all these things, Detective McClain."

The fire truck arrived and began spraying water immediately, when three police cruisers pulled up. Mike, Erica and Hunter made their way around to the front of the house; two officers were approaching them for questioning. They heard more sirens in the distance; it was probably the ambulance and more fire trucks coming.

The neighbors were stopping to see if they could do anything. The police had to direct them to move on.

"Are you folks, alright? I'm Sgt. Baker. Are there any more people inside the house?"

"No one is in the house. Chief Calabrese and another officer were in the explosion in the back of the house. I can't tell you what conditions they are in."

Two other officers circled around to the back of the house to check it out.

"Do you know what caused the explosion?"

"Erica said that she smelled gas, but I am not sure. I don't know what caused the explosion," Mike answered. "This is Detective Hunter McClain. He came to our place with Chief Calabrese and Lieutenant King."

"What was going on here, Detective McClain?"

"Chief Calabrese had a lead that there was a large amount of drug money in a crawl space at this address. He brought Lieutenant King and me to check it out," Hunter replied.

"Did you have a search warrant?"

"No, we didn't, and when Mrs. Trainer questioned Chief Calabrese about a search warrant, he completely flipped out," Detective McClain said. "He pulled his revolver and became really mean. He suggested that Mrs. Trainer shut the fuck up, or he would blow her brains out. He had us all at gunpoint and ordered us to the back of the house, so that he could check the crawl space. I believe he had intentions of killing all of us and keeping the drug money for himself."

"That is quite an accusation, Detective McClain," Sgt. Baker said, as he pulled the detective to the side. "Actually, Chief Calabrese had been acting strange lately. No wonder FBI had developed interest in him, they suspected corruption, and believed that he had connections with Briccio Cadmen Donovan and his illegal drug operation."

"I don't think he was playing with a full deck, Sgt. Baker,"

Detective McClain said. "Lights were on but no one was home, get it."

"Gotcha."

"Thank God that Anna wasn't home to see all of this," Erica said, still in a state of shock. "We need to get hold of her, Mike. This is terrible. What are we supposed to do now, Sgt. Baker?

Take it easy Erica," Mike replied, hugging Erica and trying to calm her down. "We'll have to pick up Anna and get a room at the Holiday Inn or someplace. Fortunately, I have my wallet, and our SUV is parked right outside. Thank God." Mike then called his business partner, Howard, and asked if he could get them a room for a couple of days, possibly a suite. Mike told him that their house had caught fire, and was probably be destroyed.

"You will have to find a place to stay until your insurance sorts this out," Sgt. Baker answered, as he went to talk to the ambulance people.

The ambulance was standing by and the firemen had almost gotten the fire under control, until then, a second fire truck had showed up. The two police officers came from the back of the house and informed Sgt. Baker that Chief Calabrese and Lieutenant King, as far as they could tell, were dead. Sgt. Baker called for a *Forensic Examiner to* investigate the scene, record, analyze, and gather all the clues and evidence. The two emergency medical technicians, called for another ambulance, went around to the back of the house to check it out.

"Do you remember any huge leather bag being in your crawl space, Mr. Trainer?" Detective McClain ask.

"You can call me Mike, Detective McClain, and yes, I remember that bag being there. I thought it was gym equipment that belonged to my son, Sam. It was in my way, so I move that heavy son of a bitch to the tool shed. The next day it was gone. I think Sam took it."

"Do you think he might have moved it somewhere else, Mike?"

"That's possible. I didn't see it around after that," Mike answered.

"Oh my God, will they secure our fireproof safe that is in the basement, Mike?" Erica asked. "All of our valuables are in there."

"I'll let them know about it, Erica, I'm sure that it will be alright. It may take a while to get it out of there."

The EMTs were wheeling one of the bodies from the back of the house, and reported to Sgt. Baker that Chief Calabrese and Lieutenant King were dead. They loaded the body into the ambulance, and waited for the forensic people, as the sirens of another approaching ambulance wailed in the distance. Sgt. Baker had reporting in to the dispatcher about the fire and the two dead officers. It was 7:30 pm. It would be getting dark soon. Mike texted Anna and told her that they were coming to pick her up. The firemen were ensuring that the smoldering timbers were put out completely. The house was utterly destroyed. It looked like everything on the inside was trashed. Erica was crying uncontrollably now, all her prized possessions were gone, her furniture, pictures, computers, everything. Mike's partner, Howard Huge had called in a reservation at the Euro-Suite on Chestnut Ridge Road. Detective McClain volunteered to drive Chief Calabrese's car back to the station, but Sgt. Baker informed him that the car would have to be impounded, and because of the situation, autopsies would have to be performed on Chief Calabrese and Lieutenant King.

"You can ride to the station with me, Detective McClain, and help me finish this report and alert the press."

"Gotcha, will do," Detective McClain answered, as he walked over to Mike and Erica.

"Sorry about all of this, Mike," Detective McClain said. "Do you have any means to contact your son in England?"

"No I don't. I guess I'll have to get an AT&T international calling package to make that happen. Do you know anything about that, Detective McClain?" Mike asked, with his arms outstretched and his palms up.

"Yes, I do, you can call me Hunter, Mike. I have an international roaming calling, messaging and data plan on my phone. You can call him or text him right now if you like, although it is now around 12:30 am in England."

"It doesn't matter what time it is, Sam needs to know what is going on. Can you call him and let me talk to him, Hunter?"

"I certainly can" Hunter replied. "Let's get in your SUV, and call."

CHAPTER 33

After four and a half hours on the agonizing Liverpool Royal Golf Course, they all felt like they had been beat up. Demoralized, disheartened and having lost confidence or hope of ever becoming any kind of golfer in England.

"That's exactly what I was looking for, a challenge," Deacon complained, as he flopped down on a bed at the Holiday Inn Hotel. "I never want to play that game again. How do you freakin' see it, Zack?"

"I didn't know if I had enough balls to finish, I mean golf balls, Penny," Zack clarified. "I probably lost ten of those suckers in that heather grass. Sam and I were searching all day."

"Deacon said you didn't have any of those anyway, Zack, and mind you, I don't mean golf balls," Penny replied. "Shots fired!"

"Ouch, shots received, you got me, Penny."

They all laughed their asses off.

"I heard that," Mary Ann said. "You guys are being ornery. I remember when the wife of a well-known celebrity golfer was on The Johnny Carson Late Show. Johnny asked her what she did for her husband, when he was in the major tournaments, for luck. She said, 'I kissed his balls'. You know his golf balls."

"I'll bet that made his putter straight," Deacon exclaimed.

They all laughed hysterically.

Mary Ann yelled, "Ok, kids, enough carrying on, we have to get cleaned up and find something to eat."

They decided to eat at Lino's Restaurant Wirral, which was suggested by Daiq. Daiq was a connoisseur of food and drink. He said, "The style of this five star restaurant is very traditional, but the service is hands down the best in the Wirral. You are greeted at the door, with a little wit and back chat, which is more than welcome with me. Those people who see that as a bad thing need to go back to the soulless chain pubs and restaurants they probably prefer. The food is up there with some of the best in the Wirral. Having been here a few times before, I must say that every dish I have ordered has been decent and a good proportion of them have been exceptional."

"I didn't pick up on anything you said there, Grandfather Daiq," Penny blurted out, being a little sassy. "Besides that, what is this Wirral anyway?"

"The Metropolitan Borough of Wirral is a peninsula with water on three sides, and we are right in the middle of it," Daiq answered, pointing his finger at Penny, and saying, "If you don't behave, young lady, I'm going to kick your behind."

"Got yourself in some trouble there, Penny," Mary Ann replied, with a huge smile. "Thank you for the Geography lesson, Daiq. I don't think any of us knew that the Metropolitan Borough of Wirral was a peninsula. I know we crossed that River Mersey when the limousine brought us over here to the Holiday Inn Express."

"And the River Dee is on the other side, it makes this a peninsula, in a separate borough, but, I believe this entire area is considered to be Liverpool in Northern England, This area would be Liverpool Hoylake, in the Borough of Wirral peninsula, or just the Wirral. Get it!" Daiq explained.

"Yes, they have the same thing in the United States, with all the boroughs and townships, it's confusing at times," Ben said, calling for the Holiday Inn shuttle van to pick them up. "Let's get over to the restaurant."

"I think you need to apologize to your grandfather, Penny, for being so contrary," Sam suggested.

"I'm so sorry, Grandfather Daiq," Penny said. "Just kidding, I've always thought of you as being a saint, you are heaven-sent, okay? I love you"

"Don't get carried away there, sweetie, I'm no saint," Daiq answered, hugging her.

Daiq, Fuge, Ben and Mary Ann took the Holiday Inn shuttle van to the Lino's Restaurant, and the other four walked to Lino's. It was only about two and a half blocks. It was 5:30 pm, as they were walking, Deacon shouted, "Isn't it time for that piece of crap, Hunter, to be texting, to harass us some more? What can he possibly come up with today?"

"Good question, Deacon, he has tried everything to get us upset. Chief Calabrese must really be turning the heat up on him; we have to stay cool though. And that too, unconditionally because we know he keeps making shit up. How do you see it, Sam?" Zack yelled, as they all slowed down so that Sam could answer.

"I just hope he doesn't text me while we are eating, he usually sends a text around noon, Morgantown time, which would be 5:00 pm here in England. That will definitely make me nervous while we are eating."

"Just ignore it until we have a chance to look at it, Sam, that's all," Penny commented, as she put her arm around Sam's waist. "Hunter's just trying to make this trip miserable for you. He's just hoping that you three just get completely fed up, and tell them where the money is located, ya think?"

"That's how I'm seeing it too, Penny. Now, let's eat," Sam agreed, as the pulled the door open at Lino's, which was located between two shops, Hoylake Holistic, and Rowe Fitted Interiors. Lino's Restaurant was family-owned and was running for over 30 years, serving delicious, award-winning Mediterranean cuisine. They were treated like royalty when they entered the restaurant. Everything that Daiq mentioned was true, it was beautiful. They joined the other four at a large table and seated themselves. Daiq and Fuge had already had a quick glass of wine, and were sipping on some beer, and were feeling pretty good. Ben and Mary Ann were enjoying an expensive bottle of wine. Penny, Sam, Deacon and Zack ordered colas. They all looked over the menu and made their choices according to Daiq's suggestions. Menus perused, all of them opted for the pasta and a dessert. For the main course, we had the gnocchi in bolognaise sauce and it was splendid, very tasty. They all shared some cheesy garlic bread, which was nice. Dessert was Nutella Chocolate Cheesecake with salted caramel ice cream and pour cream. Everything was fabulous.

"In wine there is wisdom, in beer there is freedom, in water there is bacteria," Fuge stated, quoting Benjamin Franklin, as he was finishing up his second beer. "I guess that quote, pretty well, speaks for itself."

"Is that why you never drink water, Fuge?" Sam replied. "Too bad Mimi isn't here to enjoy that quote. She loves your sayings, doesn't she?"

"I always heard that marriage is psychological, Sam," Fuge said. "One spouse is psycho. And the other is logical. Who do you think is the logical one here?"

Everyone burst out laughing.

"I wouldn't touch that one, if I were you, Sam. That is a loaded question." Deacon responded, as he put his arm around Sam's neck. "Your Mimi will hurt you, for sure."

"You would never say that around Mimi, would you, Fuge?" Sam shouted.

"No way, I wasn't born yesterday, you know. I was born at night, but not last night. I'm new but I'm not brand new. Your Mimi would turn that around in a minute, I would be the psycho one, Right, Penny?"

"I'd leave that one alone, Fuge," Penny shouted. "I'd leave that one alone."

They all laughed again, hysterically.

They all got up, ready to leave. Ben paid the check and called for the holiday Inn shuttle van to pick them up. Penny, Sam, Deacon and Zack began walking back.

"What do you think, Sam, did Hunter decide not to text us today, or is he racking his brain trying of think of some incredible story to tell us?" Zack laughed, giving him a fist bump.

"To hell with that asshole, I saw some goodie fridges in our rooms, six-pack in each one. I feel some partying coming on, what do you think?" Deacon said, clicking his fingers, dancing, and singing some of the words to Penny's new song…"I see myself as your student…and you as the teacher so wise…"

Zack chimed in, "Yeah! My mind is wide open…"

Sam joined in, "Not to mention my eyes…There are no two ways, baby…"

Penny finished, with her arms wide open, "There is only one way into my heart, yeah, baby, only one way into my heart."

"You guys are something else, Sam," Penny shouted. "You are totally bad."

Zack yelled, "Roaming these streets like this, reminds me of those four young lads from Liverpool, who were propelled to dizzying heights of fame and fortune. What a rush."

"Hell yeah! I'm feeling it," Deacon yelled, pumping his fist, up and down.

"Okay, you three Liverpool lads." Penny exclaimed, as she drag Sam by the arm, running toward the Holiday Inn. "It's getting dark, and we can't drink a lot of beer, Deacon, because tomorrow, we have to get up super early."

They all gathered again in Penny's room, and they decided to have one beer …period.

"I've got to tell you guys about the weird dream I had last night, you aren't going to believe this, it may have been because of the beer probably, but anyway. We were all in some sort of church; I was standing directly in front of the altar, where in a Christian church the bread and wine are consecrated in communion services. Zack, you were on my left, and Deacon, you were on my right. To the right of Deacon, and the altar, in a line, were Daiq and Ben, in long robes, as if they were saints. And you, Penny, had the wings of an angel, naturally. Each one of you had a halo, indicating a holy or sacred figure. Behind the altar, there was extreme brightness and a glowing image of a man, but the image wasn't clear. I didn't know what I was going to see, Darth Vader, the Wizard of Oz, or the coming of Christ, you know how dreams are. I was looking intently at the face, it began to come clearer, and clearer, I could see his face, it was Riley. It was Riley G. Van Lorne. He was a glowing supreme being, like Grandfather Fuge always alluded to. I jerked out of there and woke up. It took me a minute to come clear, but that was one of those crazy dreams."

"Damn, Sam," Deacon complained, spitting out the words. "That scared the crap out of me."

"Ditto," Zack exclaimed, as he crossed himself. "That was spooky as hell."

"I am totally blown away," Penny said. "That was a nightmare, if you ask me. That did it for me ever going to sleep tonight, Jesus."

They had to leave for the John Lennon International Airport at 6:00 am the next morning, and their flight to St, Andrews departed at 8:00 am, it was a little past 12:00 am when they decided they would part and go to their own rooms when Sam's phone rang.

CHAPTER 34

"What the hell is going on here? It's Hunter's phone, he apparently wants me to answer. I'm not answering. Piss on him."

"It's bad enough getting a text from that piece of shit," Deacon complained, trying to get his own shit back together. "Let alone talk to him. Leave it, Sam."

"I agree, leave it go, he'll come back with a text, believe me," Zack said, putting his hands over his ears.

"What if it's something urgent, Sam?" Penny asked. "I don't know, damn it, I don't have an international call plan on my phone, but my dad and Grandfather Daiq have it. If it is something important, we can get my dad up. Let it go to message."

"Not from Hunter, forget it, Penny. It can't be important. He'll send a text."

Detective McClain had just punched in Sam's number and was waiting for a response to the call. No one answered, Hunter turned to Mike and said, "They either are sleeping or they are waiting for a text. They won't pick up phone mail. You know how those kids do their phones. If you don't text them, they don't answer."

"Tell me about it. You are preaching to the choir, our kids never answer," Mike responded. "Maybe we can just text them."

"I don't think they will answer the text, unless they have an international calling and messaging data plan on their phone; and you usually don't purchase a plan unless you are going to be gone for a long period of time. It's kind of expensive. I only have it because of my investigating. You tell me what you want to say."

"I'm not good with that, and Erica is too shook up to text. Just tell them that you are with us and that our house has burnt down. Get hold of us as soon as possible," Mike replied, reassuring Erica that everything was going to be alright. "Are you alright, Erica?"

"Am I alright? Your guess is as good as mine. Our house just burnt down, and it's a blessing in disguise that Hunter is here helping us out of it."

"Okay, here we go, you don't want me to say anything about Chief Calabrese or Lieutenant King, am I correct?"

"No, not now, we'll tell them about the gory details later."

Detective McClain texted: "I don't know if you are sleeping, or you are just not answering your phone, my friends. Something terrible has happened on the home front here. I am sitting with your mom and dad, Sam, in their SUV, in front of their home, which has unfortunately exploded and burned to the ground. I am very sorry to be the bearer of bad news. Your parents and your sister are okay, but everything was completely destroyed, Sam. If there is some way that you can contact me or your dad, please do so. This is for real, Sam, I know it's late, but you have got to contact us. This is Detective McClain, Morgantown Police Department."

It was 12:40 am, and Sam was finally receiving a text, he punched the key to receive the message. It was from Hunter. Sam read the message and immediately screamed, "That son of a bitch! Hunter, what is this shit? He says he's with my mom and dad in their SUV, and that our house has burnt down. What else, McClain? What else are you going to come up with, you bastard?"

"Let us take a look at the text, you have to settle down, Sam," Penny said. "They'll be calling this room. We'll figure this out."

"Sam, that doesn't look like Hunter's regular bullshit. This one is a sincere message," Zack threw in, "Maybe something did happen. It wouldn't hurt to check on this one."

"He's crying wolf, he's alerted us too many times, to some freaking danger that actually wasn't there, for his own amusement. He's trying scare us," Deacon interjected. "We can't trust that son of a bitch, he's a liar, a backstabbing piece of shit. How do you see it, Sam, come on."

"I don't know, Deacon." Sam said, pounding his fist down on the bed. "I'm just pissed. Hunter is a scumbag. What do you think, Penny?"

"I know this," Penny said. "We all would feel terrible if a fire really broke out. Especially at your mom and dad's house, Sam. I don't like ignoring it, and you are right, Deacon, that little pest is a fly by night character, very unreliable. But I certainly agree with Zack, in order to put that dirt bag in his place, you need to confront him directly. This may be another prank, but I wouldn't really take that chance. We'll get my dad and mom up, they don't care. He has an international call plan. We can use his phone to contact the Morgantown Police Department. They will know if there was a fire, right? Let's go get em' up."

They all walked out of Penny's room, her mom and dad were across the hall, and down about five doors, in Room 330. Penny tapped on their door and quietly called for her dad. Mary Ann opened the door with concern and asked Penny what was going on. Penny told her the situation, that Sam got a text saying that his mom and dad's house had burnt down, and that they had no way of following up. Mary Ann stepped out in the hall and asked, "Who was the text from?"

"It was from a Detective McClain, of the Morgantown police," Sam whispered. "He said that he was with my mom and dad. We need to contact the Morgantown Police Department to check it out."

"OK, come on in the room, I'll get Ben up," Mary Ann said, as she opened the door and let everyone in. It was a suite, and they all waited for Mary Ann to get Ben up.

Sam thought about the old adage, *let a sleeping dog lie*, and was hoping that this would not result in trouble or complications. They waited a couple of minutes and Ben was standing there, half asleep and yawning, he said, "Are you guys still having fun? What seems to be the problem, Penny? Did you four run out of beer? I saw the tab from The Hilton where you raided all the snack cabinets."

"Yeah, okay, dad," Penny answered, giving him a hug. "We have a situation that you may have the answer to. Sam received a text from a Detective McClain of the Morgantown Police Department, saying that Sam's parents' house had burnt down. Detective McClain said he was with Sam's mom and dad, and asked if we contact them. We thought maybe we could use your phone to call and verify it. We may have to make a change in our itinerary."

"What time is it, 12: 55 pm? It's about 8:00 pm there. I have no problem with doing that, Should we just contact this Detective McClain. We would have to find out the number of the police station, you know, do you have his return number, Sam?" Ben asked.

"Yes I do," Sam replied, thinking that that was not what he was expecting. He didn't want to talk to Hunter. Damn it. "That should work. I hope he is still where he said he was."

"Maybe Ben could talk to your dad, Sam," Zack commented.

"I'll put my phone on speaker, that way we can all hear what happened," Ben said. "You can put the number in when you are ready, Sam, If Detective McClain answers, I'll do the talking, I'll ask for your dad."

Deacon thought: *This better not be a prank, because if it is a prank, I will hurt that asshole if I ever see him again*

Suddenly, there was a tap on the door.

"Oh my God, It's the hotel security, no doubt," Mary Ann said, as she went over to the door. "We'll probably have to quiet it down a bit."

She opened the door and it was Fuge and Daiq.

After Mary Ann explained what was going on. Fuge asked Sam, "I wonder why Detective McClain didn't just call and talk to you directly?"

"He did," Sam answered his Grandfather Fuge. "I didn't get it soon enough, that's why he sent the text."

"Did he leave a message on phone mail?" Daiq asked, just being curious.

"Nope, Just the text."

Then, Fuge and Daiq looked at the text.

"I say call that detective back, Ben, I have no idea about those phones and international devices, so I definitely couldn't help you with that call," Fuge said. "The one thing you shouldn't do is try to tell a cab driver how to get somewhere. I'll just listen."

"Good thinking, Fuge," Sam punched in Detective McClain's number, put the phone on speaker, and they all listened to the scruffy voice intently.

"Detective McClain."

"Detective McClain? This is Benjamin Daiquiri, I'm speaking for my daughter and her three band friends. They say that they received a message from you saying that Michael and Erica Trainer's home was exploded and burnt to the ground this evening. We are on a speaker so that we all can hear, Detective McClain."

"We can hear you clearly," Detective McClain stated. "We are on a speaker also."

"Are you lying about Sam's house burning down?" Deacon exclaimed.

The lying son of a bitch

"Whoa, we can't have that, if we're going to talk," Detective McClain said.

"Hold it down, Deacon, Please," Sam said, pulling him back. "Ben's got it."

"Samuel. Are you there, I'm sorry, honey. Our house burnt and we lost everything. It's probably my fault for not having that crawl space checked for leaking gas, and I believe that is what caused the fire, I'm so sorry," Erica cried, as she was using roll of paper towels, wiping her eyes constantly.

"Sam, this is dad, what your mom is saying is true. The house is gone. Your mother and I are entirely shook up. We will try to recover our fire proof safe from our basement that contains all of our valuables, thank God. So we're letting Detective McCain tell you what happened, okay?

"Sounds good," Ben agreed. "Go ahead, Detective McClain."

"Chief Calabrese received…

"Don't mention Chief Calabrese's name. Damn!" Deacon exclaimed.

"Deacon, you have to stop it, my friend, we need to find out what is going on. Stop it, please."

"One more time and I will have to end this conversation. Understood?" McClain said.

"We're cool," Ben said.

"Chief Calabrese received an anonymous text, telling him that there was a huge bag of drug money, about two and a half million dollars, stashed in the crawl space, in the rear of the Michael Trainer's residence on Laurel Road. Chief Calabrese chose to take Lieutenant King and myself with him to recover this money from an illegal drug operation bust that is in progress in Morgantown and Fairmont. However, we did not have a search warrant and therefore, Chief Calabrese had a screw coming loose. Both Chief Calabrese and Lieutenant King are dead; they were killed in the explosion and fire. Do you have any questions?"

"Chief Calabrese was never the sharpest knife in the drawer. You telling us he finally flipped out?" Sam questioned. "What else have you got, Detective McClain?"

"He pulled out his weapon and started ordering everyone around, he paraded all of us to the rear of the house. He even had Lieutenant King and I under siege, the whole group was under his control. I believe that we were all in line to be eliminated. Execution style, no doubt, that's the way I saw it. How did you see it, Mike?"

"I think we were all about to die."

"I can answer that one," Erica blurted out. "That animal was lucky I didn't have a knife, he would have been dead before the explosion and fire. He was completely out of his mind. You'll have to tell us what your plans are, Sam, so we know when you are coming home. We probably need everyone's help right now. You have to come home, Sam. This is going to be hard on your sister."

"We will let you know on that one, mom," Sam said. "Has anyone heard anything about our Hispanic friends, Roberto and Mateo, What's up?"

"I've got nothing, Sam," Detective McClain replied. "They're still missing."

"Do you think that Chief Calabrese hurt them?" Sam asked.

"Don't know?" Detective McClain answered.

"He said that there would be consequences, didn't he?"

"Still don't know. Your guess is as good as mine, Sam." Detective McClain said. "You will have to check it out when you return, I can't help you on that one."

"It really doesn't matter how those two toads died," Deacon yelled, he seemed visibly agitated by this disquieting news, about Roberto and Mateo. We have to talk about what we are going to do, I'm ready to go home, Ben and Mary Ann. Tell Hunter goodbye and let your dad know that we will contact him, okay Sam?"

Ben politely told Detective McClain to let Mike and Erica know that we will contact them as soon as we produce a plan, he said, "Detective McClain, Thank you for your help."

They disconnected.

Deacon thought: "Screw you, Hunter, you piece of shit."

"What was that all about, Deacon?" Ben asked. "I believe that you directly insulted Detective McClain. We're not that kind of people."

"I'm very apologetic for everything, I hate that toad," Deacon blurted out.

"Dad, mom, it's late, Sam will explain everything that has been going on the last week and a half, and it was excruciating, I mean extremely painful to all of us, causing intense suffering. That is why Deacon began coming apart at the seams. We need to get something together about how we can fly directly from Liverpool John Lennon international to the United States. Detective McClain has been a real pest. We'll talk."

"We need to make some quick decisions about how we can get everyone together," Ben demanded. Ben turned and said to Deacon, apologetically, self-deprecating. "I'm sorry Deacon. I didn't mean to come down on you, buddy. We'll all have to talk. Fuge, dad, you need to get hold of mom and Judith. Tell them I will book a flight for them as soon as possible, probably departing from Heathrow International Airport to Liverpool John Lennon Airport at dawn. Okay, there, 9:00 AM. I actually booked it, on my phone, while I was talking. Liverpool Airlines.

"I got it," Daiq answered. "I am calling right now."

"Hello," Liz answered. "What's up, Daiq?"

"You and Judith have to do some packing, for yourselves, and for Fuge and me. You will be at Heathrow International airport to catch the 9:00 am flight to Liverpool John Lennon International Airport. Liverpool Airlines. Pick up the boarding passes, and make sure you have your ID's. Flight should take about an hour. Pack heavy because we are flying to the United States as soon as you get here. Bye. I love you. We will meet you at the baggage claim."

Daiq yelled at Ben, "Done deal."

Ben was canceling things in St Andrews and having all the golf clubs sent to the Pines Golf Club in Morgantown, and alerted the luxury jumbo jet pilots of the flight to the United States. The pilots would make the preparations and alert Ben when they would be ready to fly, probably a little past noon.

Sam, Deacon, Zack, Penny and Mary Ann sat back on the suite furniture, and watched it all happen. It was amazing.

"I'm so sorry, guys. You know what a hot-head I am. Shots received, I am such a drone." Deacon said, pointing his finger at his head, as if he had a gun.

"You are quite a character, Deacon, we're getting some duct tape to put over your mouth, At least we can clear all this up now," Sam said, crossing his fingers.

"You can catch us all up on the plane, Sam, nothing to worry about. Alright?" Mary Ann commented, patting Sam on the back.

"Yup," Sam answered, trying to stay awake. Zack was sound asleep, sitting in a chair.

"Yup," Penny agreed, laying her head on Sam's shoulder.

"This certainly describes the three types of people in the world. Ben, Daiq and Fuge, making things happen, the four of us, watching things happen, and Zack will be wondering what happened," Deacon said, as he pointed at Zack, who was half asleep.

"Shots fired," Sam replied.

"Shots received," Zack grunted, with one eye half-open.

CHAPTER 35

"Okay," Ben ordered, acting like a person in charge would. They all had loaded into a stretch limo with their luggage and backpacks. They had gotten very little sleep. It was a forty-five minute ride from the Holiday Inn at the Wirral. They were all dropped off at the baggage claim for Liverpool Airlines at the Liverpool John Lennon International Airport, to meet Liz and Mimi. The entire luggage that Liz and Mimi had brought would be transferred to the executive staging area, where the luxury airliner was waiting for them. Ben said, "We are scheduled for departure around noon, according to our pilot, Captain Simon McArthur."

It was 10:30 am. They decided to have a late breakfast or a brunch at the Covered Bridges Restaurant at the check-point. They all sat and put in their orders.

"You didn't have to handle any of that luggage, did you, Mimi?" Ben chuckled.

"Are you kidding? Daiq's driver, Adrian, was right there at the house, carried and loaded the entire luggage. He smoothly escorted us with all of his protective guidance and courtesy. Quite the gentleman. You know what I mean? Then the sky-cap attendants and security took care of everything when we checked in at arrivals. Life is good," Mimi said matter-of-factly, sipping some of her coffee.

"You are something else, Mimi." Mary Ann laughed. "I see where your entire family got their humor. You are so precious."

"That's our Mimi," Sam said, dipping his toast in his over-easy eggs. "You never know what clever thing is coming out of her next. Fuge doesn't stand a chance around her."

"I resemble that remark," Fuge blurted out, looking over at Mimi.

"You can say that again," Mimi replied. "But I love you, Fuge. We always enjoy picking on each other."

"We all love Fuge," Sam repeated.

"Your nicknames are hilarious. I never knew my grandfather by anything but Daiq, which is just short for his last name, Daiquiri," Penny replied. "Right Daiq?"

"Wouldn't have it any other way, sweetie," Daiq answered, as he threw Penny a kiss.

"Alright," Zack said. "I'm anxious to get back on that executive airliner. What do you say? That's how we roll."

"I'm with you, brother, we are shittin' in high cotton, let's go," Deacon answered, giving Zack a high-five.

All of them were transported and escorted to an exclusive waiting area where they were served coffee, fountain drinks, or water. Deacon watched out of the window as all the luggage was transported over to the huge 747 airplane, and placed them on a conveyor belt leading to the storage area of the private executive jumbo jet. At 11:45 am, the attendant alerted them that it was time to board.

Daiq wasn't feeling well, so Liz said that they would probably not be able to go on the trip to the United States, and said that she and Daiq were going to stay in England, and return to their home. They would make arrangements to fly back to the Heathrow International Airport. The attendants removed their luggage and acquired their boarding passes. They all said their goodbyes, with hugs and kisses. Daiq and Liz were transported back to the Liverpool John Lennon International Airport to board a Liverpool Airlines jet, and fly back to their home in London, UK.

"Repeating what I said flying over here to England, I plan on catching some shut eye, Penny," Sam said, yawning. "I think Deacon and Zack probably feel the same, what do you say, guys?"

"You have some explaining to do, Sam, before you even think of sawing logs, my sleepy sweetheart," Penny stated. "So get yourself ready. Think about what you are going to say to Ben and Mary Ann, and to your grandparents. Deacon and Zack can go crash. We don't want Deacon there again, do we?"

"I don't think so, we would be there for hours," Sam answered. "I guess the ball is in my court, you can help me through it, Penny. I only hope they don't think we were unconditionally stupid, which we were."

"We'll be just fine," Penny said, giving him a big hug.

The eight of them boarded the giant palace, and again, greeted by Captain Simon McArthur and his assistant co-pilot. The stairs were removed, and the Captain guided them to the facilities seating area, where their attendant, Jackie Fernandez, was waiting to welcome them. She instructed them to take the eight available seats and to buckle up until the plane was in the air and leveled off. Ben released Jackie so that she could get belted in herself, along with two others in her crew. When the airliner leveled, they were told that they could maneuver around and do whatever they pleased. They were all fascinated with the entire luxury all over again. Not a thing missing.

Sam told Deacon and Zack, "Go back to the private room with that huge television that we had claimed as sleeping quarters. Penny and I have to clear some things up with her parents, and my grandparents."

Deacon closed the door, his hand clutched the knob as he listened to the murmur of Sam's voice beyond the closed door. He noticed a stenciled sign inside the door, it read: LIVING WELL IS THE BEST REWARD…He said, "Look Zack, that sign says, 'where the rich people live'. Get it! This is the best thing since sliced bread was invented. How do you see it?"

"You bet, but we're like two pairs of brown shoes in a tuxedo world, Deacon," answered Zack, "Geez, Sam has quite a task explaining everything out there. Let's listen to some music.

Sam and Penny were standing in front of Ben, Mary Ann, Mimi and Fuge, who were seated on the exclusive leather furniture. The inner flying mansion exuded luxury, filled with the finer things in life, that brings pleasures so freely and easily that one could say without the slightest hint of sarcasm, "life is good".

"I guess I have a story to tell," Sam began, "on Saturday, May the 21st, a day after my 18th birthday, I, Deacon and Zack had set up an interview with Penelope Daiquiri, to possibly bring her into our band. We decided to get in 18 holes of golf that morning at the Pines Country Club. We got signed in and had our clubs on the carts and started to play. On the third hole, Deacon, on his second shot, hooked his ball into the woods and thinking he could probably hit his ball out of there, we went to look for it. Zack was looking next to Barrowby Road, we call it 'Butt-Hole Road', and he spotted something going on in the woods."

"Okay, none of us knew that road had an actual name. We thought that it was nothing but an old logging road," Ben said. "Learn something new every day, huh? Go on with your story."

"Anyhow, the three of us went to investigate, and these three dudes ran and jumped into a black pick-up and left there like a bat out of hell. On a closer look, those three thugs had shot a man who was digging a hole to bury something. There was a huge leather duffle bag that Zack looked into, and the bag was full of money, a shitload l of money. We're talking C-notes. That's referring to the Roman numeral 100, which was printed on $100 dollar bills."

"Just tell the story, Sam, you don't have to define everything," Penny complained in irritation.

"I think it's cute how he explains things, Penny, leave him alone," Mary Ann whispered, making a shushing sound. "We're mid-flight and he has eight hours to explain what happened."

"Please don't encourage him, Mom, he'll take it to heart. We have to get some rest," Penny exclaimed, waving her off. "Finish the damn story, Sam."

"Samuel is sounding like Fuge now, making a long story go on for a longer time," Mimi announced.

"Yeah, right," Fuge said.

"Alright, here it is in a nutshell," Sam said. "We figured that we couldn't leave the money, because our fingerprints were all over it, and hoped that those thugs didn't get a good look at us. We carried the leather bag so we wouldn't leave behind any trail. We got back to the clubhouse, threw our clubs in Deacon's dad's car, put the leather bag in the back seat, and got the hell out of there, and then headed for Fritz's."

"You turned it over to the police?" Fuge asked, shrugging his shoulders.

"No, and that's not the end of the story. That was just the tip of the iceberg, Fuge. On the way to Fritz's, you know, Deacon's dad's Sport's Bar. The black pick-up, somehow, picked up our trail and began following us, actually wanting to kill us and take the money. Deacon, in an attempt to lose those suckers, zoomed away and went on the ramp toward I-79 south."

"And the pick-up kept following you?" Fuge questioned, leaning closer, in anticipation.

"Tailgating, I mean they were tailgating us. He was right up our butt, Fuge. Deacon cut off on I-68 east and was driving about eighty or eighty five mph, and just before the Cheat Lake exit, the pick-up pulled up like it was going to pass, and guess what? The passenger side window rolled down and Deacon was looking at a double–barreled shotgun. In a state of panic, I told Deacon to slam on the break. He jumped on the brake with both feet, and started a total vehicle crashing havoc behind us. The black pick-up, probably being shocked, veered off to the left across the grass median and somehow crashed and burned. We were unhurt and I told Deacon to continue driving, get off at Coopers Rock exit, and go to my mom and dad's house."

"You didn't wait for the police?" Fuge asked.

"Hell no," yelled Sam. "We were scared shitless, and how would we explain the duffle bag full of money? Besides that, we had reason to believe that the Morgantown Police Department was involved in these drug dealings, at least the top crust, Chief Anton Calabrese, Chief Investigator George Oliver and Sparrow Alexander. The man that was digging on Barrowby Road to bury the leather bag, Sgt. Earnest Maxwell, was also a corrupt police officer. The newspaper report was unreal, which came from Chief Calabrese saying Maxwell was digging a shallow grave to bury a body, and the body turned up missing. We believe that the police made up that story. We believe that Sgt. Maxwell was a bagman picking up the corrupt law enforcement protection payoff and got greedy. He was looking at a nice retirement. Maxwell's lovely wife's body was found in the crashed and burned pick-up, on I-68 east, along with three of Donovan's gang members. What do you say, Penny?"

"My father said that he suspected that there was some hanky-panky going on because there were no convictions for drug distribution, trafficking and manufacturing in all of Monongalia County, targeting corrupt law enforcement dealings."

"This is getting interesting. Quite an experience, Sam. What else?" Fuge asked.

"That is not the end of the story either. Our lives were still in danger."

"How's that, Sam?"

"Not only are the police involved," Sam said. "I had a run-in with that totally unforgiving piece of crap, Briccio Cadmen Donovan, a drug lord, who lived and owned almost everything in Fairmont, West Virginia. He was married to Roberto's older sister, Cleopatra. Roberto is a member of our band, you know? Anyway, Donovan was the worst person that ever existed. And the sad part is if you went after him, he would find some way to legally kill you. He was shaved bald and as strong as an ox, and had mean tattoo designs. He belonged to the Aryan Brotherhood which was founded by two white supremacists, Mills and Bingham in 1964 at the San Quentin state prison. He's the one that ran me off the road on I-68, and trashed my van."

"Go on," Fuge said.

"Around that time, people started dying." Sam continued.

"Oh my God," Mimi cringed, crossing herself. "This is terrible."

"Chief Investigator, George Oliver, got in Briccio Cadmen Donovan's way and was found dead, shot execution style. The new chief Investigator, Sparrow Alexander, knocked dead with a set of oriental non-chuck weapons. Drug Lord, Briccio Cadmen Donovan, and his wife, Cleopatra, killed in an explosion and fire. Three more of the Donovan gang members died in the same explosion and fire. It was later found that all five were shot before the explosion and fire, execution style, in the head. The explosion was, unconditionally, detonated a safe distance from the house. All those people were eliminated last week, pursuing the bag of money that is in Penny's gun safe, in your utility room, Ben. Those people were involved in the huge drug operation bust that just happened recently in Morgantown, which now brings us to Chief Calabrese and Hunter McClain."

"What do you think about the corrupt police officers, Dad?" Penny asked.

"We expect our police officers to be wise and honest. Their integrity and impartiality are the absolute bedrock of the entire community, including the city and state systems. We trust them to ensure our safety, to protect the rights of our citizens, and also to oversee the orderly flow of justice."

"Absolutely," Penny agreed.

Ben continued, "But what happens when a law enforcement officer bends the law or takes a bribe? It is certainly rare, but it happens."

"Indeed," Sam said, moving his head up and down. "The love of money is sometimes the actual root to corruption. In Chief Calabrese's case, the bribes didn't seem to be enough. Especially when he was backed into a corner, and his hungry mind was being driven toward a bigger treasure. With his drug lord friend Donovan out of the way, you could bet your last dollar that Calabrese was overly anxious to get his grubby hands on that bag of drug money, and actually escape to the islands."

"I'll bet that hurt the drug world when Donovan went down, Sam. What do you think?" Fuge asked, gritting his teeth.

"Oh yes, it was very crippling to their whole illegal drug operation, especially with all the drug paraphernalia that they confiscated, and his entire trucking company," Sam said.

"So what went on with Chief Calabrese and Detective McClain?"

"First of all, that Lieutenant King, who died with Chief Calabrese, was a part of the police corruption, just another piece of crap taking bribes."

"I'm so sorry that happened to you three, also including Penny, Roberto and Mateo," Mary Ann commented. "That must have been horrible, No wonder you poor souls needed a vacation."

"It was total hell. Chief Calabrese had hired Detective McClain to negotiate with the three of us, with some blackmail payoff in exchange for the bag of money. He offered the three of us one hundred and fifty thousand, tax free dollars, in the exchange, get it? He told us that if we didn't conform, there would be consequences. He would arrest the three of us for concealing the drug operation evidence and punish us to the full extent of the law. We agreed that it would all go down when we came back from vacation, giving us some time to come up with a plan to get out of that mess. We figured we were all history if Chief Calabrese found out where that money was hidden."

"That is when Detective Hunter McClain began harassing Sam, sending texts, with threats about Roberto and Mateo, threats about Sam's sister's safety, and then the topper about his parent's house burning. He was a total pest, being pushed by Chief Calabrese. That's why Deacon went off when he heard Detective McClain's voice in that phone conversation. Deacon had major plans of beating

Hunter to a pulp, isn't that right, Sam? There is a big difference between a human being and being a human. Only a few people really understand that."

"Deacon wanted to throw him into the Monongahela River. I'm thinking that Chief Calabrese had plans of keeping that money for himself. There is no way of tracking the money in that leather duffle bag and I really didn't think that Chief Calabrese would hesitate killing us for it," Sam remarked.

"Alright, that is enough, let all of that sink in, you guys," Penny said to the elders, holding her arms out to her sides, with her palms up. "Sam and I have to get some rest. We're going back to our favorite space in this adorable flying palace, and join Deacon and Zack, Good night, we love all of you."

"Good night, honey, we will alert you when we are ready to land," Mary Ann responded.

"If you get hungry. Jackie will get you something to eat," Ben added.

"Good night," Mimi said. "We love you too."

"Good night," Fuge said, as he and Mimi retired to the sleeping quarters they were occupying.

CHAPTER 36

"What about Weed and Mateo?" Deacon asked. "Do you think Chief Calabrese hurt them? Do you think he might have killed them? I'm worried sick about both the guys."

"Ditto, I am totally upset also," Zack said.

"We have to believe that our Lord will keep them safe, Deacon. Zack," Penny said.

"That is the first thing that we are checking out, once we get my parents settled," Sam exclaimed, "But until then, all we can do is pray."

Deacon finished sewing something on his jogging pants.

"Weren't you in the Boy Scouts, Deacon?" Zack asked.

"I had a long track record in the scouts, building character and self-esteem."

"How long were you a scout?"

"I achieved the prestigious rank of an Eagle Scout."

"Is that where you learned to sew so nicely?" Zack asked, with a little taste of teasing.

"No, but that's definitely where they taught me how to kill a man with a thumb to the eyeball."

"I guess we learn by doing," Zack replied, crawling inside himself. "What else you got?"

"Stop it you two." Penny exclaimed. "Do you guys ever quit?"

"Shots fired, Deacon. Let's try to get some sleep," Sam suggested.

"Shots received," Zack said, stretching out on one of the couches. "Goodnight."

This flight was definitely going to bring on some jet lag. They departed at noon, from England, United Kingdom, which was 7:00 am, on the east coast of the United States. The eight hour flight would make it 8:00 pm, in England, and their arrival time in the United States would be 3:00 pm, in the afternoon, go figure.

They all got some rest before Mary Ann and Jackie had alerted all of them that they had to get up, and get themselves seated, because Captain Simon McArthur was getting ready to land. They all got belted into their seats, as the plane circled and prepared to land, they could fill the wheels grabbing the landing strip as they slowly came to a stop. The huge luxury airliner was directed to the executive area, where stairs would be attached, and they would all exit the airplane. They were escorted to the waiting area, as their luggage would be transported to where the private helicopter was stationed. Ben Daiquiri's helicopter was being prepared for their flight to Morgantown, West Virginia.

While all of that was happening, Mary Ann and Penny took the opportunity to go to the restroom to freshen up. They entered a walked down a long corridor to a sign that pointed to the right. Then, there was a short corridor to the ladies room. When they reappeared and walked to the corner where it made a turn, a person grabbed Penny from behind. He was dressed in authentic-looking black cotton/poly blend attire, with a hood and a face mask. The terrorist, apparently a man, was pointing his Glock at Penny's head. He yelled at Mary Ann, "Keep moving down the hallway, bitch. Don't try to interfere or get in my way, I will blow this girls brains out."

"Don't hurt my baby," Mary Ann pleaded.

"Just shut up, and go back out the way you came in. Your 'baby' is coming with me."

When Mary Ann was out of sight, the terrorist maneuvered Penny toward the other end of the corridor, stopped, pushed open a door of what looked like an office. The first thing Penny saw in the office was the blood-smeared bodies of two security guards, lying on the floor. She screamed and said, "What do you want?"

"I'm sure your lady friend has alerted security that you are being held hostage by now."

"That lady was my mother! Again, what is it that you want? Is this about money? What's up?"

"I have an informant who tells me that your boyfriend, Samuel Trainer, is holding a huge amount of unmarked cash money and the way I see it, he is going to retrieve that money, and bring it here. I suggest that you do as you are told. I am in charge. We are going to communicate with security using that iPhone of yours, and if everyone cooperates, no one will be hurt. I'm sure everyone will agree to re-fuel that private jumbo jet out there, and do all the safety checks. You know, and have it ready for another long trip. That way, your boyfriend, you and I will be flying out of here, with me instructing the pilot. That way I will have the proper funds to complete my mission, killing your president."

"What? Why would you tell me all that stinking crap? That means that you're planning on killing me, too?"

"That's right. If you don't do as you're told. Okay, we are contacting your boyfriend right now."

"I know where the money is, I can take you there, and there is absolutely no need to get my boyfriend involved in this."

"Forget it, bitch. Again, do as you're told, or a lot of people are going to die."

"Don't have a cow. What do you want me to do, just say?" Penny exclaimed, being scared out of her wits.

"Text your boyfriend and let him know what I expect. Have them put the money in two separate suitcases. Got it? Then dial his number and let me talk to the security."

Penny texted Sam: "Sam, tell the security not to try anything stupid. Please. All this man wants is the drug money that you are holding, in my safe. Just have my dad, Deacon, and Zack go get the money, put all of the money in two suitcases, and bring it back here."

"Good girl, now call his phone, tell him that I want to talk to the security."

Penny called Sam and told him to put security on phone. She put it on speaker.

"Security Matt Donata here, how can I help you?"

"Hold on," Penny said.

"Security, Donata. Listen up. Don't be busting my chops or this will be your worst nightmare. I have a few things I need for you to do, or the girl dies. I am in charge here. First, that executive jumbo jet that just arrived will be re-fueled, inspected, and made ready for another long flight. Do you understand?"

"Got you, go on."

"Next, Sam Trainer, the gentleman whose phone you are using, will somehow produce two suitcases full of money, and bring them here to me in this security office. I will check the suitcases first. If everything is to my liking, Sam, I and his girlfriend here, will be departing for parts unknown, on that executive airliner. I will direct the pilot after we get airborne from the Pittsburgh International Airport. Get it?"

"Sir, this is Donata. The air traffic controllers are saying that what you want to do is not advisable or desirable. You have to have a destination point, to bring the aircraft down, it should be programmed like that."

"I don't think you understand the gravity of the situation. I am in charge here, Donata. I suggest that you and whoever is involved in this, just do as you're told."

"Sir, air traffic controllers are people trained to maintain the safe, orderly, and expeditious flow of air traffic in the global air traffic control system. Please be aware of that, for the sake of your own safety," Donata said. "This may take some time. We will stay in touch. I'll get back to you."

"Just do it, and contact me once the suitcases arrive."

Security director, Matt Donata, immediately got together with Sam, Ben, Deacon, and Zack, to come up with some kind of plan to make it all happen. The security team said that there was no response from the security officers that were located in that security office that the terrorist and Ben's daughter were in. Ben insisted that he take his helicopter to his home in Morgantown, West Virginia, with Deacon, Zack, and one of the security police to pick up the money, transfer it to two separate suitcases, and return to the airport. The airport security could maybe think of something else to do, while they worked that magic. Sam would stay with Director Matt Donata.

"You need to keep my wife, Mary Ann, and Sam's grandparents comfortable while all of this is happening." Ben suggested as he was preparing to board the chopper. "Actions speak louder than words. Let's go, guys."

"No problem, Mr. Daiquiri," Director Donata said. "We understand, that is your daughter that is being held hostage. It is totally devastating. We will work with you and try to come up with some solution. How long will the flight to West Virginia take?"

"We'll be back in a little more than an hour," Ben replied, fearing that something bad was going to happen.

Ben cranked up the chopper and they all fastened their belts. They lifted off and ascended up quickly from the helicopter pad and were on their way, he said, "This shouldn't take too long, we're moving as fast as this baby travels well."

It was a quick flight, Ben, Deacon, Zack and the security policeman got prepared to land. The helicopter was descending toward the private landing pad at the Daiquiri's house. As soon as they were down and settled, Deacon and Zack jumped out and ran to the garages where the utility building was. Ben and the security policeman ran to the house to pick up two suitcases. Zack unlocked the utility building and they hurried over to the gun safe.

"We have to transfer all that money to these two suitcases as quickly as we can, and get on our way back. I don't want that terrorist son of a bitch getting too -anxious. No telling what that asshole will do when there is such an uncertain outcome," Ben shouted at the security policeman.

Deacon used his key to open the safe. The door swung open, but Deacon and Zack were in for the shock of their life. There was no leather duffle bag in there. It was gone. Zilch. Nothing.

Deacon yelled, "What the fuck is going on. The sum-bitch is gone. What the hell are we supposed to do now, Zack? Damn!"

Deacon pulled out his iPhone and punched Sam's number and texted: "Sam…the money isn't here, the bag is gone…"

Sam texted: "Don't screw around, you two…this is serious…"

Deacon texted: "No shit, Sam…gone…the bags gone…"

Sam texted: "Put something in those suitcases… anything…this terrorist isn't playing…we'll have to fake it…there's no other way…"

"Holy crap, we have to stay calm, Deacon," Zack exclaimed, trying to settle Deacon's ass down. "What the hell, we have to take something back in those suitcases."

Ben and the security policeman burst in through the door with the suitcases. Deacon and Zack were standing there, dumbfounded.

"What's going on guys," Ben asked. "Where's the bag of money?"

"The son of a bitch is gone," Zack yelled.

"What?"

"How the hell is that possible? No one knew where that money was. That terrorist is going to kill Penny. What should we do, Ben?" Deacon shouted, sounding a little out of control, presenting a counter argument, like the devil's advocate.

"We need to settle down a little, Deacon. We don't need all of that. There is a pile of newspapers over by the door leading to the garages. Start stuffing those papers onto the suit cases."

"Got ya," Zack yelled.

Deacon grabbed one of the suitcases, opened it, and started cramming the newspaper into it.

"Stuff a lot in there, those suitcases have to be pretty heavy, 30 to 35 pounds," Ben said, as he grabbed the security policeman by the arm, "Leave yours about half empty, Zack. I have about fifty thousand dollars in our home safe, and I want this officer to witness that there was no bag of money here, and me putting my own money in that suitcase. Are we on the same page here, officer?"

"You can count on me." The officer replied.

"We leave the suitcase with my fifty grand unlocked, and tag it for Sam, he can show the terrorist. Lock the other one tight. That should help us pull the wool over the terrorist's eyes as a means of deceiving him. Come on boys, let's do it."

Everything went to plan as they had intended, the suitcases were loaded into the chopper, everyone got on board and buckled up, the chopper lifted off the pad and ascended into the air. They were on their way back to the Pittsburgh International Airport.

CHAPTER 37

Sam waited with baited breath when the helicopter returned and was being guided to the landing pad. He was aware that the ball was now going to be in his court. He would deliver the money down the hallway to the security office. There was an anxiety rising in his heart; he wanted to go. Ben informed Sam that the tagged suitcase was unlocked and contained actual money, and that the second bag, locked securely, contained nothing but newspaper, a whole bunch of newspapers. He could show the terrorist inside the tagged suitcase. Sam was preparing to make this journey; he was lifting the suitcases, and setting them down, getting used to the feel. They waited about ten minutes, and Security Director Donata punched in Penny's number and informed the terrorist that Sam was coming with the suitcases. He suggested that he quickly check them, and that the executive jumbo jet was ready for boarding. The terrorist peeked out the security office window and the pilot, a security officer, could be seen through the window of the cockpit. He answered and ordered Sam to be sent.

"I suggest that you people don't try to deceive me, because you have my word, I will shoot the girl, enough said. Send him in."

Sam walked toward the building and into the hallway, his hands and body were shaking uncontrollably, He was scared shitless. He walked past the sign pointing to the woman's restroom, as he then approached the door to the security office. The terrorist pulled him inside. Sam was set back when he saw the two dead bodies of the security officers on the floor. The sight almost made him throw up. He put his arm around Penny and gave her a hug. He grabbed the suitcase with the tag on the handle and quickly opened it. The terrorist took a closer look.

"What the fuck are you trying to pull here? This was supposed to be C-notes."

Sam Thought: *When you are extremely desperate you need to take drastic actions.*

"Oh no, sir, that money was in all different denominations. That's why those sum-bitchin' suitcases are so heavy, no shit," Sam said.

"He's telling the truth. Please," Penny said, holding her head in a down position.

"Okay, close that son of a bitch, and let's get this show on the road," said the terrorist, as he punched Sam's number to talk to security.

"Security Donata here, how can I help you? Are you ready to board, sir? The stairs to the aircraft are in place."

Security Director Donata had a conversation with Ben Daiquiri and had informed him that there were two sniper shooters that would have their crosshairs on the terrorist's head. If they saw a safe opening, they would drop him.

"We are coming out. The girl will be in front of me, Sam behind me, carrying the suitcases. My weapon will be pointing at the girl's head the whole time. If I find anything suspicious, I will shoot the girl, point blank."

Deacon and Zack snuck into a room full of traveler's golf clubs. Deacon pulled a Ping Pistol putter out of one of the golf bags, threw the cover off and said to Zack, "Here's my equalizer. Grab something, Zack."

Zack found a large crescent wrench on a shelf and secured it, slid it into his pocket and said, "I got mine."

Deacon and Zack went to a door that was closest to the stairs leading to the airplane and waited. Everyone was hiding and watching.

"It is safe to come out," Director Donata said to the terrorist. "No one will interfere, and you can ascend up the steps and enter the airplane."

They came out single file with Penny leading and Sam behind, carrying the suitcases. They made a path to the bottom of the stairs leading up to the plane, emotions were high and Penny guessed anything could happen. She quickly made a superior "Sonkal" move, (a "Sonkal" is the Taekwondo name for a move similar to a "Karate chop") pushing the weapon up and her open hand came crashing down to make an impact on the terrorist's neck. Sam took advantage of the terrorist while he was down on one knee. He aimed a kick at his chest, but failed to catch him directly, and barely managed to knock him off balance. Sam reached and grabbed the arm that was holding the weapon, but before he had secured it, a shot rang out. Penny was now facing them and her hair puffed up and she went down, backwards and rolled over face down.

"You son of a bitch," Sam screamed still having a firm grip on the arm. A knee came up out of nowhere and drove super hard into Sam's crotch, taking his breath away. The pain was excruciating, and he lost his grip on the terrorist's arm, and stumbled back. Deacon and Zack burst out of the door they were next to, and were running out to check on Penny. Director Donata was screaming his lungs out, telling the two dumb asses to get back. Another shot rang out and Zack dropped to his knees and fell forward to the concrete, the crescent wrench flying from his hand. Deacon reached Penny, still holding the Ping putter. Sam again closed in on the terrorist, but he pushed Sam off and tackled him around the knees. He scrabbled on top of Sam, straddled him and was sitting on his stomach. He drove his fist down at Sam's face. Sam turned his face away and the fist grazed off his ear. The terrorist brought his right hand up and made a double fist holding the weapon, ready to smash Sam in his face. That was going to fucking hurt. Before the terrorist could start the down swing, Deacon plunged the pointed end of the Ping Pistol putter into the terrorist's back. Almost simultaneously, a loud shot went off, the back of the terrorist head peeled off from a sniper's bullet, and the terrorist dropped to the side.

"Sum-bitch, Sam, that terrorist was kicking your ass, man."

"Thanks for the sympathy, Deacon," Sam said, as he looked up and saw Penny and Zack standing there, looking at him. "Oh my God, I can't believe it. Are you two alright? I was thinking the worst. Thank God for small favors."

Everyone was crowding around, Mary Ann was hugging and holding Penny, Mimi and Fuge were elated that the nerve racking havoc was over. Security Director Matt Donata was giving Deacon and Zack all kinds of hell for running out like that. Zack was limping. He had taken a shot just above the knee. Penny had a flesh wound to the neck. There were plenty of ambulances to deliver everyone around. Ben, Deacon and Sam were looking at the terrorist's body, and Sam reached over and pulled off the rest of his mask, and had the absolute shock of his life.

"Hunter, that terrorist was Hunter McClain." Sam exclaimed.

"Hunter? That no-good piece of shit! One more money hungry bastard just bit the dust. Holy shit," Deacon yelled, hacking up and spitting at Hunter. "Bastard."

"Hunter McClain," Zack cringed. "That freaking worm!"

"You mean that Detective Hunter McClain that we were talking to on the phone while in England, Sam?" Ben asked.

"That's the one. Hard to believe, isn't it?"

"Whatever doesn't kill you really does make you stronger, Sam. We thought we were going to lose you. Time will heal all of this that has happened. We have to give time some time," Fuge said in his usual fashion.

Penny went over and kicked Hunter, "That's for calling me a bitch."

Mary Ann kicked him also, "That's double from me, you toad."

Michael and Erica Trainer, Sam's mom and dad, showed up

while all of this was going on. His sister, Anna, stayed with a friend. Sam said, "Boy, do I have a story to tell you guys."

"I can't say that I'm sad because that evil bag of money disappeared, and I hope forever. It had definitely been a curse from the word go," Penny said. "I don't even care where it disappeared to. I'm so glad your mom and dad got here. I feel so sad that they lost their home. They need some special comforting also, Sam. This has been quite a journey, these last two weeks, and it's not over yet. We still don't know what happened to Weed and Mateo."

"Yup," Sam agreed.

The huge 747 luxury jumbo jet was being prepared to be returned and staged at the Pandora JFK Airport, and its owner. Ben, Deacon, Sam, Mimi and Fuge were boarding Ben's helicopter for a relaxing flight back to Morgantown, West Virginia. Life Flight was transporting Penny, Mary Ann and Zack to Allegheny General Hospital, where they would be treated for their wounds and trauma. Mike and Erica were driving across to Allegheny General to pick them up.

Mike was receiving a text. One of his foremen, Lloyd Browning texted: "Mike, I hate to deliver the bad news, but Howard, took the big one, man. I mean a massive heart attack… doesn't look good… he is at Ruby Memorial Hospital… (304) 598-4000…he may have cashed it in, my friend."

Mike texted: "Hang in there, Lloyd… we are in Pittsburgh. I will call the hospital."

Mike punched in the numbers and saved it to his contacts, and the hospital answered immediately, "Ruby Memorial, how can I help you."

"Can you connect me with the intensive care unit?"

"One moment."

"Intensive Care."

"This is Michael Trainer, Howard Huge was just brought in and I need to know his condition."

"Are you family?"

"I'm his business partner at Huge Structural & Home Improvement, in Morgantown. I need to know his condition, please."

"Mr. Huge has passed away sir, I'm sorry."

"Oh my God, Thank you." Mike said and ended the call. He turned to Erica and said. "He's gone, Erica. Howard and I were just talking about that. He has no known family, and he was turning everything over to me if something happened to him. It's in his will. He is worth ten million dollars."

"What, He left it to you?"

"It's written so in his will."

"Holy Jesus, Mike, we're rich, I'm going to have a heart attack."

"We can't say anything yet, until it's all sorted out, but you are so right. We're rich."

They pulled into the parking lot at the emergency room. They went inside and found Mary Ann. She said that they were working on them, "We'll have to drive back to Morgantown, thank you for everything, and I'm so sorry about your house."

Erica thought: *We are going to own a beautiful home, and Samuel is going to Yale*

"We had a little bad news driving over here, Mary Ann. We were told that my business partner, Howard Huge, passed away."

"How sad, I'm so sorry," Mary Ann answered.

CHAPTER 38

Everyone got together at the Euro-Suites Hotel, on Chestnut Ridge Road, in Morgantown, after everything was settled at the Pittsburgh International Airport. There were tons of questions from airport security, the local police, and whoever needed to know something. There would be more inquiries, you could bet on that. Deacon and Zack went to their homes to explain everything to their parents. Sam, Penny, Ben, Mary Ann, Mimi and Fuge were at the hotel.

"Mary Ann informed me that your business partner passed away. Don't be backward about asking me for any help, Michael. Let me know if I can do anything at all. I am totally crushed by what has been going down. Your home burned, the corrupt law enforcement, Chief Calabrese and Detective Hunter McClain causing havoc, the missing Hispanic's, Roberto and Mateo, and the unexplained missing drug money. This is a situation that is unpleasant but must be accepted. It's quite a bitter pill to swallow. Do you and your family have a place to stay until all of this is sorted out, Mike? You are welcome to stay at our place otherwise. We have plenty of room."

"Howard and I had an empty three-bedroom apartment that Erica, me and the kids will rent or just get cozy in, until we can rebuild. Now that Howard has passed, I will be the sole owner of the business, rest in peace my dear friend and partner for years. I texted our lawyer, Ethan Rockefeller, and he informed me that it's perfectly clear in the will. I am to take over our business and all of

Howard's worldly possessions, including his bank account, which is huge, as were his name and body, Howard Huge. Erica and I will be pretty much taken care of for the rest of our lives."

"Wow," Sam exclaimed. "What about me going to Yale Law School then?"

"That is another surprise, Samuel." Erica said, being elated. "We received a letter saying that you are receiving a full scholarship from Yale Law School, with recommendations from the Daiquiri's and the President of the United States, all inclusive."

"That settles it, dad. That is where I will be attending law school too. What do you say?" Penny exclaimed.

"What can I say, sweetie," Ben smiled. "That is your choice."

"Done deal," Mary Ann agreed. "Both of you are going to Yale."

"That was easy, wasn't it?" Mimi exclaimed, with a big smile. "Everything that the Daiquiris do is somehow sent straight from heaven. I believe that there is a connection to God himself. How do you see it, Fuge?"

"Everything can change in the blink of an eye, but don't worry, God never blinks," Fuge announced. "I'm proud of both of you, Sam and Penny."

"Thank you, Ben, for all that you have done for all of us," Mike said, giving Ben and Mary Ann a hug. "We can never repay you."

"Okay," Ben concluded. "Let's all try to get a little rest tonight, the jet lag is catching up, I am beat."

The next day at noon, Deacon, Zack, Sam and Penny planned to meet at Fritz's to try to figure out what happened to their friend's, Weed and Mateo. Sam was driving to Fritz's in the Mercedes Van, and he thought: *What if Chief Calabrese was holding Weed and Mateo captive, and they are still alive somewhere?* Everyone was deceased that would even know. They would have to just wait and watch.

Sam swung the Mercedes into the parking lot, climbed out, locked the doors, and headed to the entrance of "The Fritz". He entered, gave a thumbs up to the Stop, Drop and Roll sign and saw that was there - Penny, Deacon, Zack, and even Francisco, Deacon's dad. They all hugged and high-fived.

"How we doing, Mr. Fritz?" Sam shouted, shaking his hand. "Looks like everything is back to normal, except for Weed and Mateo."

"Life is good," Francisco spat out. "Sorry about your Hispanic friends, very strange, everyone is presuming that they had met their maker. I don't know? You don't have to call me Mr. Fritz, Sam, call me Francisco, okay?"

"Thanks, Francisco. We appreciate what you said about Weed and Mateo. You're right; it is strange about what happened to those two," Sam said, as Francisco went about his business.

It seems that no one can explain the disappearance. They were both seen at Fritz's eating and having a couple of beers. They left for a while and then returned. When they left the second time they disappeared, their motorcycles were still in the parking lot. No one had seen them since.

"I'm worried that Francisco is right. Chief Calabrese undoubtedly eliminated those two, they wouldn't have taken any crap off of him, **or** his cohort's. You know that. I'm afraid they are dead, Sam," Penny said, giving him a hug.

"We may have to face that," Zack agreed. "Chief Calabrese was desperate, and time was running out for him. He had to get out of town fast."

"Those heartless sons of bitches. I hope they all rot in hell," Deacon said, as he pounded his fist on the table.

"We all feel the same about it, Deacon, but, life goes on, my friend," Sam replied.

"What about Hunter McClain? Was that a shock too?" Zack laughed, as he slapped Deacon on the back.

"That was the poorest impersonation of a threatening terrorist I have ever seen, saying that he was going to kill our president", Penny laughed. "I don't know what he would have done, if we would have taken off in that jumbo jet. Yikes. That just wasn't going to happen. I knew that. I knew that they were going to pick him, **or me,** off with a sniper's bullet. Believe me when I say I was scared out of my wits. And then you two heroes entered the scene. Oh my God."

"We saved your life, lady," Deacon remarked, as he acted like he was insulted. "You would have been dead meat."

"Yeah," Zack agreed, giving thumbs up.

"Yeah right, Zack," Penny exclaimed. "You and I were face down on the concrete. How were you going to help? Was that a giant crescent wrench that you were carrying?"

"Yes it was. I could have done some damage with that. Besides, I was just playing dead," Zack complained, crossing his arms.

"So was I, Zack. Believe me," Penny agreed, tilting her head and sticking her tongue out.

"Listen girl," Deacon countered. "I plunged the pointed end of that Ping Pistol putter deep into that assholes back, or Sam wouldn't be here now. What do you say, Sam?"

"I have to agree, he would have split my head wide open with that weapon, if he didn't jerk back from the blow of that putter, for sure. Then the back of his head exploded, when sniper dropped him. No shit about it, you saved my ass, Deacon."

"Damn straight," Deacon said, winking at Penny.

"All I have to say is that we are certainly a team, watching each other's backs, like the WW1 fighter pilots. You know, like, 'I got your back, man'." Sam reminisced, being nostalgic. It seems sad that the four of us are going to be split up. Penny and I are departing and going to the 'Yale School of Law' and you two will be going to the 'West Virginia University School of Law'. We actually have the rest of this summer to put together Penny's song and see where it goes. I'm sure that it will go to the top of the charts. I'd lay money on that one. How do you guys see it?"

"The way I see it guys, we will always be together in our hearts and minds," Zack muttered sadly.

"Hey, who started this sad stuff?" Deacon demanded. "We're all going to Francisco's house, on Downwood Drive, in Downwood

Manor, and we are going to tie one on. I mean get drunk out of our sculls, and discuss our futures. What do you say? Everyone can stay overnight."

"Count me in," Zack agreed, getting up from the booth, before anyone changed their minds.

"Let's do it," Sam and Penny said, simultaneously, at the same instant.

The next morning, Penny, Sam, Deacon and Zack, a little hung over, drove out to go see Weed and Mateo's parents. They had changed their address and were now living at "The Crossing", a top notch sub division, in new, exclusive homes. They no longer lived in their mobile homes at Country Squire Mobile Home & Park. They really had nothing to add to what they already knew about Weed and Mateo. Their parents didn't seem to be too shook up about their sons being missing, possibly dead. The boys and Penny said their goodbyes and headed back to Fritz's.

CHAPTER 39

Sam's father had saved the newspaper clippings about the explosion and fire at their home, and about the deaths of Chief of Police Anton Calabrese and Lieutenant Bernard King. Their fireproof safe was recovered unharmed from the basement with all of their valuables intact. Mike had moved his family into the three-bedroom apartment which he now owned due to the death of his business partner, Howard Huge. Mike and Erica were in the process of looking for a lot and examining the house plans for the future home that they were going to build until the Daiquiri's came up with a deal that was rather hard to resist. Ben and Mary Ann decided that they were going to take up residence in New Haven, Connecticut, near the Yale University. They were moving out of their million-dollar home in Morgantown and, if the Trainers would have been interested, they could purchase it for five hundred thousand dollars, all inclusive of furniture and other interior decorative.

"Ben, that is one hell of an offer," Mike said. "But we can't just accept such charity, especially since we have come into a windfall of unexpected monies."

"What are you talking about charity?" Ben replied. "I need these deals in order to set off my taxes, Mike. I would give you the home if I could. I have to show some sort of huge loss. It would be perfectly legal for me. I will collect twice as much as the house is worth. What do you say? Do we have a deal, Mike?"

"I'll answer that one, Ben, we have a deal," Erica exclaimed, cupping her hand over Mike's mouth. Then turning towards Mike she said, "These things happen very rarely, Mike. These happen once in a blue moon."

"You're right, we are receiving two hundred and fifty thousand dollars from the insurance for our home, I would have never even dreamt of living in such an exclusive home. You are making things very comfortable for us. You are saving us the agony of building a new home. We are forever indebted to both of you."

"Thank my father Michael. He's the one that gave me one hundred and twenty five million dollars as a graduation gift when I graduated from college," Ben explained. "It will take us a week or two to get our personal things out of the house. Mary Ann, Penny and I will stay at our apartment in Washington, DC, until we purchase a home in Connecticut. Sam will be able to visit us while he and Penny get ready for law school this fall. You and I can take care of the paperwork, Michael. I can handle all the transaction myself."

"One thing," Mary Ann demanded. "You have to keep a couple of those bedrooms open in case Penny and I feel an urge to play golf at the Pines Country Club."

"No problem," Erica replied. "You will always be welcome in this home."

"When we get settled in Connecticut," Mary Ann said. "You will certainly be welcome there, too."

The Morgantown Police Department seemed to be a little more upbeat. The new Chief of Police seemed to have a firm grip over the organization. For starters, they had filled all the vacancies. A strong police force had been created and the drug trafficking seemed to have slowed down considerably, if not disappeared. State cleanups were happening with the closure of the meth labs in West Virginia, Pennsylvania and Ohio. Law enforcement officers in Morgantown were still abiding to their previous code, before and during the corrupt invasion of their police department, by corrupt perpetrators who carried out acts that were harmful, illegal, and immoral.

The code: *Law Enforcement is any system by which some members of society act in an organized manner to enforce the law by discovering, deferring, rehabilitating, or punishing people who violate the rules and norms governing the society.*

An entire fleet of more than 80 trucks and vans was confiscated from Donovan trucking and a couple of them were torn down to find how drugs were being transported. They found that large amounts of drugs were being inserted inside the spare tires so they could be easily be recovered when they reached their destination. This was the reason why drug-detecting dogs were unable to pick up the scent.

Seth and Ethan Rockefeller, being concerned about what their legacy would be, had donated thirty million dollars to the Department of Health and Human Resources of West Virginia, which would create approximately one thousand more crisis and detoxification beds for the nearly thirty thousand West Virginians who were already in drug rehabilitation and treatment programs. The Governor of West Virginia would authorize the Department of Health and Human Resources to ensure that the treatment beds were available in the highest priority areas throughout the state. Data showed that the treatment programs were effective for many people who completed them.

Seth and Ethan also turned the Rockefeller Towing Services over to their cousin, Liam Hercules, lock, stock, and barrel, to operate it completely on his own and enjoy all of the profits.

Within a few months' time, the "No Two Ways…Rock 'n Roll Band", created a music album, which included Penny's song, and Penny was looking for a single song contract publisher for her specific song; *The Single Song Contract is probably the most basic publishing agreement a songwriter can enter into. If a songwriter has written a song, and a publisher thinks it can be placed on an artist's album, or perhaps in a film or TV program, the two parties can sign a single-song agreement.*

"What is my best bet for getting single song contract?" Penny asked a song publisher, Jennifer West, whom she was considering for placing her song.

"I have seen and heard your band's music, as well as your songs. I would certainly be willing to move on it, Penny," Jennifer commented. "Sometimes a single song deal, if the song is placed, can help you get the position of a full-fledged staff writer from the publisher. If the song becomes a major hit, of course, you can earn tremendous royalties. But even if the song is not a hit, but is on a big-selling album, the income can be substantial. You have already sent me a sample of your work and I believe something can be worked out. I am prepared to offer you a $20,000 deal because I believe that you are a potential 'hit maker'."

"Is there a possibility of a known singing artist, such as Celine Dion, performing and actually promoting my song?" Penny asked.

"Yes, that is totally possible. For example, if I thought your specific song could be placed with an artist such as Celine Dion, under that contract, the songwriter usually assigns 50% to 100% of the publishing rights of the song to the publisher for a certain period of time, usually between 12 and 24 months. If the publisher secures a placement with an artist during this period, then the publisher becomes a permanent copyright owner of the song. See how it works."

"I sort of like the $20,000 deal, Jennifer, How do you see it?"

"That's an excellent choice, Penny. We can complete the contract and you will be on your way."

Penny was elated and excited to tell Sam and the guys about the deal that she had just cracked. Sam had already signed a contract for their new album "No Two Way" The music publishers were all excited about the new contracts, and were ready to get everything placed.

"I'm crazy about it," Zack exclaimed, as he gave Deacon a high five. "We have this thing completely covered in the most effective and efficient way, from A to Z. The whole nine yards, baby!"

"Yeah, baby," Deacon replied. "That money might help out on

our educations. I freakin' love it. I just wish Weed and Mateo were here to enjoy all of this."

"This is all wonderful. I'm just so entertained by all these things," Sam said.

"I believe we've got something here, Sam. Jennifer said that even if there is no future offer, it is often surprising how much money can be made from having just one song placed. If my song becomes a major hit, look out, there will be tremendous royalties. She said that even if my song is not a hit, but on our big selling album, the income can be substantial. You could knock me over with a feather."

The production cost for the creative process and marketing of a hit, approximately $1,000,000. Considering the explosive profit potential that a hit has, it is actually surprising that it is "that cheap". It seems the only pro in this deal that isn't guaranteed to get paid is the artist themselves. The rest of the people in the mix get paid either way (though it is possible that their careers will die if they don't produce results very often). It makes a person curious as to the percentage/fixed take, of those producers and writers.

Penny's song became a hit, immediately, quickly climbing the charts in popularity. The "No Two Ways" album, also took off like a rocket. The money began rolling in and the royalties were rising tremendously, going through the roof. Deacon and Zack were in an ecstatic frenzy of intense, overpowering emotions when they realized that they had made it to the top. Things were good.

CHAPTER 40

Two years had passed, and the Trainers were pretty much settled into their new home on Anchor Avenue. Michael and Erica and taken the master bedroom. Sam and Anna had their choice of the other seven bedrooms. Anna became very popular at the University High School and her cheerleader friends were delighted to come to the exquisite estate where she lived. They had constant pajama parties, practiced all of their cheers in a detached sunroom with a fireplace, and lounged at the indoor pool and spa. The grounds featured mature, manicured landscaping, fencing, patios, fire pit, and a flat yard, privacy and plenty of parking in the driveways. Anna was making excellent grades and was planning on attending the West Virginia University School of Law. Deacon and Zack had already begun working their way through the WVU School of Law.

Michael Trainer became a success-story taking over the Huge Structural & Home Improvement business as he came up with expectations adequate enough to compete and participate with the other contractors. He was now able to take on contracts that involved building huge apartment complexes. He now employed about 120 construction workers with full benefits. Mike also took over Howard's membership at the "Lakeview Golf Resort & Spa", which was set on 500 acres overlooking Cheat Lake, the golf resort is 8.5 miles south of the Pennsylvania border and 7.4 miles from West Virginia University.

Erica was now a Grievance Officer as the Director of Social

Services at the Ruby Memorial Hospital. The Board of Directors designates the Hospital Grievance Committee as the committee to have oversight of the Complaint and Grievance process and the authority to review and resolve the grievances. This group was led by the Director of Human Resources and the members included the Hospital Risk Manager, Chief Nursing Officer, Compliance Officer, Director of Social Services and Quality Assurance Director. Meetings are held on a regular basis in order to identify risk management trends that translate into institutional learning and improvement with the hospital. They handle both the complaints and the grievances.

A "complaint" is defined as an expression of dissatisfaction brought to the attention of hospital personnel. A complaint can be resolved by the appropriate department or with the assistance of Human Resources. A complaint is not initially considered to be a grievance. All complaints received by the Human Resources will be documented in the patient complaint/grievance system.

A formal "grievance" is defined as a written or verbal complaint that is made to the hospital by a patient, or the patient's representative, regarding the patient's care (when the concern is not resolved at the time of the complaint by staff present), abuse or neglect.

Sam had moved to an all-expenses paid apartment in New Haven, Connecticut, and was attending Yale Law School at the Yale University. Penny Daiquiri was planning an exclusive wedding for the two of them. Penny was also attending the Yale Law School. Ben and Mary Ann Daiquiri had purchased a home in Milford, Connecticut, on the Woodmont Waterfront nestled in a private upscale location surrounded by magnificent gardens and trees with a sweeping front lawn to the water's edge and private beach. A splendid New England style 7-bedroom home, meticulously cared for, which boasted panoramic views. It had an open floor plan with two fireplaces, a marvelous glassed in wraparound porch overlooking beautiful Long Island Sound. The second level veranda offers a hot tub with breathtaking views and a master suite that's for royalty.

Sam and Penny would return to Morgantown periodically and meet at Fritz's with Deacon and Zack, and Zack's new girlfriend, Sydney Madison.

Riley G. Van Lorne had become a Rhodes Scholar and now, through the encouragement of the President of the United States and Benjamin Franklin Daiquiri, he was now being nominated for the Ambassador to the United Kingdom, awaiting approval from the Senate. Riley was working on the 2020 Campaign Committee Staff for re-election. Britain was always used to wealthy Americans being awarded the most coveted job of ambassador to the Court of St James. There were six wealthy businessmen in a row who had filled the post before Riley.

The position was regarded as one of the most prestigious positions in the United States Foreign Service. The ambassador and the embassy staff at large work at the American Embassy in Governor Square, London. The official residence of the United States' Ambassador is Winfield House in Regent's Park. He answers to the Secretary of State, who is the senior official of the federal government of the United States of America, and also the head of the U.S. Department of State.

The ambassador's main duty is to present American policies to the Government of the United Kingdom and people and to report E British policies and views to the Federal government of the United States. He serves as a primary channel of communication between the two nations and plays an important role in treaty negotiations.

The ambassador is also the head of the United States consular service in the United Kingdom. He also directs diplomatic activity in support of trade. He is ultimately responsible for the services and for the provision consular support to American citizens in the UK. He also oversees the cultural relations between both the countries.

Riley G. Van Lorne, who had been educated in top fashion at the Georgetown University and as a Rhodes Scholar who studied at the University of Oxford, together with the strength, the ability and the intelligence, was the President's pick, to mold and structure the pre-existing "Stop the Nuclear War" coalition in England. The coalition is an alliance of political groups and countries joining together for a common purpose. Riley G. Van Lorne was to lay the cornerstones for global disarmament of all nuclear weapons. In the almost fifty years in the nuclear age, defacto nuclear proliferation had led to nine nations definitely having nuclear weapons, these nations being the U. S.A., Russia, England, France, China, India, Pakistan, Israel, and North Korea. The Nuclear Non-proliferation Treaty was signed on July 1968 and entered into force in March 1970.

The Treaty on the Non-Proliferation of Nuclear Weapons is an international treaty whose objective is to prevent the spread of nuclear weapons and weapons technology, to promote cooperation in the peaceful uses in nuclear energy, and to further the goal of achieving nuclear disarmament and general and complete disarmament. Central to the treaty is the concession of the Non-Nuclear Weapons nations to refrain from acquiring nuclear weapons and in exchange, the nuclear weapons nations to make progress on nuclear disarmament and provide unrestricted access to nuclear energy for non-military purposes.

CHAPTER 41

Penny and Sam agreed to meet with this gentleman that was claiming to be Mateo, along with Deacon and Zack at Fritz's at 2:00 pm on May 6, 2020. They were all waiting at their favorite booth when the door opened and a man entered, gave thumbs up to the Stop, Drop and Roll sign and walked toward the booth. When he came closer, they could see that it was indeed Mateo Martinez. Penny screamed, jumped up and through her arms around him, and exclaimed, "Mateo, I can't believe it. Where have you been? Where is Weed? I can't believe that you're alive!"

Everyone jumped up and greeted him in amazement, because they all thought that Mateo and Weed were dead.

"I guess I have some explaining to do. Let me sit down and get a beer and I'll try to clear all of this up."

At the drop of a hat, Deacon ran to the bar and pulled five Coors Light's out of the cooler and brought the over to the booth. Everyone popped them open, and waited with bated breaths for Mateo to begin.

"There are a couple things that I have to tell you," Mateo explained. "Weed and Cleo are both dead, they both died, along with Weed's girlfriend, Mia, when his plane went down in the Atlantis Ocean. Cleopatra did not die in the fire and explosion with Donovan. That was their maid, Maria, who had a very close resemblance to Cleo."

"That is strange. That was never changed in the paper, about Cleo," Zack said. "And when did Weed buy an airplane?"

"Let me start at the beginning," Mateo replied, as he took a big swallow of his beer. "I'll tell you about the eerie part first. On a day in May, two years ago, Weed, myself and Cleo had just finished eating at the Fernandez's house. We were relaxing and watching some TV, when something strange happened. The three of us could feel something entering our bodies, something invisible. Something that was supernatural, extraterrestrial and sort of like a holy spirit. A voice came from nowhere saying, 'Your journey has begun'. Naturally we were scared shitless and began asking, 'What journey?', or 'What kind of journey?' The voice came back saying, 'To end the evil corruption, we will guide you'."

"You are totally blowing me away, Mateo," Penny yelled, as she wrapped her arms around herself. "That is too weird."

"So what happened then?" Deacon asked.

Mateo continued, "The next day Weed and I were riding our Trail bikes on a couple of trails and we spotted a man digging a hole like he was going to bury something. A couple of minutes later a huge black Ford pick-up, with dark tinted glass, zoomed up and made a quick stop. Three men jumped out and ran into the woods where the man was digging, and shot him many times in the back. They heard someone coming. It was the golfers. They got spooked and left. That's when you three made off with the bag that the man was burying."

"You watched us take the duffle bag?" Deacon questioned.

"Yup."

"The black pick-up came back and saw that the bag was missing and took off again."

"That is when those thugs picked up our trail, chased us, and ended up crashing and burning on I-68 east," Zack concluded.

"If you remember, Briccio Cadmen Donovan was absolutely certain that Chief Calabrese had stolen his drug money, and he was threatening to waste Calabrese if his money wasn't returned. That is when Weed and Cleo executed Chief Investigator George Oliver, with the intention that Chief Calabrese would take that as a warning from Donovan."

"Weed sent an anonymous text to Donovan saying that there were some golfers involved in taking his drug money as well," Mateo continued.

"Did you three kill Donovan?" Deacon asked.

"The three of us were completely brainwashed, some supernatural power was driving the three us and we just did as we were told. Weed and Cleo had affixed tons of explosives at the Donovan Complex. Cleo had set up a misappropriated money account and embezzled millions of dollars from Donovan. Cleo knew how to launder money and to relocate it into a family business account through Nassau Life. The amount was close to twelve million dollars. Weed had acquired a valid pilot's license to fly light propeller aircraft, after taking flight training while we were working at the Morgantown airport. He purchased a six-passenger, Cessna Citation 525, twin-engine aircraft and began flying from island to island. The three of us purchased an already established Nassau Bahamas company, which was renamed Cleodo Enterprises."

"What kind of business was it?" Zack asked.

"Cleodo Enterprises had an extensive collection of unique diving equipment and scuba gear that were sold throughout the islands, using the already established sales representatives. Scuba diving was extremely popular in the Bahamas. Weed was flying from island to island to deliver our products. Weed and Cleo also had intentions of eliminating all the known drug lords and distributors by means of execution."

"I'll bet you bought new Harley Davidson's, Mateo?" Deacon commented, shrugging his shoulders.

"We bought two Harley Davidson Sportsters immediately, Deacon, and Cleo bought herself a Corvette Z06 to cruise around in."

"You said Weed, his girlfriend, and Cleo were killed in a plane crash, so are you keeping the business?" Sam asked.

"I plan on maintaining the business. I'm living in a condo that Cleo purchased. It is located in the gated complex of San Marino on Paradise Island. I met and married my lovely wife, Ivanna, and we now have a son, Roberto. He is a year old now. We are doing well, financially."

"That's wonderful! And you called him Roberto, how precious," Penny exclaimed. "I can't believe that you were keeping these things at bay. We had no hopes of ever seeing you again. So what happened at the Donovan Complex?"

"Weed and I went to the Donovan Complex early that morning, Cleo let us in. Donovan was still asleep. Weed and Cleo were carrying handguns as we combed the entire complex looking for the gang members. Arnold Cress had fallen asleep sitting up in a chair in the recreation area. Weed pointed his Glock 23, which was suppressed with a Silencerco Osprey 40 Silencer, and shot Arnold in the back of the head. The handgun made a slight whistling sound and Arnold was silent. They found Roscoe Dashon and Marco Anthony, in separate rooms, sleeping. Cleo and Weed went in each room and blew their heads off. Cleo told us that the maid had a close resemblance to her, and that the police would possibly think that it was her. The maid had fallen asleep on the living room couch and they wasted her there. Cleo actually woke Donovan up and at gunpoint, made him sit in one of the living room chairs. Donovan pleaded for mercy, as Cleo pointed the Glock 23, with the silencer at Donovan's forehead and said, 'This is for being such an asshole', and pulled the trigger. Cleo asked if we had all of the detonators for the explosives. We told her that they were all in the car. There were enough explosives planted in the complex to take out a small city. Nothing would be left of the place. The three of us climbed into the Weed's Jeep Cherokee that he borrowed from his father, and drove about two miles away from the Donovan Complex. We flipped all the switches on the detonators and there was an enormous explosion. It was as though a fist of orange flame had decided to punch its way out of the complex. An instant later, there was a blinding flash, like sheet lightning, and a huge ball of varicolored fire shot up. Needless to say, the Donovan Complex was totally leveled and destroyed. We immediately hit the road and by the time we reached I-79 north, we could hear the sirens and the fire trucks were now passing us, headed towards the Donovan Complex. Cleo stayed at the Fernandez's house and Weed and I met the four of you here at Fritz's. Donovan was a piece of shit. How do you see it, Sam?"

"What goes around comes around," Sam answered. "Karma will come after everyone eventually if they 'screw with people'. That's how it works. The universe has served Briccio Cadmen Donovan with the revenge that he deserved."

"Good riddance to the bad garbage," Deacon replied. "This was long time coming for him."

"Anyway, Weed took the opportunity to snatch Deacon's keys to the Utility room at Penny's house, and to Penny's safe. We were being directed to secure that transport bag of money and that the three of us, Cleo, Weed and I, would anonymously disappear to the islands."

"So that's what happened to my keys," Deacon exclaimed, giving Mateo the evil eye.

"Chief Calabrese seemed to be in hot water with the Feds, and was pressurizing the three of you to give up the bag of drug money, now that Donovan was no longer a threat to him. He was using Hunter McClain to negotiate and Weed and I feared that you were going to break down and turn the money over to Calabrese. When you put Chief Calabrese off until after your vacation and were well on your way to England, we decided to take action. Cleo picked up Weed and we met at Fritz's. In her father's Jeep Cherokee, we drove to the Pittsburgh International Airport and rented a vehicle, which Weed drove, and we headed back to Morgantown. Cleo dropped Weed and me back off at Fritz's with the airport rental, and we ordered a beer. Weed sent an anonymous text to Chief Calabrese telling him that his bag of drug money was in a crawl-space at Michael Trainer's house on Laurel Road. We wanted to keep Chief

Calabrese occupied while they went to pick up the actual Transport bag of money at Penny's house. Weed and I yelled and bid adieu to everyone to bring it to their attention that we were leaving. Cleo picked us up in the airport rental and we headed for Penny's house, intentionally leaving our motorcycles in the parking lot. We entered the utility building and opened the safe. Cleo had brought three smaller transport bags that we would transfer the money into. We filled the bags and loaded them into the rental's trunk. Cleo would have them sent and laundered. We locked everything back to the way it was, and were on our way to the airport. We had packed overnight bags for the airplane. We then also purchased some new clothes."

"What a fantastic story, Mateo," Sam commented. "We had no idea what happened to the bag of drug money."

"Were you aware that Chief Calabrese and Lieutenant King were killed in an explosion and fire at Sam's dad's house?" Zack asked.

"Our parent's told us about it. We were in contact with them," Mateo answered.

"That explains why they didn't seem too upset that you and Weed were missing when we went to see them," Deacon said.

"Is that when you left for the islands, Mateo?" Penny asked.

Cleo had made reservations at the Hyatt Regency, Pittsburgh International Airport, for that night. She had a flight scheduled for 9:00 am, departing the Pittsburgh International Airport, and arriving at the Nassau Lynden Pindling International Airport at 2:10 pm. She made unlimited reservations at the Comfort Suites at Paradise Island until we could get organized. It was a thirty-minute taxi ride from the airport. The Comfort Suites were absolutely beautiful. We spent an entire week just basking in the luxury, the huge swimming pool and the continuous entertainment. Cleo had already acquired an unlimited credit card with a credit line of two million dollars in her new name, Camila Isabella Lopez. We started calling her Cami-lo. Weed and I were shocked that we were only eight minutes away from the downtown Nassau Harley Davison dealership, just across the Atlantis Bridge/ Sir Sidney Poitier Bridge from our Comfort

Suite on Paradise Island to downtown Nassau. Weed and I wasted no time and immediately purchased two Harley Davidson Sportsters with Cleo's credit card. We acquired the motorcycle registrations and 10 year license plates right at the Harley Davidson dealership, a far cry from American dealings for motorcycles. Weed and I rode our Harley's to the Odyssey Aviation Airport where Weed purchased his six-passenger, Cessna Citation 525, twin-engine aircraft, which the Odyssey Aviation would look after, and he could fly to designated small aircraft airports throughout the Islands. Weed was totally elated. Cleo purchased a harbor-front condo located in the gated complex of San Marino on Paradise Island. It was a two-floor unit with five bedrooms and had spectacular views from both of its balconies. Weed met a girl named Mia Jimenez, whom he fell totally in love with. She moved into the condo, and we all liked her very much. That was when Cleo bought her a bright yellow Corvette Z06. Both the girls traveled around and did plenty of shopping. Cleo and Mia were crazy about flying to all of the islands on Weed's airplane."

"What were you saying about Weed and Cleo executing the drug lords?" Deacon asked.

"In the almost the two years that we were in Nassau, Weed, Cleo and I were investigating the illegal drug trafficking moving through the Bahamas on go-fast boats, small commercial freighters, and small aircraft. We were gathering names of corrupt dignitaries who were accepting bribes from the Columbian drug smugglers, and names of notorious cartel members and drug lords."

"With the intent of executing them?" Deacon asked.

"We were still being mysteriously controlled, Deacon. We hoped that it was holy spirits."

"Oh my God, how awful, go ahead and finish your story, Mateo," Penny said, sadly.

"The Bahamas is not a drug-producing country, but it stays a transit point for illegal drugs bound for the United States and other international markets. The Bahamas' closeness to the coast of Florida as well as its location on Caribbean shipment routes made it a natural conduit for drug smuggling. Small sport fishing vessels and pleasure crafts move cocaine from the Bahamas to Florida by blending in with legitimate traffic that travel those areas. Turks and Caicos Islands are used as a critical transit point for drug trafficking between countries such as Haiti, the Dominion Republic and the Bahamas. Smuggling was enabled and accompanied by organized crime, gang activity and corrupt dignitaries. Our mission was to stop this corruption."

"How did that work out?" Sam asked.

"Our first target was a man at the Turks and Caicos Islands that Weed had heard about in his airplane travels. His name was, Lucas Salvador, who was taking bribes from undercover agents to ensure a safe passage of drugs by permitting a safe stopover to re-fuel drug flights from Columbia to the Nassau Bahamas and the United States. Needless to say, Lucas Salvador is now pushing up daisies, and for him, the stopover no longer exists. Similar executions were carried out throughout the Turks and Caicos Islands and many traffickers were eliminated. Weed, Cleo and I rented small motorcycles and trail bikes to get around finding our targets and later eliminating them. Weed found a place that sold magnetized explosives that we could carry to the airports and boating docks to destroy boats and planes used for trafficking. With us continually eliminating traffic routes and doing away with at least 25 drug cartel gang members and drug lords. Along with 22 corrupt dignitaries on the take, our job had taken effect."

"How's that, Mateo?" Sam asked.

"Newspaper columns and 'opinion editorials' were expressing that the drug trafficking throughout the islands seemed to have slowed down, or completely stopped. It was noted that many deaths of noted officials had occurred."

"How did that make you feel?" Zack asked. "Was there any glory to be had?"

"We did a lot of high-fiving and patting each other on the backs."

"How sad," Penny exclaimed. "You three were like super heroes who got no recognition."

"When and where did Weed crash his plane?" Deacon asked. "Were their bodies recovered?"

"One month ago Weed, his girlfriend Mia, and Cleo were returning from a pleasure flight, southeast of Nassau, and there was some kind of malfunction in Weed's twin-prop airplane and they went down and crashed into the Atlantic Ocean, Cleo and Mia's bodies washed up on shore the following day. Weed's body and part of the plane were never found. More than likely swept out further into the ocean. Ivanna and I had Cleopatra and Mia cremated and the Cremation Urns were entombed in a beautiful Mausoleum niche at a Catholic Cemetery on Paradise Island. We had a marble bench made and placed in front of the Mausoleum niche with their names Cleopatra Fernandez, Roberto Fernandez, and Mia Jimenez, inscribed into the marble edges. On the top and in the middle of the marble bench was inscribed in large letters 'Weed'."

CHAPTER 42

They all met at the Trainers house so that everyone could relax and enjoy the afternoon. They spent the entire afternoon sitting around the pool and enjoying a few drinks. Penny let Mateo know that their album and her solo single had made it to the top. Mateo was elated.

"No, Mateo," Penny shouted. "I mean we owe you and Weed for your participation in the band. We'll figure something out."

"You owe me nothing at all, I am very wealthy now. You can thank Weed in your prayers. Life is good. I appreciate your thought, but no. Just being together again makes me very happy."

Later, Anna joined them with her cheerleader girlfriends and invited them to come in swimming.

"You girls go ahead and enjoy yourselves, and maybe I'll join you later." Penny said.

Deacon and Zack were saying goodbye to Mateo, and wishing him a safe trip, as he was preparing to return to his island paradise. Before leaving, he had informed Sam and Penny that he had another mysterious occurrence when an actual visible spirit appeared before him and related to him that weapons were only used because God knows that you can't fight evil with tolerance and understanding, and that his journey was over. He felt the emptiness in his body and he knew that he was free from his burden. He felt fresh and had a clear self-consciousness about himself and everything that had happened. Sam and Penny hugged him dearly and made sure that he and his wife, Ivanna, were coming to the wedding on September the 16th, of 2020, in New Haven, Connecticut. Mateo promised that they would definitely be there and that he would stay in touch. He gave Penny his address.

"I can't wait to see little Roberto," Penny screamed, as she kissed and hugged Mateo, as he was sliding into his airport rental to return to the Pittsburgh International Airport. He would stay at the Hyatt Regency at the airport. He had a 9:00 am flight in the morning. "I will send you and Ivanna a beautiful wedding invitation."

"Ciao! Te amo, mucho!

"We love you too, Mateo," Penny shouted.

Sam and Penny were staying over with the Trainers for a couple days. They let Sam's parents know that Mateo was still alive, and what had happened with him and Roberto. They were all extremely sad about Roberto, his girlfriend, and Cleo dying, when Roberto's plane crashed into the Atlantic Ocean. They were equally pleased to hear about Mateo being married, with a son, Roberto, and having a home on Paradise Island, avidly running a functional business, with great interest and enthusiasm."

"I want to live on Paradise Island," Anna exclaimed. "That definitely sounds like my kind of place."

"Don't we all?" Penny agreed, giving Anna a big hug.

Penny, Sam, Zack and Deacon sat around reminiscing about all the things that went on in Morgantown. Being nostalgic and casting their minds back, remembering with pleasure all their times at Fritz's, the golf course, the leather bag of money, recalling Hunter McClain impersonating a terrorist very poorly, and their cut-short vacation to the United Kingdom.

"Now that we are all together again, I have to tell you about my latest dream. This one was really out of sight, and you must remember, 'The Lord travels in mysterious ways'," Sam said.

"Don't be scaring the crap out of us, Sam. Like you did the last time," Deacon laughed.

"This dream was so real that when I woke up I was too confused to go on... It was almost too real… Everything was exceptionally unblemished, impeccable, unsullied. Things that were said in this dream, were completely flawless, clear, and untarnished. Once again, I was in a church that I couldn't identify. I was standing on an immaculate marble floor, directly in front of the altar in a Christian church, where the bread and wine are consecrated in communion services. Zack, you were on my left, and Deacon, was on my right. To the right of the altar, were Daiq and Ben, we were all in long robes, as if we were saints, facing the fixed tabernacle, which is the liturgical furnishing used to house the Eucharist outside of Mass. Penny, you and my sister, Anna, were on the left side of the altar, in long robes, also facing the tabernacle. Each one of us had a halo, indicating holy or sacred figures. While we were praying, heaven was opened, the altar became extremely bright, and a glowing spirit descended upon us like a dove. He was in a bodily form. I looked intently at the face, and it became clear. It was Riley Giuseppe Van Lorne. He was dressed in a white robe with his arms outstretched. He was naming the twelve disciples of Jesus, who were the foundation of Jesus' church. Several wrote portions of the Bible… Peter… James, the son of Zebedee… John… Andrew… Phillip… Bartholomew… Thomas… Mathew… James, the son of Alpheus… Thaddaeus… Simon… and Judas Iscariot. With all the courage that I could muster, I asked, 'What are we to do, o Holy Spirit? Why are we communicating like this?' The supreme glowing image of Riley, in an echoing voice, said, 'All of you already are, or are going to become Attorneys, and you will then become my soldiers. You will join me and help me with my journey. 'Advantageously, Daiq spoke up and ask, 'What journey would that be?' Demanding authority loudly, the glowing image of Riley replied, 'To save mankind from any nuclear confrontations. You are the one that built me as the human savior, Benjamin Franklin Daiquiri, now you and your son must help me. This may be the most dangerous time in human history. The Treaty on the Non-Proliferation of Nuclear Weapons is an international treaty whose objective is to prevent the spread of nuclear weapons and weapons technology, to promote cooperation in the peaceful uses in nuclear energy, and to further the goal of achieving nuclear disarmament and general and complete disarmament. Polarization among non-proliferation parties has reached new heights, especially with many non-nuclear state parties…frustrated with the pace of nuclear disarmament… supporting negotiations on the treaty to ban all nuclear weapons. The president's administration must take steps in support of its non-proliferation Treaty's, Article VI, obligating to pursue nuclear disarmament, and explore ways of deterring abuse of the withdrawal provision. Nuclear disarmament refers both to the act of reducing or eliminating nuclear weapons and to the end state of a nuclear-weapons-free world, in which all the nuclear weapons are completely eliminated.' With his arms still outstretched, he began naming us as his soldiers, 'Daiq… Ben… Penny… Anna… Sam… Zack… Deacon. You are the forces that I need to form the cornerstones for global disarmament of all nuclear weapons.' As I said before, this dream was so real that when I woke up I was too confused to go on... Absolutely too real…"

"Holy crap! I don't know what's going on, but a chill just shot threw me like a double-edged sword, and I don't mean shots received. I honestly feel like something entered my body!" Deacon exclaimed, holding his hands over his stomach.

"Same here," Zack agreed, as he stood there openmouthed and awestruck. "I am totally awestruck."

"Something definitely happened there," Sam replied. "I felt the chill myself, what do you say, Penny?"

"For real," Penny answered. "I hate to say it, but I believe we have been entered by spirits. It was something supernatural. Have you noticed that the area that we are standing has a more vivid color than our surrounding area, and the unusual temperature change, a sense of enhanced energy. I've read about these things, Sam, we may have stumbled across an energy vortex which houses spirits or inter-dimensional portal."

"I've heard of that myself, guys, when I was watching a

supernatural episode on TV. Every home is believed to have at least one of these portals, an entry avenue of spirits. I believe that we are now included into a spiritual journey with Riley. Anna will work on a Bachelor of Science in Foreign Services, and join us at a later date," Sam responded,

"This is surreal, I guess we don't always need a plan, sometimes you just need to take a deep breath, put trust in what you're doing, let go. And see what happens. Right, Penny?" Zack asked.

"A spiritual journey is the unlearning of fear," Penny told Zack, "and accepting whatever comes our way."

"This is how I describe a spiritual journey," Deacon said, with his own theory. "You can't be a wine taster, you have to become a total drunk, I mean really into it. You follow? We have stepped into a zone. Riley, Daiq and Ben, and five professional lawyers who are familiar with foreign affairs will surely get the ball rolling. The four of us will receive our Bachelor of Science degrees, pass the bar exam, and join them. Anna will follow up when she finishes her studies at the WVU School of Law. That makes us twelve."

"We may become a big part of history, Sam," Zack said, as he crossed himself.

"Riley has been a part of history from the day he was born, Zack. We'll have to just wait and watch."

No Two Ways…about it!

The End

Printed in the United States
By Bookmasters